THROUGH THE EYES OF A SHEPHERD

KENNETH A. WINTER

WildernessLessons

JOIN MY READERS' GROUP FOR UPDATES AND FUTURE RELEASES

Please join my Readers' Group so i can send you a free book, as well as updates and information about future releases, etc.

See the back of the book for details on how to sign up.

* * *

Through the Eyes of a Shepherd

Published by:

Kenneth A. Winter

WildernessLessons, LLC

Richmond, Virginia

United States of America

kenwinter.org

wildernesslessons.com

Edited by Sheryl Martin Hash

Cover designed by Dennis Waterman and Terry Pedigo

ISBN 978-1-7328670-9-3 (soft cover)

ISBN 978-1-7328670-8-6 (e-book)

Library of Congress Control Number 2019905349

DEDICATION

I do not cease to give thanks for you ....
Ephesians 1:16 (ESV)

* * *

With a grateful heart:
to my wife, life partner and best friend, LaVonne,
for your steadfast love and faith throughout the journey;
to my family,
for your encouragement all along the way;
to Sheryl,
for enabling me to express my thoughts in a much better way;
to an advance reading group of dear friends,
for graciously challenging me as iron sharpening iron to write a better novel;
to Dennis and Terry,
for your creativity and artistic touch;
and most importantly,
to my Good Shepherd,
for Your grace, Your mercy and Your love, and for being worthy of all glory
forever and ever. Amen.

CONTENTS

From the author xi

Preface xiii

Chapter 1 1
Chapter 2 9
Chapter 3 20
Chapter 4 26
Chapter 5 36
Chapter 6 42
Chapter 7 49
Chapter 8 61
Chapter 9 71
Chapter 10 81
Chapter 11 92
Chapter 12 100
Chapter 13 108
Chapter 14 116
Chapter 15 124
Chapter 16 132
Chapter 17 142
Chapter 18 150
Chapter 19 158
Chapter 20 166
Chapter 21 176
Chapter 22 187
Chapter 23 194
Chapter 24 201
Chapter 25 209
Chapter 26 220
Chapter 27 232
Chapter 28 241
Chapter 29 251
Chapter 30 261
Chapter 31 270
Chapter 32 283
Epilogue 293

Please help me by leaving a review!   297
Through the Eyes of a Spy   298
Timeline   299
Listing of Characters   303
Scripture Bibliography   308
Other Books Written By Kenneth A. Winter   322
About the Author   328
Please join my Readers' Group   330

FROM THE AUTHOR

A word of explanation for those of you who are new to my writing.

* * *

This word of explanation only applies to the Preface and Epilogue of this book. i do not impose this personal conviction on the characters in this novel.

You will notice whenever i use the pronoun "I" referring to myself, i have chosen to use a lowercase "i". It is not a typographical error. i know this is contrary to proper English grammar and accepted editorial style guides. i drive editors (and "spell check") crazy by doing this. But years ago the LORD convicted me – personally – that in all things i must decrease and He must increase. And as a way of continuing personal reminder, from that day forward, i have chosen to use a lower case "i" whenever referring to myself. Because of the same conviction, i use a capital letter for any pronoun referring to God. The style guides for the New Living Translation (NLT) and some of the other translations quoted in this novel do not share that conviction. However, you will see throughout the novel, i have intentionally made that slight revision and capitalized any pronoun referring to God in all quotations of Scripture. If i have violated any style guides as a result, please accept my apology, but i must honor this conviction.

Lastly, regarding this matter – this is a *personal* conviction – and i share it only so you will understand why i have chosen to deviate from normal editorial practice. i am in no way suggesting or endeavoring to have anyone else subscribe to my conviction. Thanks for your under-standing.

* * *

PREFACE

"But these are written so that you may believe that Jesus is the Messiah, the Son of God, and that by believing in Him you will have life." [1]

This work is a fictional novel set in the midst of true events. At its core, it is a story of redemption. A fictional story line has been created to weave certain parts of the narrative together. The narrator and main character of the story – the shepherd Shimon – is fictional, as are the members of his family. However, the **principal** character of this novel is the Lord Jesus Christ. The story begins prior to His incarnational birth and concludes on the Day of Pentecost, as recorded in the Book of Acts. You will recognize many of the other characters who have been included in the story line from the Gospel accounts of Matthew, Mark, Luke, and John.

Each of the Gospel writers was writing to a specific audience and had a different focus. Matthew was writing as a Jew to Jews about a Jew. He took great care in presenting Jesus as the long-awaited Messiah. Mark directed his Gospel account to a Roman readership reflecting Jesus as a

Servant, ministering to the physical and spiritual needs of others. Luke, the physician, was careful to document the humanity and compassion of Jesus as the Son of Man. John, the beloved disciple, wrote to help us understand, through an account of those events he personally witnessed, that Jesus was and is God in the flesh. He wanted us to fully understand the deity of the incarnate Son of God.

In those instances where i have included an event that is recorded in more than one of the Gospels, and where different details have been included in those accounts based upon the writers' individual perspectives, i have endeavored to use a narrative that blends together all of those accounts.

Throughout the novel, many instances of the dialogue are direct quotes from Scripture. Whenever i am quoting Scripture, you will find it has been italicized. The Scripture references are included in the back of this book. Those remaining instances of dialogue and teaching that are not italicized are a part of the fictional novel to help advance the story line. i have endeavored to use Scripture as the basis in shaping that dialogue as well.

There are numerous instances in the Gospels the writers under the anointing of the Holy Spirit chose to omit details. Those details are not of paramount importance to the Gospel message. The fictional story line of this novel is built around some of those silent points. For example:

• It is possible some of the shepherds in the fields of Bethlehem on the night Jesus was born, were still living during His earthly ministry as an adult, as well as His crucifixion and resurrection. How might they have connected the dots between those events?

• When Herod the Great ordered his soldiers to kill all the boys ages two and under, living in and around Bethlehem, how would those families have dealt with that grief and pain? Did they have any idea why their child was being murdered?

• How might individuals have been inspired to join in the zealot movement of the day? And what did that movement look like?

• How would Jesus' actions, such as the cleansing of the Temple, have impacted the common people of the day? How might they have reacted?

This novel looks at these points – and others – and attempts to create a fictional story line that runs through them. In the midst of the story, you will hear and see the gospel as it unfolds. Prayerfully, nothing i have written detracts from the integrity of the gospel.

Some scholars advocate that during Jesus' day, shepherds were at the very bottom of the social order, perhaps slightly above tax collectors and dung sweepers. Though i make no effort to contest their position, i also do not see overwhelming evidence to support it. In the Old Testament, from the days of Jabal in Genesis 4 through the Patriarchs and even the shepherd King David, we see shepherding presented as a noble occupation, and there is not any definitive proof or reference in the New Testament of a change in that view. Therefore, i have chosen to present shepherds in this novel as a part of the unpretentious, hardworking and honorable working class of village life in the early first century, all of whom were looked down upon by the religious leaders of the day.

Also, in the back of the book is a listing of the characters portrayed in the story. i have noted whether they are fictional or not, and in the case of those who are not, i have noted any assumption i have made regarding the individual about which Scripture is silent. i have also noted other fictional details i have attributed to them as a part of the story line.

My goal – and my prayer – in writing this novel is that you, as the reader, see Jesus – and the events that surrounded His incarnational life and ministry – through the eyes and the life of a shepherd – one who first saw Him as He lay in a manger, and one whose life was forever transformed as a result. It is a story of redemption – the redemption of a shepherd – and the redemption of each and every one who responds to the voice of the Good Shepherd.

i pray the novel stimulates conversation, so i have established a discussion group inside of Facebook for that purpose. If you are on Facebook, i invite you to join the **Through the Eyes of a Shepherd** group and i look forward to hearing from you there.

May the grace of the Lord Jesus Christ be with you.

* * *

1

But you, O Bethlehem Ephrathah, are only a small village among all the people of Judah. Yet a ruler of Israel will come from you, one whose origins are from the distant past. [1]

* * *

The sun was casting its late afternoon shadows across the Samarian Hills. Our unlikely band of fourteen was in our respective positions. Any minute now, our intended prey would come into view. As I crouched behind the rocks overlooking the passageway, a drop of sweat ran down my forehead into my right eye. My body involuntarily shuddered with a sense of foreboding.

I was used to rescuing sheep who had strayed into rocks like these, but I had never been in the hills for a reason like this. The odds were overwhelmingly against us. But that didn't matter if our cause was right. But was it right?

. . .

Was this truly who I had become? Was our cause truly just or had I become nothing more than a common criminal? Who were we – against trained Roman soldiers? We were going to die today. What would our deaths accomplish – for anyone – let alone for my family?

I had convinced myself this was my opportunity for vengeance. But was vengeance enough? And was this truly vengeance? As I waited for the soldiers to come into view, my mind raced back to all that had happened to bring me to this point.

It was a sunny, spring day in the village of Bethlehem. The grass was starting to peek through the rocky soil on the hills. Though it wouldn't last long, the landscape was being transformed from barren dunes into rolling green hills budding with the beginnings of a new season.

Sitting atop an enormous aquifer, Bethlehem was known to have the best-tasting water in the region. As a matter of fact, some of King David's mighty men had risked life and limb by crossing through the Philistine battle lines to get him a cup of water from the Bethlehem well.[2]

Bethlehem had been one of the fortress towns when it was built. It originally was a defensive military installation designed to safeguard the water supply that also fed Jerusalem and surrounding villages. Now under Roman rule, it was less of a fortress and more of a sleepy village away from the commotion of Jerusalem. Its fertile soil produced some of the best almonds and olives in the region.

There was great demand for lambs in Jerusalem, and Bethlehem – with its good water supply, rolling hills, and fertile soil – was an ideal place for raising sheep. Lambs were the principal sacrifice offered in the Temple throughout the year. And during the feasting days, Jerusalem was filled with pilgrims from all over the land who weren't able to bring their own animals. They relied on the lambs and birds available at the Temple to use as sacrifices. This provided shepherds in and around Bethlehem with a reliable source of income.

Moshe was one of those shepherds. His father had been a shepherd, just like his father's father. As a matter of fact, his family had been shepherds as far back as anyone knew. They could trace their ancestry back to the shepherd king himself – David – who had once been a shepherd in these very same hills. Moshe's father had taught him from the time he was a boy that shepherding was the most honorable of trades.

The Torah spoke of Abraham. He was a shepherd whom God richly blessed with livestock, herds, and flocks of sheep. And everyone knew that God had created him to be the father of their great nation of Israel. Moses, for whom Moshe had been named, was a shepherd watching over the flocks of his father-in-law Jethro, when God called him to lead the people out of Egyptian bondage. Yes, being a shepherd was a noble and honorable trade, and God had blessed Moshe and his ancestors through the years.

Like his father before him, Moshe raised a broadtail variety of sheep, which had large fatty tails and a thick fleece. The rams were horned, and the ewes were not. They were docile animals that were completely at the mercy of their environment and predators. Sheep cannot defend themselves; they do not have sharp fangs or claws and they can't run. They are helpless and completely dependent upon their shepherd.

It was an ongoing challenge for Moshe to teach the sheep to know his voice and obey his commands. They were his livelihood, though, so he took tender care of them, even giving them names to which they responded.

In the spring, Moshe would lead his flock from the sheepfold to graze on the fresh, succulent growth in the nearby pastures. This was the season when the new lambs were born, and the size of the flock increased. It was also the season when he would shear the winter fleece from the sheep. This was an occasion to celebrate!

After the fields near the village were harvested, Moshe allowed his sheep to graze on new shoots and on grain left among the stubble. When summer heat set in, he moved his flock to cooler pastures on even higher ground in the hills. For days on end, he worked and slept outdoors, allowing the flock to graze on the steep green slopes.

He and the other shepherds took turns spending the night to guard the sheepfold gate. At times, Moshe needed to shelter his flock overnight in a cave, where they would be protected from jackals and hyenas. If the howl of a hyena panicked the flock of sheep in the dark of night, his reassuring voice would calm them.

Each evening, Moshe counted his sheep and checked their health. In the morning, he would call, and the flock would follow him out of the sheepfold to the pasture ground. At midday, he led the sheep to the cool pools of water to drink. Because of Bethlehem's aquifer, these pools never dried up. However, when he was away from Bethlehem, Moshe would guide them to a well and draw water for them.

When the cold rains began, he would shelter his sheep in a cave. Otherwise, they could perish in the lashing rains, hailstorms, and snow. From November until spring, Moshe, like all the other shepherds, would not graze the flock in the open fields.

In return for the shepherd's care, the animals provided the necessities of life for him and his family – milk and meat for the table. The fleece and skins were used in trade for making clothing and bottles. And, of course, the primary source of income for Moshe was the sale of unblemished lambs to the Temple.

The sheep were his livelihood. His father had taught him a good shepherd must be diligent, dependable, and brave. He must be willing to risk his life to protect the flock. And one day, Moshe would train his sons to do the same.

Moshe was also a husband. He and Ayda had been married now for a little over a year. Though he had not known her well when they first became betrothed, God had blessed him richly with his beautiful bride. Truly the writer of Proverbs had been correct when he wrote, *"The man who finds a wife finds a treasure, and he receives favor from the Lord."* (3)

She was fifteen years old when they were married, ten years younger than Moshe. But Ayda had demonstrated a maturity well beyond her years. She was energetic and strong, always up before dawn after working late into the night. But she also was tender and always willing to extend a helping hand to her neighbors and those in need.

Moshe knew, though he would never admit it, that she was cleverer than he was. But she never belittled him in any way, and always honored him – in the presence of others – and when they were alone. She reminded Moshe of the woman by the name of Ruth whom he had heard about in the synagogue – a most beautiful and devoted wife. He truly was blessed by God!

And last week, Moshe was even more blessed when he became a father. His wife had given birth to a beautiful baby boy. His son! His firstborn son! A son whom he could mentor and teach. A son whom he could train up in the way he should go. A son he could be proud of. A son who would care for him and Ayda in their old age.

And I was that son!

As my father looked down at me, lying in the cradle, he could see himself in my dark brown eyes.

"What a handsome boy you are!" he exclaimed with a twinkle in his eye.

Even then I seemed to be looking at everything, taking in all the sights around me.

"You have your mother's mouth, always turned into a natural smile. And look at that amazing head of hair – dark brown – just like mine," he continued.

As my father studied me, he marveled at my ten tiny fingers and ten tiny toes. He thought about how those toes and feet would guide the flock all over the hillside in the years to come, and how those fingers and hands would gently – but surely – care for the flock when any of them needed to be lifted up.

• • •

"I am so proud of you, my son, and I am thankful to Jehovah God for this great gift. I prayed for a son, and God heard and answered my prayer."

Because of that, he and my mother had decided to name me Shimon – meaning "heard." God had heard their prayer!

Today was the eighth day since I was born. In accordance with the Law of Moses, my parents traveled the three miles to the Temple in Jerusalem to present me to the Lord and to be circumcised.[4] The Law stated, "*If a woman's first child is a boy, he must be dedicated to the Lord.*"[5] Accordingly, my parents had selected a one-year old lamb from their flock and brought it to the Temple to be sacrificed as a purification offering. As they arrived at the Temple, they presented the lamb to the priest at the entrance.

Upon entering into the Temple, they saw a woman off to the side worshipping God. They would later learn her name was Anna. She was a widow, who had been married for only seven years before her husband died. Ever since his death, she had remained in the Temple day and night, worshipping God with fasting and prayer. She was now seventy-four years old.

When she saw my parents, she walked over to them and admired their beautiful baby boy.

"God told me that one day I would look upon the face of the promised King who would come and deliver Jerusalem from bondage," she explained. "Until then, I will continue to faithfully worship God and wait for those days to be made complete."

· · ·

Her face radiated as she spoke of the coming Messiah. Before she turned away, she reached down and gently touched my head and quietly spoke this prayer of blessing over me:

"Lord God Jehovah, bless this little child and guard him.
Show him favor and be gracious to him.
Show him kindness and grant him peace.
Grant that he will see the Savior who You will give to all people.
Grant that he will have a heart to receive the Savior and know Him.
And grant that he will follow the Messiah when He comes as one of Your mighty men."

After I had been presented and circumcised, my parents and I began our journey back home. Along the way, my parents talked about Anna and how the Spirit of God had quickened their hearts as she prayed over me. Could it be that God had an even greater purpose for my life than what they could imagine? Would my eyes see the Messiah – the One whom the prophets foretold? Would I possibly be one of the Messiah's mighty men?

Again, they thanked God for the gift of their son and, as they did, they released me to God to become the man He intended me to be – a mighty man who would serve and follow the Messiah.

* * *

2

At that time the Roman emperor, Augustus, decreed that a census should be taken throughout the Roman Empire.[1]

* * *

In the years that followed, God continued to bless my parents, and our family grew. My sister Hannah was born when I was three years old, followed two years later by my brother Jacob. Right after I turned seven years old, my sister Rachel joined the family.

My mother was now expecting her fifth child. Though my father was thankful for all of his children, he secretly hoped for another son. His sons would eventually be able to help him shepherd his flocks. Though he would never admit it to anyone — including my mother — he considered sons to be an even greater blessing from God. So, he asked God to bless them with another boy.

By now I was a typical ten-year-old and loved to shadow my father as he attended to his flock. My father was my hero, and in many ways, I favored him in temperament and appearance. I was big for my age, and people often mistook me to be two or three years older. Since I was reflective and quiet, everyone decided I had a very serious disposition, like my father.

I wanted to be just like him in every way. Each day he would patiently teach me how to be a good man, and specifically, how to be a good shepherd. He even taught me about the specific clothing I would need to wear.

"A shepherd's clothing needs to be simple but rugged," he explained. "To protect you from rain as well as the cold night air, your mother has made you this mantle made of sheepskin, with the fleece turned inward."

Against my skin, I wore a tunic. Sandals protected my feet from sharp rocks and thorns, and my father showed me how to wrap my head in a woven, woolen cloth.

He instructed me in the importance of each and every tool I would need. And on my tenth birthday, he gave me my own set of tools.

"Take good care of these tools," he said, "and they will take good care of you."

They included a scrip, or leather bag, which I would use to carry food such as bread, olives, dried fruit, and cheese. My rod was in many respects a weapon — three feet long with a sharp piece of slate embedded in the bulbous end. My other weapons included a knife as well as a short-bladed sword.

"This sword belonged to your grandfather, and it was given to him by his father," he explained. "One day perhaps, you will pass it along to your son.

"Your most important tool will be your staff," my father instructed. "In addition to aiding you as you walk along uneven terrain, you will use the blunt end of the staff to jab a wandering sheep in the ribs and nudge it back in the direction of the flock."

He taught me how to use the crook of the staff to lift a sheep that had fallen into a pit or ravine, or to help catch or better inspect one by hooking it by the neck or leg. During lambing season, he showed me that if a newborn lamb became separated from its ewe, I should use my staff to hook the lamb, pick it up, and carry it to the ewe. I must never touch the newborn lamb because my scent on the lamb would keep the ewe from suckling it.

He also gave me a personal water container he had made for me. It was a collapsible leather bucket that enabled me to draw water from deep wells when needed; and a sling, which he taught me to use to lob stones near straying sheep to frighten them back to the flock or to drive off prowling wild animals. Lastly, he gave me his prize possession – his reed pipe – which he taught me how to play to entertain myself on long days and nights in the field, as well as to soothe the flock.

Throughout our time together in the fields, my father was always teaching me. Whenever he told me or showed me something new, I would carefully ponder it and ask him questions. I was not content to accept anything at face value. I always sought to know the why and how of anything new I encountered. I probably favored my mother in that regard. I was able to learn quickly. I excelled in Beth Sefer (elementary school). I already had memorized long passages from the Torah, and my understanding of Hebrew was beginning to surpass that of my father's.

People told me I inherited my mother's tenderness toward others. Because I was big for my age, I was often told I was a "gentle giant." Whenever I attended to the newborn lambs that strayed from their mothers, I would gently steer them back where they belonged. In many respects, I demonstrated that same behavior in my role as a big brother toward my younger siblings.

Every evening just before going to sleep, my parents would lead us in reciting the Shema prayer as a confession of our faith in God and a reminder of who we are as His chosen people:

"Hear, O Israel: The Lord our God, the Lord is One. You shall love the Lord your God with all your heart and with all your soul and with all your might. And these words that I command you today shall be on your heart. You shall teach them diligently to your children, and shall talk of them when you sit in your house, and when you walk by the way, and when you lie down, and when you rise. You shall bind them as a sign on your hand, and they shall be as frontlets between your eyes. You shall write them on the doorposts of your house and on your gates."[2]

These were busy days in Bethlehem. The Roman emperor had decreed a census be taken throughout the Roman Empire. Jerusalem had been conquered by the Roman general Pompey in 63 B.C. In 40 B.C., Judea was formally established as a province of Rome under the Roman client King Herod the Great.

. . .

Herod, in his capacity as King of the Jews, did what the Roman emperor told him to do. But Herod was a pretty savvy politician. He apparently had the right mixture of pride and obsequiousness, self-importance and humility to be placed in his position by Augustus, and yet still be somewhat respected by the Jewish citizenry. Of course, having half of a legion of Roman soldiers at his command didn't hurt, either.

The decree for the census required that all people return to their family's original homestead to be registered. Soon, our little village was inundated with people coming home to comply. Lodging accommodations in Bethlehem became scarce.

I was out in the fields with my father watching the sheep. Even from there, the increasing activity and noise in our normally sleepy town was apparent. Though I found it interesting, I was glad to be in the fields away from it.

I had other things on my mind. My mother was about to give birth at any moment now, and I was hoping – and secretly praying – that the baby would be another boy. There was an equal number of boys and girls in our family, including my parents, and I was hoping for a male majority with the next addition. Though I loved my sisters, I wouldn't mind another helping hand in the fields. Like father, like son!

My father was rounding up a stray sheep, and I was rescuing a lamb that had caught his hoof in a rocky crag when I heard someone shouting off in the distance. When I looked up, I saw my sister Hannah running toward me. As she approached, I could hear her shouting,

"Shimon, the baby has arrived! It's a baby boy! We have a new baby brother! Come quickly and see!"

I knew we could not abandon our sheep, so I told her to run on and tell our father who was just over the ridge.

In a few minutes, I saw our father walking toward me with the stray sheep over his shoulders and Hannah walking beside him. He had a smile on his face from ear to ear! As he approached, my father said to me, "Shimon, let's lead the sheep into the sheepfold and go meet your new baby brother!"

My father called out to his sheep and they began their walk to the rocky enclosure. God had answered our prayers — baby Eliezer was the newest addition to our family. I could not think of any happier news! God had again blessed our family! The birth of a baby was always a joyous occasion, but this time it seemed doubly so. After the sheep were safely corralled in the sheepfold for the night, the three of us hurriedly headed home to meet Eliezer.

Our family reveled in the birth of this little one. Each child in our family was a blessing from God, but somehow little Eliezer seemed to bring even greater joy to us all. My parents sensed he would be their last child. The words of the psalm by King Solomon echoed in their hearts: "*Children are a gift from the Lord; they are a reward from Him. Children born to a young man are like arrows in a warrior's hands. How joyful is the man whose quiver is full of them!*" [3]

Two nights later, I was again with my father in the fields outside of Bethlehem watching over our sheep. It was a still night without a cloud in the sky. My father and I were both reflecting on the goodness of God. My father was thanking the Lord God Jehovah for blessing him and my mother with five healthy children. I was telling my father about all the ways Jacob and I would help him train up little Eliezer to be a good shepherd. All of a sudden, a figure, like that of a man but surrounded in a bright light, appeared in front of us.

I quickly moved to stand beside and slightly behind my father, staring at this startling sight — not knowing what to do. Should we run? Should we stand and fight? The other shepherds in the field seemed torn with the same questions. They wanted to run, but they too were being drawn to this light. They began to approach from the other parts of the field – momentarily forgetting about their flocks. As they did, a voice spoke in a calming and reassuring way from the midst of the light: *"Don't be afraid! I bring you good news of great joy for everyone! The Savior – yes, the Messiah, the Lord – has been born tonight in Bethlehem, the city of David! And this is how you will recognize Him: you will find a baby lying in a manger, wrapped snugly in strips of cloth!"* [4]

My father and I, along with the rest of the shepherds, were still trying to understand who and what this being was, when suddenly the sky was filled with a vast heavenly host. We all fell to our knees in unison, fearful, and shielding our eyes from the brilliance that radiated above. We quickly concluded we were witnessing a host of angels – the armies of heaven – who had come to bring us great news. The angelic host began praising God, saying:

> *"Glory to God in the highest heaven,*
> *And peace on earth to all whom God favors!"* [5]

As the angels proclaimed their news, it was as if time stopped and everything stood still. Even the sheep seemed to bow low. No one – and no thing – could move. Each of us was overwhelmed by the sight and enraptured by their news. Not one of us could tell you how long the angelic host remained in our midst. In some ways, it felt like an eternity; but, in others, it felt like a fleeting moment. It was a sight – and a sound – that was forever imprinted on our hearts.

Just as quickly as the angels appeared, they disappeared. And for a few moments, we continued gazing into the heavens. Gradually, we began to look at one another. Almost in unison, we said: *"Come on, let's go to Bethlehem! Let's see this wonderful thing that has happened, which the Lord has told us about."* [6] Then we did something shepherds never do! We left our flocks unattended in the field. We didn't stop to secure our sheep in the sheepfold. Somehow we knew they would be all right. We didn't hesitate for one moment. We ran to the village to the stable where the angels had directed us.

As we approached the site, we expected to find a large crowd of people gathered to worship the baby Messiah. We expected all of the religious leaders would be gathered to give praise to God – and perhaps even King Herod himself would be there. This was a great night of rejoicing in celebration and worship. Glory to God in the highest!

We were dumbfounded when we arrived at the stable and found no one but the baby's mother and father – and a few animals – gathered around the baby wrapped in strips of cloth and lying in a feeding trough. Surely this wasn't the place! Where was everyone? Why weren't the streets filled with celebration? The rest of the village seemed to be asleep like it was an ordinary night.

I wanted to get a closer look at the baby. I looked at the baby's mother for permission, and she smiled and nodded her head. She wasn't much older than I was. I turned my head and looked up into the father's eyes. He, too, gave me a permissive nod. As I looked at the baby's parents, I realized their expressions were similar to those I had seen on the faces of my parents just two nights before, when my brother Eliezer was born. They were expressions of love, thanksgiving, and blessing.

But I – and the shepherds around me – sensed there was something more. There was an atmosphere of worship and adoration there in that stable. I told the baby's mother about the angelic host. I told her what they had said, and why we had all come. She didn't say anything in response. She simply gave me a tender smile and, with a knowing look, nodded her head. Immediately, each of us fell to our knees and worshipped the baby lying in the manger.

Again, time seemed to stand still. No one wanted the moment to end. Our hearts were so full we couldn't utter a word. And the reality of all we had heard and were now seeing became clear. The Messiah whom the Lord God Jehovah had promised through the prophets of old had now come. The message of His arrival had been delivered to us – a group of shepherds on a hillside. The Messiah for whom generations had watched with anticipation was now lying there before our eyes in a manger. God had made the announcement through His angels to us! He hadn't made it to the religious leaders or the King, He had made it to us! He had entrusted the good news of the angelic message to us! And the rest of the world seemed to be sleeping right through it.

Eventually my father softly reminded us that the baby's mother was tired and needed her rest. So quietly, we stood to our feet and reverently backed out of the stable. I was the last to get up. As I did, I continued to stare into the baby's eyes. His eyes were dark brown, just like mine. But His eyes had a unique quality about them – particularly for a newborn baby. His eyes were inviting and gentle. They were eyes that welcomed me in and made me feel safe. But they were also eyes that seemed to look right into my very soul. I remained there for only a moment locked in that gaze, but it was a gaze that would remain with me forever.

As I followed my father and the rest of the shepherds back to the fields, we began to talk excitedly about all we had seen, heard, and experienced. Our joy began to bubble over, and the few passersby we encountered stopped to ask us what was happening. We explained what had happened and what the angel had said to us.

They appeared to be amazed by our report, but none seemed interested enough to seek out the newborn for themselves. Perhaps the thought that angels would announce the arrival of the Messiah to a group of shepherds was just too astonishing for them to believe, because the word didn't spread beyond us. But we knew what we had seen and heard, and that truth was etched in our hearts forever!

The next morning, I ran to the stable to see the baby again. But when I arrived, no one was there. The baby, His mother, and His father were gone. None of us had thought to ask the family's names. None of us knew where they were from. They had probably come to Bethlehem for the census. And though I asked some people nearby, no one seemed to know who the family was or where they had gone. All that remained in the stable was the manger where the baby had lain, the animals that had surrounded Him, and the memory of a holy moment. I slowly walked back to the fields to tell my father what I had found.

Five days later, our entire family traveled to the Temple for the presentation and circumcision of my baby brother, Eliezer. Though I knew it was too soon, I was hoping we would see the baby and His parents from the stable. But they were not there.

. . .

However, we did meet a curious man named Simeon at the Temple. He ran over to us as we entered, looked at Eliezer, shook his head, and walked away. His actions seemed very odd to our entire family. My mother told us he must be searching for one of his own family members, so no one gave his actions any more thought. Little did we know that Simeon, too, was looking for the Messiah and in two days his faith would become sight.[7]

* * *

3

A cry of anguish is heard in Ramah – mourning and weeping unrestrained.
...[1]

* * *

Like many other children, my education began at age four in Beth Sefer. Both boys and girls attended the class in the synagogue. The teaching included the writings of the Torah (the Law), the Nevi'im (the Prophets) and the Ketuvim (the Writings). The emphasis was on both reading and writing the Scriptures. My goal was to memorize the six hundred thirteen precepts and commands recorded in the Torah by the end of my studies.

Now age twelve, I was in my final year of preparation before I would be permitted to fully participate in the religious life of our synagogue. At that point, I would take part in a ceremony where I would formally take on the yoke of the law and become a *bar mitzvah* or "son of the commandment." This was a crucial turning point in every Jewish boy's life. It was the day I would become a man.

. . .

I looked forward to that day with great anticipation. I used much of my time in the fields to recite Scriptures, practicing them word for word. My education was a priority to my father; however, my grandfather had not had the same conviction. My father had spent more time in the fields than in the classroom, so I already knew more Scriptures than he did.

I particularly savored the words of the prophets – and specifically those regarding the Messiah. I knew the Messiah had come. I had seen Him in Bethlehem! He now would have been approaching two years of age, just like little Eliezer. I wondered where the Messiah and His parents had gone. I wished I could have seen the baby one more time.

Since I was practically a man now — according to Jewish law, anyway — my father trusted me to watch over our sheep by myself. Most days I would come home from school and watch the sheep until evening so my father could rest. My seven-year-old brother, Jacob, would help sometimes, but he would often wander away to explore in the hills.

On this particular day, I was in the field watching over the sheep and reciting Scripture. Jacob was off wandering again, and our father was home resting. Off in the distance, I saw a contingent of soldiers on horseback racing toward the village. The setting sun glimmered off their breast plates and helmets, and their flags were streaming in the breeze.

Their horses were far more majestic than the work horses we had. Theirs galloped with heads held high, snorting with pride. The approaching cavalry made for quite an impressive sight as they entered the village. I wondered why they were coming to Bethlehem. I had seen such a sight only twice before, and on both occasions, they were escorting King Herod as he traveled through the region. But I did not spot the king today.

Just then I heard a loud bleating. One of the sheep had gotten caught in a thicket and was entangling itself even more as it attempted to break away. Sheep were experts at getting themselves into trouble. I made my way to the thicket and placed one arm around the sheep to calm it and hold it steady. With my other hand, I gently pulled away the constricting branches.

As I finished freeing the lamb, I could hear shouts and loud noises coming from the village. Those sounds were soon joined by loud wailing that echoed through the hills. I wanted to run into the village to investigate, but my father had entrusted me with watching the sheep and I couldn't leave them in Jacob's care – he was just too young. Other shepherds in the field were also straining to see what was going on. We were all curious to know what was happening.

Off in the distance, I saw my sister, Hannah, running toward me. The last time she had run into the fields like this was when Eliezer was born. But this time I could tell she wasn't coming with good news. Even from a distance I sensed she was terrified. I knew I needed to go to her.

"Jacob," I shouted, "watch the flock!" Then I turned and raced toward Hannah. As I got closer, I could tell she was weeping uncontrollably. Beyond my sister, I saw the soldiers riding out of the village as rapidly as they had arrived. They moved like men on a mission, charging toward their next assignment. Apparently, whatever purpose had brought them to Bethlehem had been completed. But the shouting and the wailing from the city had not ceased; in fact, it seemed even louder than before.

"Shimon! Shimon!" Hannah was screaming at me but I couldn't understand what she was saying. Finally, between her sobs, I heard these words: "They killed Papa! And they killed Eliezer!"

My heart skipped a beat. Surely Hannah was mistaken, and my father and brother were fine. But I needed to get home quickly so I could see for myself. I told my sister to go further up the hill, find Jacob, and stay with him until I returned. I didn't give Hannah the opportunity to object. I ran past her and just kept running. I ran faster than I had ever run before.

As I arrived at the outskirts of the village, the shouts and the screams were deafening. I saw mothers holding their young sons in their arms, weeping unconsolably. And I saw blood.

Everywhere I looked, I saw blood.

When I arrived home, I saw my mother — bent over, kneeling on the floor, with her back to me. But I could tell she was holding something, and someone was lying on the floor in front of her. And she, too, was making wailing sounds the likes of which I had never heard ... sheer pain and overwhelming grief. In the corner of the room, my sister Rachel stood screaming.

As I approached, I saw the blood. My father was lying there lifeless, his clothing now stained a bright, crimson red. Then I noticed my mother holding Eliezer's limp little body in her arms. He, too, was covered in blood.

I began to reel. I could not imagine what had happened to my father and little brother. And as much as I wanted to ask questions, all I could do in that moment was embrace my mother. And then I began to weep uncontrollably.

Eventually, my mother struggled to speak between sobs. "The soldiers killed Eliezer! They killed my baby! They said it was by order of the king! The king killed my baby! Your father tried to stop them. He drew his sword to stop them. And they killed him, too! The king killed my husband and my baby! Why would the king do that? Why would he send his soldiers to kill my husband and my baby? What did they do?"

"A cry of anguish is heard ...
weeping and mourning are unrestrained.
Mothers weep for their children,
refusing to be comforted – for they are dead!"[2]

My father was dead. A good man, an honorable man, a man who loved and cared for his family. He had loved God and obeyed His law. He honored those in authority and obeyed their laws. The most honorable man I had ever known had just been killed by the king's soldiers. And his only crime was trying to protect his little son!

The king's soldiers, in one brief moment, had taken the life of my father and my baby brother. And for what? Why had they ridden into town to kill baby boys ... and my father? Then left, like it was nothing? Eliezer, like all the other babies, was an innocent. These children weren't old enough to have done anything wrong. Eliezer was a gentle toddler. There was no reason for their deaths ... and there would be no comfort from anyone!

Where had God been? God had protected Moses as a baby from Pharaoh's soldiers. Why didn't He protect Eliezer? How could He let this happen? Eliezer was a blessing from God. He was an answer to our prayers. Why had God allowed him to be killed? I would never trust God again! My father and my brother were dead. And God had allowed it to happen!

Soon, some neighbor women gathered in our home to console my mother and baby sister. I turned and slowly walked out. I needed to return to the fields to find Hannah and Jacob. I realized I was now the man of the house. I was responsible to provide for and protect my family.

I would find time to grieve later, but now I had to learn to care for my family. My father was no longer here so that responsibility now fell to me. I would honor my father by not allowing any further harm to come to my mother, my sisters, or my brother. God had failed to protect our family. I could no longer depend on Him to protect us! As I returned to the fields, I made a solemn oath on the dead bodies of my father and my baby brother to do whatever I needed to do to protect my family.

* * *

4

Herod was furious when he learned that the wise men had outwitted him. He sent soldiers to kill all the boys in and around Bethlehem who were two years old and under....[1]

* * *

None of us understood why King Herod the Great had ordered the massacre of the children. It remained a mystery for many years. I later learned it was because he was fearful his reign, personally and through his line of succession, was being threatened. He had heard about a baby born in Bethlehem who was the promised Messiah. He feared if that news were true, then the Child, not Herod and his sons, would one day sit on the throne.

And this king was not going to let *anyone* usurp his or his sons' positions on the throne. He decided infanticide was his only course of action. Since he didn't know when the baby was born, he directed his soldiers to execute all male children under the age of two living in and around Bethlehem.

. . .

There were nineteen other children murdered that day in the village of Bethlehem, bringing the death toll in our village to twenty-one, including Eliezer and Moshe. The soldiers never knew why they were massacring innocent children — they were just following orders. Herod and his advisers never explained the reason. But this vicious attack wasn't out of character for Herod. During his reign he ordered the killing of his own wife, his brother-in-law, three hundred military leaders and three of his own sons.

One of those sons, aged two, was actually killed at the same time as the massacre in Bethlehem to appease those who would criticize his actions. Supposedly, Roman Emperor Augustus was once overheard to say, "It is better to be Herod's pig than to be his son," referencing the fact that as a Jew, he would not kill pigs but had no hesitancy about killing his own children.

Soon after the massacre, Herod contracted an excruciatingly painful illness that caused his body to putrefy. The pain became so great he attempted to take his own life on more than one occasion. Some speculate his death resulted from one of those attempts.

When King Herod died, the rule of the provinces of Judea, Samaria, and Idumea was granted to his son Herod Archelaus by Caesar Augustus in accordance with Herod the Great's wishes. The remainder of his kingdom was divided between his son Herod Antipas, being granted rule over the provinces of Galilee and Perea, and his son Herod Philip II, being granted rule over the remaining provinces of Ituraea, Trachonitis, Gaulanitis and Paneas.

When the news reached me that Herod the Great had died, I felt no grief over his death. But neither did the news satisfy the ache in my heart for my dead father and brother. And by association, I had no regard for our new ruler Archelaus, Herod's son. This new puppet king of Rome would be no better than the former. Life continued on, but the massacre had forever cast its shadow upon our lives.

As the years passed, I became more and more hardened by my grief – not toward my family or neighbors – but toward our Roman rulers whose soldiers had been the executioners, toward our puppet king and leaders ... and toward God. I went through the motions of attending synagogue and reciting Scripture for the sake of my mother, but it was an empty ritual.

Attending synagogue was as much a part of our small village life as working, eating, and sleeping. I did so because I knew it was expected, particularly now that I was the man of our home. But I no longer considered myself to be a follower of God. I didn't believe I was abandoning Him; He had abandoned us in our hour of need.

I tried to be a good brother, and an even better son to my mother. I did everything I knew to do to provide for and protect my family. I made the decision not to seek a wife. I did not want anything or anyone to distract me from my oath to care for my mother and siblings. I worked hard. I tried to live up to all I believed my father would expect of me.

Eventually, a new normalcy developed in our lives. Gratefully, over time, a smile returned to my mother's face. Laughter never returned to my heart, but a calmness did. At least on the outside – though a rage still burned within me.

As Jacob grew older, he was able to help me and take on more responsibility for tending the sheep. As time passed, we were able to grow our flocks and each year multiply the number of newborn lambs, which provided more income for the care of our family. My sister Hannah was now married, and she was expecting a child of her own. Rachel was not only a loving daughter, but she also had become a trusted companion to our mother. She was my mother's "Ruth."

Jacob and I were in the fields one afternoon when we saw a Roman cavalry unit approaching the village. In the twenty-two years that had passed since the massacre, we had seen soldiers passing through on numerous occasions. Each time brought back the horrific memories of that day. Even now, as we stood there watching, another wave of fear and panic washed over us. Why are they here? What is about to happen?

Today, however, they passed through the village without stopping. Apparently, they were on a mission that did not include Bethlehem. The entire village felt a collective sigh of relief, combined with a renewed sadness, as the soldiers continued on their journey.

I also felt a renewed anger. How dare the soldiers come through our town to demonstrate their presence, their power and their control! Several of the men in the village were talking about a growing group of men who referred to themselves as Cananaeans. Others referred to them as zealots. These men were actively seeking independence from Roman rule by whatever means necessary. I decided to learn more about this group.

In the fall and spring, just before the major feasts, we always sold a portion of our growing flock to the Temple merchants in Jerusalem, just as our father had before us. The outer Court of the Gentiles in the

Temple had become a bustling marketplace under the leadership of a priest named Annas.

Annas had served as high priest for nine years, and during that time had become a very powerful man. He was so powerful that one of the first actions of the new Roman Prefect Valerius Gratus was to remove him from that position and replace him with a series of his own puppets. However, over time the prefect succumbed to the pressure of the Jews and named Annas' son-in-law, Caiaphas, as high priest. One of Caiaphas' first actions was to place responsibility for the Temple merchants and treasury under the supervision of Annas.

The market had originally been established outside the Temple as a place where visiting Jews could exchange their money for temple currency and purchase animals to be sacrificed. But in recent years, under Annas' leadership, the priests had become more critical of whether an animal was suitable for sacrifice and disqualified many due to "blemishes." This meant the Temple merchants maintained an even greater stock of animals in their pens to provide for the increased demand. Increased stock required increased space, so they set up tables and stalls inside the Temple courtyard as well.

It had become a very profitable enterprise for Annas, the priests, and their merchants, and the whole affair was under the overall protection of the High Priest Caiaphas. It had become quite a family affair! Though the priests and merchants sold the animals at high prices, they kept the price they paid us low. However, we were still able to make a good living. As long as we could continue to increase the size of our flock each year, our income increased, as well.

It was late September and the Feast of Tabernacles was approaching. It was time for me to take the sheep to the Temple. But on this trip, I had another matter on my mind. The last time I was at the Temple, I had met a man named Barabbas, who was in his late thirties, a few years older than me. He was the son of one of the members of the Sanhedrin.

The Sanhedrin was seventy-one rabbis who were appointed to sit as a tribunal ruling on matters of national significance related to religious life. Under Roman rule they were empowered to adjudicate matters within the parameters laid down by biblical and rabbinic tradition, as long as they did not violate Roman law. These were the most powerful, and in many instances, the wealthiest religious leaders of the day. But Barabbas no longer shared his father's view as to the best way to deal with Roman tyranny.

During our last meeting, Barabbas had expressed opinions regarding Roman rule that aligned with my growing beliefs. He had been a part of a band of rebels that had seized control of the armory in Herod's palace two years ago. The rebels had been defeated, but he and a few others had escaped, most notably Judah the Galilean, who had led the band. They were bitterly opposed to the heavy-handed oppression of Roman rule, which basically equated to slavery, as well as the tyrannical actions of the Herodian leaders. Some of the rebels had fought for religious reasons; others, like Barabbas, were more motivated by the opportunity of unbridled power and financial gain.

I entered Jerusalem with our sheep through the Sheep Gate, specifically earmarked by the ancients for the delivery of animals for sacrifice to the Temple. The Temple merchant offered me a much lower price for my sheep than I had received on my last trip, so we began the long process of haggling.

In the midst of our negotiations, Barabbas walked over to greet me. Barabbas was an intimidating man, not only in physical size but also because of his rough demeanor. Immediately the merchant's appearance changed. I saw fear in his eyes. I did not completely understand the reason for his fear, but apparently the two men knew one another.

Instantly, the merchant increased his offer to me. By the time we were done, he had given me a price that was higher than any I had ever been paid. As we concluded our business, the merchant continued to keep a wary eye on Barabbas. He seemed relieved when we left and headed off to find an inn where we could enjoy some good food and private conversation.

I was pleased with my unexpected profit and I knew I had Barabbas to thank for it. So I wanted to express my gratitude by treating him to a meal. As we ate together, it became obvious our shared hatred for Rome had not lessened since we last talked.

"Shimon, my friend, I have important news to tell you. There is a growing faction of men across the provinces that shares our views. Some are seeking to overthrow Roman rule based on religious reasons. They consider us to be the Chosen People of God, that He alone is our Leader and Master."

Barabbas went on to explain these men believed it was contrary to God's Law that we be subjected to the rule of an idolatrous empire that accorded divine honors to its emperors. They considered the Roman empire to be the antithesis of our spiritual beliefs and our way of life as Jews. They also believed that very soon God would send His Messiah to lead the people out of enslavement, overthrow Roman oppression and establish a new government in which the people would enjoy complete freedom.

．　．　．

But others, including Barabbas, by his own admission, were less religiously motivated and were more self-serving in their motivation. They sought the wealth and the power the Romans and the Herodians enjoyed. But regardless of their motivation, they were united in their cause.

My interest in this talk of rebellion didn't align with either of those camps. My motivation was revenge driven by my hatred for the lot of them – and in order to achieve that end, I would happily unite with this group.

As we ate, a man entered the inn whom Barabbas greeted and invited to join us. The man's name was Simon and he, too, was one of the zealots. He was not physically intimidating, but he was passionate and spoke with deep conviction. He wasn't a bully looking for a fight; he was a man that truly wanted to be a part of changing things for the better. He was mild-mannered and soft-spoken, but he had fire in his eyes. Simon was from the province of Galilee, and as he told his story, it became obvious his was a religious motivation.

Simon gave me more insight regarding this growing movement.

"There are two principal leaders of the zealots," he explained. "One is Zadok the Pharisee. He believes the Messiah is coming soon and we need to be better prepared for His arrival. The Messiah will lead us to overthrow the tyranny of Rome. The other leader is Judah the Galilean. He believes God helps those who help themselves. We must show we are no longer willing to bow to Roman oppression. He espouses that though we can't overcome Rome's military might, we can perhaps break her resolve by continuing to strike at her heel through raids like he led on the armory."

. . .

Simon went on to tell us he had heard a group of Greeks discussing the fact that every Jew could be identified as being an adherent of one of the four different prevailing philosophies within Judaism – each having a foundation in their religious belief.

"The first philosophy," he said, "is that of the Pharisees, espousing the unbending legal tenets of the Mosaic Law and the rabbinical teachings. The second is that of the Sadducees. Though their beliefs are also rooted in the Mosaic Law, they do not adhere to the oral rabbinical teachings, and neither do they subscribe to the belief of resurrection. They firmly believe death is the end. Their philosophy has been influenced over time by the Greek teachers." I already knew that the Sanhedrin – our religious ruling body – was made up of representatives from both of these two groups and their philosophies.

"The third philosophy is the Essenes," Simon continued. "They abstain from Temple worship but are much stricter than the Pharisees. They agree the soul lives on after death, but not in bodily form. Accordingly, they do not believe in bodily resurrection. They often lead a celibate life and choose to live in abject poverty – many in the desert caves that overlook the Dead Sea. They also follow strict water purification rituals.

"The fourth philosophy that has most recently emerged is made up of people who think like we do – the zealots. We are characterized by our passion for liberty. We show zeal for God, and believe we are acting on behalf of God to keep Him from punishing our nation. Many have vowed to kill or root out all offenders – either from the outside – or from within. Some of us hold strong religious conviction, while others can better be described as 'a group of bandits and robbers.'"

I couldn't help but notice Barabbas give a subtle smirk to that last comment. Simon concluded his lesson to us by saying, "The two founders – Zadok and Judah – represent the two extremes of the movement."

Simon and Barabbas also clearly reflected these two extremes to me. Simon planned to return to Galilee to be discipled in the philosophy and the planned rebellion by Zadok and Judah. Barabbas had already spent time listening to both men and had followed Judah for a while. But now he was growing weary of all of the talk. He preferred action.

I shared the zealots' passion for rebellion, and I determined that day I would join with them. I decided the best way I could truly care for my family was to take action to protect them from those who were our enemies. I would no longer be Shimon the quiet shepherd, minding my own business. I would become Shimon the zealot, who would proactively work to bring about change for our people.

The next morning, I returned home to Bethlehem to make arrangements to transfer responsibility for our flock to my brother Jacob, and to seek his agreement to care for our mother and sister. The added money I had received this time from the sale of our lambs would provide him with a greater financial reserve as he undertook his new responsibility. Then I would join Simon in Tiberias, in the province of Galilee.

5

It was ... the reign of Tiberius, the Roman emperor. ... Herod Antipas was ruler over Galilee; ... Annas and Caiaphas were the high priests... . Some time ago there was that fellow... Judah of Galilee. He got some people to follow him. ...[1]

* * *

Tiberias was a newly constructed city located along the western shore of the Sea of Galilee. It had been built within the last five years by Herod Antipas to be the capital of his realm in the province of Galilee. Herod had named it for Tiberius, the current emperor of Rome.

The city had absolutely no connection with Jewish history. Thus, the Jews viewed Tiberias as a strictly pagan city. No religious Jew would willingly step foot into the city. Accordingly, as Antipas was building his palace there, he had resettled many non-Jews from rural Galilee and other parts of his domain in order to populate his new capital. In the eyes of the Jews, the city represented all that was wrong with

Roman and Herodian rule, and quickly became a magnet for the growing number of zealots gathering from throughout the land.

Every day Herod Antipas did something to further alienate the Jews — both through his offenses against Jehovah God and his growing deference to Rome. As a result, more were drawn to the ranks of the zealots each day. Zadok the Pharisee and Judah the Galilean welcomed their growing numbers with open arms. They were both charismatic leaders who inspired great zeal. They rallied the young men who were drawn to them with the cry that "God alone is our Leader and Master." Though I no longer felt I could follow God, I agreed the Romans and the Herodians were most definitely not my leaders.

When I arrived in Tiberias, I quickly located my newfound friend, Simon. Together we sat under the teachings of Zadok and Judah. As we listened to Judah, we clearly heard his radical plea for rebellion against Rome. Judah's "an eye for an eye" teaching promoted unbridled aggression, theft, and murder – all for the sake of the resistance.

He not only encouraged aggression against the Romans and Herodians, but also against other Jews, particularly those who were deemed to collaborate with Rome. The Sadducees – which included our High Priest Caiaphas, his father-in-law Annas, and most of the members of the High Council – were viewed as being some of the chief collaborators since they seemed to profit the most from Roman and Herodian rule.

As Simon and I listened to Judah, we became more convinced his approach was merely being used as a justification for violent lawlessness and was as repugnant to us as the behaviors of our Roman and Herodian enemies. It appeared that the solution being espoused to counter Roman and Herodian pilfering, extortion, violence, and

murder was for the zealots to do the same in return. And though
Simon and I could not continue to tolerate those actions by our
enemies, we had no intention of adopting those same behaviors to
counteract them. Though Judah used words like "God alone is our
Leader and Master," his response was just as godless as the actions of
our enemies.

Zadok's response was indeed more measured. He often told us, "The
long-promised Messiah is coming soon, and when He does He will
lead His people to overthrow the treacherous and godless rule of Rome
and establish His rule over us. We must all be prepared to join Him in
the rebellion and follow Him when He arrives. In the meantime, we
must stir the hearts of rebellion within the people and strike at the heel
of our Roman and Herodian enemies." He explained we would do that
by raiding their treasuries for provisions and carrying out other kinds
of disruptive activities to foster our efforts.

So, a raid was planned for Caesarea Maritima. Herod the Great had
built the city on the coast of the Mediterranean Sea. The first structure
he built was a majestic palace situated on a magnificent promontory
that jutted out into the sea. The city was built as a major commercial
port – constructed as the largest, artificial harbor built in the open sea.

Just like Tiberias was the seat of Herodian power in Galilee, Caesarea
Maritima was the seat of Roman power in the province of Iudaea.
Valerius Gratus was the current Roman prefect to govern the Iudaean
province. The year was 20 A.D. and he was now five years into his
rule. The role of prefect was a military appointment, not a political one.
He was primarily charged with maintaining peace within the province
and making sure Rome's voracious appetite for taxes continued to be
satisfied.

. . .

Taxes collected throughout that region of the world were ultimately brought to Caesarea Maritima to be shipped to Rome. There was no naval force that could compete with Rome's, so the cargoes were safe as they traveled by sea; however, the sizable treasure was vulnerable on land. Since all roads that "led to Rome" from that region passed through Caesarea, the rebels knew that was where we needed to go to strike at our enemy's heel and fund our rebellion.

Zadok enlisted Simon and me to be part of a planned raid. He told us the raid was to be led by Judah, and to the surprise of Simon and me, our "friend" Barabbas would be assisting him. Judas explained that Barabbas' experience in previous raids, together with his unique skill set, would certainly be valuable for this effort. And Barabbas had specifically asked that Simon and I be part of the raiding party. We reluctantly agreed to do so.

A Roman centuria of eighty soldiers guarded each collection being transported to Caesarea. The majority were local men who had been conscripted into the army or had been enticed by the wages and the perceived power. Roman discipline of its soldiers was unbending, and death was often the remedy for insubordination or failure.

But, as we soon learned, every man has his price. And Barabbas apparently had the ability to find the "right" men at the "right" price. He was able to recruit six of Caesar's eighty who would be guarding the collection on the day of our raid. They agreed to willingly help our rebel force in exchange for a generous payment.

Simon and I, together with twelve other men, all led by Judah and his "lieutenant" Barabbas, made up the raiding party. Along with our six confederates from the Roman military, we were tasked with overpowering the remaining seventy-four soldiers and escaping with the tax collection. The odds weren't in our favor, but the element of surprise was. Judah was confident of our success and he instilled that confidence in each one of us.

As the Roman guard drew closer to Caesarea, they passed through the Samarian Hills prior to entering the Plain of Sharon. The Samarian Hills provided cover for our raiding party and, at one point, created a narrow passage through which the Roman soldiers would travel. Our plan was to create a natural barricade that closed off the passage. The soldiers would have to clear the rocks and boulders so their wagons could pass through. As they were distracted by that effort, we would attack.

Our plan would have been successful if the Roman centurion had not discovered the disloyalty of his six men. They had been overheard boasting about their plan before they left Jerusalem. Once en route, the centurion had his remaining soldiers arrest and interrogate them. After they had extracted the information they needed, the soldiers executed the traitors. The other soldiers actually cast lots for the privilege of executing the intended betrayers. So, when the remaining Roman guard entered the pass in the Samarian Hills, they knew exactly what was awaiting them, and we had already lost our six confederates as well as the element of surprise.

Judah had determined that part of his force would attack the Roman soldiers from each side of the pass, and the third portion from the rear. Simon and I were part of that rear force being led by Barabbas. Judah and another man were leading the other two groups.

As I nervously waited for the moment to attack, my mind replayed memories leading up to this very moment – and most poignantly the day when my father and brother were massacred. I vividly recalled the evil deeds of the soldiers. I remembered how they had shown no mercy to the children, to their families, or to my father. In my mind's eye, I could still see the blood that had been shed. I thought about the lives that had been taken … and the tragic pieces that were left.

This was my opportunity to avenge the deaths of my father, my brother, and the nineteen other little boys who had been senselessly murdered that day. The deaths of these soldiers would be rightful retribution. Or would it? Was there anything truly right about this?

It was doubtful that any of the soldiers I was going to attack today had taken part in the murder of my loved ones. And even if they had, how was what I was preparing to do any different from what they had done? All of a sudden, I could no longer justify the soldiers' murder for my revenge. I realized the soldiers who had murdered my family were just following orders.

These thoughts were still colliding in my mind as the Roman guard entered the pass. The shadows cast by the afternoon sun had continued to lengthen, but I could still see clearly as I watched the soldiers dismount from their horses to clear the barrier. I knew what we were about to do was wrong. If there was truly a God in heaven, how could He possibly forgive me for this heinous act? So, I prayed, "God, if You are truly there, show me what You would have me do!"

* * *

6

… Judah of Galilee … got some people to follow him, but he was killed too, and all of his followers were scattered. … John son of Zechariah … went from place to place on both sides of the Jordan River, preaching that people should be baptized to show that they had repented of their sins and turned to God to be forgiven.[1]

Immediately, Barabbas knew there was trouble. Only half of the centuria had entered the pass instead of the full centuria our six recruits had assured him would show up. He signaled to Simon and me to stay where we were. As he did, he spotted movement up over the ridge to our right and quickly saw there was movement on the ridge on the other side of the pass as well. The remaining soldiers were flanking our other two groups from the rear. Though Barabbas had not noticed any movement to his rear, he knew they would be coming from that direction, too.

Obviously, the soldiers knew of the planned raid. Our advantage of surprise had been taken away. The other two groups were caught in between the soldiers, just like they had been that day at the armory. Barabbas knew the Romans would not take any prisoners. The men would be slaughtered. Judah and the other two groups were too far away for him to signal. There was no way for him to warn them to retreat. He motioned to Simon and me to quickly and quietly move toward him, and the three of us then took cover inside the opening of a limestone cave.

Just as we entered the cave, we heard Judah give the signal to attack. But as they did, the prepared Roman soldiers advanced on them from all sides. Very little fighting actually took place. The two groups of zealots were outflanked, outmanned, and outmaneuvered within moments. The soldiers who were advancing from behind Barabbas, Simon and me, had not seen us retreat into the cave, so they thought we had already moved up into the pass. They advanced past our position and joined the others in flanking the remainder of our men, not knowing the three of us were not with them.

Judah and two others were killed in the brief skirmish. It looked like two or three other zealots had been able to outrun and escape the soldiers. As the soldiers surrounded the remainder of our now unarmed band, the centurion gave the order for them to be executed. There was nothing Simon, Barabbas, or I could do at that point to aid the other rebels. The whole affair was over as quickly as it had begun – without any Roman casualties. We had suffered an overwhelming defeat: one of our leaders had died in the attempt along with most of the men, and the few who remained had either scattered or were hiding in our cave.

Barabbas, Simon, and I remained in the cave until after the soldiers cleared the pass and moved on. Barabbas went in one direction and Simon and I went in another. Simon and I knew God had protected us that day. We knew that otherwise our dead bodies would also be lying in that pass for the wild animals to ravage. And we knew armed rebellion was not the solution to the brutality, oppression, and treacherous greed of our nation. We knew neither Zadok nor Judah had the right answer. We knew our only hope was in the promised Messiah.

Recently, we had heard about a man by the name of John, who was preaching about the coming Messiah. We determined to find this John and see what more we could learn from him.

We had heard some interesting stories about John. Apparently, his father was a Jewish priest by the name of Zechariah from the priestly line of Abijah and Aaron. Zechariah and his wife were advanced in years and had no children. Their lives were fully devoted to serving God. One day Zechariah was serving in the Temple, burning incense in the sanctuary of the Lord. Suddenly an angel had appeared before him.

It was said Zechariah had been overwhelmed with fear at the sight of the angel – I knew exactly what that was like! The angel told him his wife, Elizabeth, would conceive and give birth to a son, whom he was to name John. John would be a man with the spirit and power of Elijah, and he would proclaim the coming of the Messiah. Zechariah was allegedly struck dumb by God from that moment until John was eight days old because of his lack of faith in what the angel told him.

John's parents raised him in and around the Temple, but they died of old age while he was still a boy. John had no relatives to take him in except for Elizabeth's nephew and his wife. John went to live with them in the wilderness outside of Jerusalem, in an area known as Qumran, near the Dead Sea. He soon became very accustomed to living in the wilderness.

• • •

Most of the people living in the community were Essenes, who lived very simple, pious lives. Though his mother's nephew was married, many within the community were celibate, avoiding marriage and devoting their lives solely to God. They had very little and they wanted very little. Their diet was simple – locusts and wild honey. Their clothing was simple, too – a woven cloak from coarse camel hair with a leather belt securing it. They devoted their lives to studying the Scriptures.

John never returned to the Temple because his relatives, like the rest of the community, believed the Temple had become corrupt – not only because of the market trade carried out there, but also due to the Pharisaical embracing of the Talmud – the oral teachings. The Pharisees placed the Talmud on an equal standing with the Torah – the written law. Those who lived in and around Qumran practiced and followed the words of the Torah to the letter but did not believe the oral teachings carried any authority.

This community also expressed their piety and devotion through a purification ritual of baptism by immersion. As John grew older, he questioned whether this practice was wrongly focused on the outward act instead of the inward change it should reflect. He believed baptism was a demonstrative testimony of a heart of repentance before God, and not merely a pious ritual. That conviction would shape his ministry in the coming years.

When John was in his mid to late twenties, he left the community and traveled from place to place as an itinerant preacher on both sides of the Jordan River. From the time he was old enough to understand, his parents had told him what the angel Gabriel had announced about his birth. John knew he was to be a voice shouting in the wilderness, preparing the way for the Lord's coming. The spirit of God and the

power of Elijah were upon him, and God clearly showed him that now
was the time.

John soon earned the reputation as a man who feared God and not
men. People from all over Judea and the Jordan valley began to come
hear him preach and watch him baptize. It didn't take long for the
Pharisees and Sadducees to hear about his ministry as well. They were
always attuned to anything – or anyone – that became popular among
the citizens. And they were always careful to guard against anything
that could threaten their power over the people.

One day several religious leaders came to him when he was baptizing
– and they asked to be baptized, too. But John knew their motives. He
knew they wanted to do this simply as a pious ritual before men, so he
denounced them, saying: *"You brood of snakes! Who warned you to flee the
coming wrath? Prove by the way you live that you have repented of your sins
and turned to God. Don't just say to each other, 'We're safe, for we are descen-
dants of Abraham.' That means nothing, for I tell you, God can create children
of Abraham from these very stones…. I baptize with water those who repent of
their sins and turn to God. But someone is coming soon who is greater than I
am…. He is ready to separate the chaff from the wheat with His winnowing
fork. Then He will clean up the threshing area, gathering the wheat into His
barn but burning the chaff with never-ending fire."*[2]

The religious leaders knew they were the chaff to which he was referring. They had come that day to be recognized for their piety by the
people but instead had been unmasked for who they truly were. They
quickly retreated to plot among themselves how they would deal with
this threat to their power.

His boldness was what had attracted Simon and me to seek out John.
We came upon John that day on the west side of the Jordan River,

across the river from Bethany, just north of the Dead Sea. We stood on the bank of the river, watching, listening, and marveling as he preached.

In response to his call to the people to repent, the crowd asked, *"What should we do?"*

And he replied, *"If you have two shirts, give one to the poor. If you have food, share it with those who are hungry."* Even corrupt tax collectors came to be baptized and asked, *"Teacher, what should we do?"* He replied, *"Collect no more taxes than the government requires."* Some of the soldiers asked, *"What should we do?"* To them he replied, *"Don't extort money or make false accusations. And be content with your pay."*[3]

It seemed no one was beyond being saved, except those who thought they had no need to be saved – like the religious leaders. Everyone in the crowd, including Simon and me, was hoping and expecting the Messiah to come soon, and they were eager to know whether John might be the Messiah. But he said to them, *"I baptize you with water; but someone is coming soon who is greater than I am – so much greater that I'm not even worthy to be His slave and untie the straps of His sandals. He will baptize you with the Holy Spirit and with fire."*[4]

He also very publicly criticized Herod Antipas for marrying his niece Herodias, who was also the wife of his half brother, Herod II. Both Antipas and Herodias had divorced their spouses in order to be married to one another. John was denouncing it as an adulterous and incestuous affair. Simon and I both recognized here was a man who spoke truth. He was not fearful of the Romans, the Herodians or the religious leaders. He spoke plainly and did not seek fame or riches. He talked of the Messiah who would come after him. John was a man whom we could follow. But more importantly, he was a man who sought after and followed God. And we determined in our hearts that day we, too, would follow God and would seek to learn more about Him as disciples of this baptizer.

I knew, on that day, God had a purpose for saving my life at the pass. He had brought me to this place. So, I repented of my sin before Him. I repented of my anger. I repented of my hatred and my unforgiveness. I repented of my murderous intent. I repented of having turned my heart from God and hardened my heart toward God. I confessed to God my desire to follow Him with my whole heart. On that day, the forgiveness of God poured over me, and I was baptized by John the Baptizer – and from that day forward I would never look back.

* * *

7

The following day John was standing with two of his disciples. As Jesus walked by, John looked at Him and declared, "Look! There is the Lamb of God!" When John's disciples heard this, they followed Jesus.[1]

* * *

In the weeks and months that followed, I grew in my understanding of the Scriptures that told of the coming Messiah and His coming judgment. John's message to the growing crowds was simple – repent and be saved! The Messiah is coming! He will judge all people. And those who are not His will be cast away.

"Even now the ax of God's judgment is poised, ready to sever the roots of the trees. Yes, every tree that does not produce good fruit will be chopped down and thrown into the fire."[2]

Whenever I thought about the promised Messiah, my thoughts returned to that night thirty years earlier and that little baby in the stable. The angel had said the baby was the Messiah – but no one else seemed to know about the baby. My father, the other shepherds, and I had believed the words to be true. But there had been no evidence since then.

John was the man whom everyone else thought was the Messiah. But he continued to assure everyone he was not the One. What had happened to that baby boy? Had he been murdered by Herod's soldiers just like my little brother Eliezer? Had Herod foiled God's plan by killing the Messiah while he was still just a toddler? Should I tell John and the others what I saw that night long ago? Should I tell them it is possible the Messiah was killed as a little boy?

The number of John's disciples was continually increasing. When Simon and I arrived, there were two fishermen from Galilee who had made a point to befriend us. Their names were Andrew and John, and they had originally come from the town of Bethsaida. Apparently, their families were partners in a fishing enterprise on the Sea of Galilee. Both of these men had elder brothers who were maintaining their family fishing enterprise. That caused me to think of my brother, Jacob, and how much I appreciated the way he was caring for our family's flock.

Andrew was the one who first introduced us to John the Baptizer, and we quickly observed he was continually bringing people to meet him. John the fisherman was apparently well respected among everyone as well. The religious leaders who came to see and hear what the baptizer was preaching often knew John the fisherman, too, and they would engage him in conversation. The fisherman seemed to be approachable by people from all walks of life.

There were twenty men who were currently following John as his disciples. We were a diverse group of zealots, shepherds, religious scholars, fishermen, tax collectors, carpenters, and tradesmen. We came from near and far, and from all walks of life. But what we had in common was a hunger to know more of God, to walk before Him righteously, and to see His promised Messiah. We all looked forward to that day!

One day, as the crowds were being baptized, a Man came walking toward John. He was dressed as a humble carpenter. As He approached, the Spirit of God revealed to John the One coming toward him was the Lamb of God who would take away the sins of the world. Jesus said to him, "I have come to be baptized." But John tried to talk Him out of it by saying, *"I am the one who needs to be baptized by You. Why are You coming to me?"* Jesus replied, *"It should be done, for we must carry out all that God requires."*[3]

So, the two entered the river, and John baptized Jesus. As He came up out of the water, the heavens opened, and the Holy Spirit descended on Him like a dove. And John heard a voice from heaven say, *"You are My dearly loved Son, and You bring Me great joy."*[4]

I was watching from the shore. I had not heard the exchange between the two men before they entered the river, and I had not heard the voice from heaven. But I knew something was different about this Man. There was a radiance about Him I had only ever witnessed once before – and it was a radiance that originated from within.

At that moment, as the Man approached, His eyes locked with mine. I had looked into those eyes before — they were inviting and gentle. They were eyes that welcomed me in and immediately made me feel safe. And they were eyes that peered into my very soul. The Man didn't stop but continued to walk on by. He walked with purpose, as if

He were on a mission. But as He passed me, He smiled and said, "Shimon, you will see Me again."

Could it be? Was this Man the baby who had lain in that manger? Was He the Messiah? Was He the One whom the angel had announced? Was He the One for whom my soul had yearned ever since? Even when my heart had turned cold toward God, there was always a burning ember of hope for this One. And He knew my name! I didn't yet know His name, but I knew who He was. My heart had leapt – and it still was leaping. As I watched Him walk away into the Judean wilderness, the words kept echoing in my heart – this Man ... the Messiah – has promised that I, Shimon the shepherd – who once was a zealot – would see Him again.

Six weeks passed, and each day I looked toward the wilderness awaiting His return. I had asked John about Him, and all he would say was, *"He is the Lamb of God. I have been baptizing with water so that He might be revealed to Israel."*[(5)] As the days passed, John continued to preach, baptize, and prepare the road for Him.

None of us, including John, had any idea what Jesus was doing during those six weeks. I would later learn the Father had directed Him to go out into the wilderness to be tempted by Satan. For forty days and forty nights Jesus ate nothing, and after that time had passed Satan tempted Him. Satan couldn't touch Him as the Son of God but, perhaps as the Son of Man, Jesus would be unable to resist him. However, at every turn, Jesus defeated the tempter. So, Satan went away and awaited his next opportunity. The angels then came and ministered to Jesus.

John the Baptizer was standing that day with the two fishermen – Andrew and John – when Jesus approached from the wilderness. As

Jesus walked by, the baptizer looked at Him and declared, *"Look! There is the Lamb of God!"*[(6)] I also had seen this Man approaching from the wilderness, and was standing nearby when John made his declaration. I knew I couldn't stay where I was any longer. I had an overwhelming compulsion to follow this Man. Without stopping to say anything to anyone, I joined Andrew and John and we went after Him.

We had walked only a few steps when the Master turned around and saw us following Him. He looked at each one of us with that deep, penetrating look I had experienced just a few weeks earlier. It was as if He were looking into our souls. He asked, "What do you want?" In unison we responded, *"Rabbi, where are You staying?"*[(7)] Then with that same knowing smile He had given me a few weeks earlier, He replied, *"Come and see."*[(8)] It was four o'clock in the afternoon when we went with Him to the place where He was staying in Bethany. We remained with Him for the rest of the day.

We soon learned His name was Jesus of Nazareth, and He began to teach us by saying, *"You search the Scriptures because you think they give you eternal life. But the Scriptures point to Me! If you truly believe Moses, you will believe Me, because he wrote about Me."*[(9)] Moses wrote:

"The Lord your God will raise up for you a prophet like me from among your fellow Israelites. You must listen to Him. For this is what you yourselves requested of the Lord your God when you were assembled at Mount Sinai. You said, 'Don't let us hear the voice of the Lord our God anymore or see this blazing fire, for we will die.' Then the Lord said to me, 'What they have said is right. I will raise up a prophet like you from among their fellow Israelites. I will put My words in His mouth, and He will tell the people everything I command Him."[(10)]

Jesus then went on to teach us from the writings of the prophets explaining what the Scriptures meant. He spoke with an authority unlike anything we had heard. The hours passed quickly as He continued to explain one truth after another. Our hearts became strangely warm, and we knew He was the One about whom the prophets had written.

As the hour drew late, we left so He could get some rest. Andrew and John decided to travel to Bethsaida to tell their brothers all they had learned from Jesus. They didn't want to waste any time before letting their families know the Messiah had come! I wanted to return to my home to tell my family as well, but I decided to remain there and see if I could spend more time with Him in the morning.

Early the next morning, before the sun had risen, I saw Jesus stirring. I followed Him at a distance to see where He was going. He stopped and entered into a garden. I could not hear all of what Jesus was saying, but it was clear He was praying in a way that was more intimate than I had ever heard. It was more like a conversation: *Father, the time has come. Glorify Your Son so He can give glory back to You.*[11]

It reminded me of the late night or early morning conversations my father and I used to have in the fields while we tended the sheep. Oh, how I missed those conversations! Nothing and no one could ever replace those special times. As I watched and faintly heard some of what Jesus was saying, I knew He was having that kind of conversation with His Father. And I began to hunger to have that kind of conversation with God as well.

Several hours passed before Jesus came out of the garden. When He did, He walked straight over to me and invited me to join Him as He traveled to Bethsaida. I did not give His invitation a second thought. I immediately began to walk with Jesus.

. . .

I could tell He knew there was something I wanted to ask Him — and He was patiently waiting for me to do so.

"You were the baby in the stable that night, weren't You?" I asked.

Right after I asked the question, I felt foolish. How could a little baby possibly have known or how could a grown man remember something from when He was a baby? And yet, Jesus had known my name when He first saw me the day He was baptized.

Jesus turned to answer me with that same knowing smile I had now seen twice before. "Yes, I was. And you were there," He replied.

"How could you possibly remember that?" I asked.

"I remember everything about that night," Jesus explained. "I remember you and the other shepherds entering the stable and then you knelt and worshipped Me. And I know you returned the next morning, but we were gone. You were one of the few people who welcomed Me at My birth. And your worship was true and pure. I have anticipated this day when we would again see one another, and the Father has ordained for that time to be now."

His answer opened a dam of pent-up questions – so out they poured. I asked Jesus about where He and His family had gone, where He had grown up, and where He had been all these years. I told Him I feared He had been murdered like my own baby brother and my father.

Jesus wept with me over the suffering of my father and brother, our entire family, and all of the families who had suffered that day. He wept over the suffering that had been brought about by sin. He wept over the fact that what the Father had intended as a celebration of joy and life, Satan had attempted to overshadow with pain and death. He wept over the reality that death and despair had never been a part of the Father's plan. And though the world often blamed God for it, it was not of His making. That's why the Father had now sent His Son.

Jesus assured me my father was a righteous man who had sought after God and trusted by faith in the promised Messiah. He assured me that one day I would see my father and brother again – they were not lost to me forever. Jesus then explained that Herod had attempted to kill Him when he ordered the massacre of the little boys. Herod had feared the Messiah would take away his power and position, as well as that of his sons, and out of a jealous rage sought to kill Him. But an angel had come to Jesus' earthly father, Joseph, and told him to take his family into Egypt. There they had waited until their return to Nazareth.

Jesus explained that Joseph was a carpenter and had taught Him the trade, just like my father had taught me how to be a shepherd. And Jesus explained that Joseph had died some years ago. That meant we had something in common – we were both the eldest sons of our widowed mothers. Then Jesus explained how He must now be about His heavenly Father's business – the purpose for which He was born.

It took us three days to reach Bethsaida and along the way Jesus continued to teach me from the Scriptures. I grew, not only in knowledge and understanding, but also in my love and awe for Jesus. I began to have a deep peace and joy I had not felt since prior to the day of the massacre. I once thought I would carry the pain of the deaths of my father and brother with me forever. And though I would always miss them and be sad their lives were cut short, Jesus gave me hope, healed my heart, and took away the pain.

. . .

When we arrived in Bethsaida, Andrew brought his older brother Simon to meet Jesus. The two brothers were very different. Andrew had a gentle nature and was soft spoken. Simon, on the other hand, was brash and outspoken. They both were large framed and in good physical condition from their labors on the sea. But Simon almost seemed fearless. He was the natural leader of the two. It said a lot about Andrew's affection for his brother that the first person he wanted to introduce to Jesus was Simon.

As they met, Jesus looked intently at Simon – but, for that matter, Jesus looked intently at everyone. It was as if Jesus could gaze into your very soul and know everything you had ever done, and everything you would ever do. He looked at you like He was seeing you for who and what you would become.

He saw Simon that way, and He said, *"I will no longer call you Simon for you will be called Peter, which means 'a rock'"*.[12] He saw Simon – or rather, Peter – in a way even Peter could not see himself. And Peter, perhaps for the first time in his life, was struck silent. All he could do was marvel at this man Jesus, whom John the Baptizer had told Andrew was the Messiah.

Next Andrew took Jesus to meet Philip. Philip was a fisherman with a disarming smile. He, Andrew, and Peter were longtime friends and fishing companions, having grown up together in Bethsaida. Jesus told Philip to *"come and follow Me."*[13] And to his credit, Philip never looked back. As a matter of fact, he left to go find his friend Bartholomew, who was also called Nathanael. He too was a fisherman. He was originally from the village of Cana, but he was now living in Bethsaida to carry out his trade.

. . .

Bartholomew was a jester. He often found humor in most situations. As Philip told him, "Andrew and I *have found the very person Moses and the prophets wrote about! His name is Jesus, the son of Joseph from Nazareth.*" Nathanael immediately exclaimed, "*Can anything good come from Nazareth?*" To which Philip replied. "Don't believe me, *come and see for yourself!*"[(14)]

As they approached, Jesus again looked intently at Bartholomew, and called out to him, "*Now here is a genuine son of Israel* – a man who says what he thinks."

Bartholomew replied by asking, "*How do you know about me?*"

Jesus explained that He had seen him standing under a fig tree before Philip had gone to find him. But Jesus had been nowhere near. And Philip had not told Jesus he was going to get Bartholomew. But somehow Jesus knew.

Immediately, Bartholomew exclaimed, "*Teacher, You are the Son of God – the King of Israel!*"

To which Jesus replied, "*Do you believe this simply because I told you I had seen you under the fig tree?* You will all see much more than this! Come follow Me."[(15)]

Jesus announced that He needed to go to Cana. Peter needed to return to Capernaum to attend to his work, but the rest of us – Andrew, John, Philip, Bartholomew, and I – accompanied Jesus on His one-day journey to Cana. Along the way, He answered our questions and taught us from the Scriptures. We marveled with every step we took.

· · ·

When we arrived in Cana, we came upon a wedding celebration. Jesus' mother was there. Thirty years had passed since I had seen the young mother in the stable. Mary still had that tender smile combined with a natural beauty and grace that had only improved with age. Jesus explained to His mother that I had been the young boy with the other shepherds who visited that night in the stable. She thought back to that night and smiled, reflecting on all that had passed since. I was again reminded that I needed to return to Bethlehem to tell my own mother and family about Jesus.

But before I could leave, Jesus invited me to remain with Him for the wedding celebration. The bride was a relative of Mary's, so the family had invited Jesus' companions to join in the celebration as well. Not wanting to offend the hosts for the kind invitation – and wanting the opportunity to spend more time with Jesus – the other men and I remained.

Late in the afternoon, as the festivities continued, Mary quietly approached Jesus to tell Him that the hosts had run out of wine. Apparently other guests had also brought uninvited friends with them, so there were many more guests than the hosts had expected! Running out of food or drink was a social disgrace that would cause great embarrassment to the hosts. Mary wanted them to avoid humiliation.

But I thought it was curious she told Jesus like she expected Him to do something about it. What could He do? It's not like Jesus had any wine with Him. And their family did not live in Cana, so Jesus could not arrange to have some brought from their home.

Jesus' reply to His mother was even more curious – "*Dear woman, that's not our problem. My time has not yet come."*[16] What did He mean by "His time had not yet come"? But still, Mary told the servants to do whatever He told them to do. Obviously, she believed Jesus would do something about it.

As I and the other men with Him watched, Jesus instructed the servants to fill all six of the nearby stone jars guests had used when they arrived for ceremonial washing. The servants proceeded to refill them with water. I couldn't help but think, "But the wedding host doesn't need more water, He needs more wine. And those stone jars are an unlikely place to find it. What is Jesus doing?"

Then Jesus told the servants to dip out some of the water from one of the jars and take it to the master of ceremonies. To their credit, the servants never questioned Jesus. I, along with the others, watched in amazement. What will the master of ceremonies do when he tastes the water the servant has brought to him? Then we heard the master of ceremonies exclaim to the bridegroom, *"A host always serves the best wine at the first ... but you have kept the best until now!"*[17]

No one at the celebration knew what Jesus had done – except Mary, the servants, and those of us who had attended with Him. We had just seen Jesus do the miraculous. It wouldn't be the last time – and He would do far greater!

When the celebration concluded, Jesus returned with His mother and family to their home in Capernaum. I told Jesus and the other men goodbye and set out for Bethlehem. But we would all be back together again soon. As I made my way home to my mother and family, Mary's words kept echoing in my mind ... *"Do whatever He tells you!"*[18]

* * *

8

It was nearly time for the Jewish Passover celebration, so Jesus went to Jerusalem. In the Temple area He saw merchants selling cattle, sheep, and doves for sacrifices; He also saw dealers at tables exchanging foreign money.[1]

* * *

Life had carried on after my departure from home. My brother, Jacob, had found a wife and married, and they now had two young sons, ages three and nine months. The family's sheep trade continued to prosper under Jacob's guidance, as I knew it would. It now more than provided the means necessary for the family to live comfortably. Hannah and her husband also lived there in the village, and they had three children – two girls and a boy. Her husband worked with Jacob in the family sheep business.

The five grandchildren had brought renewed life to my mother. Rachel had recently married a carpenter – an honest and hardworking man who had come to the village from Hebron. She delayed getting married so she could care for our mother. But since Jacob had married, he and his wife had stepped into that role. Rachel then felt a release to marry – and God, in His perfect timing, had brought this carpenter into her life.

It had been three years since I had last seen my family. I had returned home after my narrow escape from death outside of Caesarea. But that visit had been brief. My friend Simon had been traveling with me, and we had both been intent on our quest to seek out John the Baptizer. My mother had seen then – and spoken plainly to me – that I was still consumed with seeking revenge for the injustice and tragedy of my father's and brother's deaths.

Though nearly twenty-five years had passed, she could see then that I was nowhere closer to finding peace. She could see that my experiences with the other zealots in Galilee had only hardened my heart even more and left me with more uncertainty. She had prayed that this "John the Baptizer" could help me find the answers and peace I was seeking.

But this time when I returned, my mother saw a different man. There was a tenderness and a peace in my demeanor and in my conversation she had not seen since the massacres – and maybe, she had never seen in me at all. I told them all about Jesus. I told them how John the Baptizer had told us that Jesus was the Messiah who had been promised. I told them about how Jesus had been the baby in the stable that night long ago. I told them how Jesus had known my name and remembered that our father, the other shepherds, and I had come to worship Him as a newborn baby that night. I told them about the miracle we had witnessed Jesus perform at the wedding celebration in Cana. But most importantly, I told them how Jesus had healed my heart and taken away my pain.

. . .

"The Baptizer says, *'He is the Lamb of God who takes away the sin of the world!'*[(2)] He teaches from Scripture with a clarity and authority the likes of which I have never before witnessed," I told them. "And my life has been transformed by Him! Where I had hatred, He replaced it with love. Where I had bitterness, He replaced it with joy. Where I had anger, He replaced it with peace."

Over the next several months, I continued to recount to my family all that Jesus had taught me. And they marveled at the difference they saw in my life. I made it clear that I was only back for a visit. I intended to be one of Jesus' followers. But in the meantime, while I was home, I helped my brother and brother-in-law shepherd the flock and savored the days back together with my mother and the rest of my family. I was enjoying being an uncle to my young nephews and nieces. There was laughter again in our home, as well as in my heart.

The months passed quickly, and soon it was springtime. It was time to deliver the sheep to the merchants in the Temple. I knew Jesus would be traveling to the Temple for the Passover, so I planned to help Jacob lead the sheep to Jerusalem. I would then remain in Jerusalem and follow Jesus wherever He went from there. To everyone's surprise, our mother announced her plans to travel with us to Jerusalem as well. She wanted to see and hear "this Jesus" for herself. She wanted to meet the One who had so greatly changed her son.

The day arrived and we made our journey to Jerusalem. As we entered the city through the Sheep Gate, we immediately began to sense a commotion near the Temple. This season was always busy in Jerusalem. Jews made their pilgrimage from all over – near and far – to come to the Temple for Passover, so the city was always filled with visitors of many languages.

. . .

We had always led our sheep to the huge colonnaded structure called the Royal Stoa, which was just outside of the holy area that was considered the Temple Mount by the priests. The stoa served as the marketplace for the buying and selling of the sacrificial animals. Occasionally, when there wasn't sufficient space in the stoa for all of the animals, some would be taken to other pavilions or pens outside of the Temple walls.

The outer part of the holy area was called the Court of the Gentiles. It was aptly named, because non-Jews could proceed no further into the Temple than this outer court. It was this area where Gentile pilgrims seeking to know more about Judaism could come to ask questions and learn. In recent years, certain priests and merchants had received permission from the High Priest Annas to also set up stalls and tables inside this holy area in the Court of the Gentiles.

Today, however, it seemed someone was driving the animals out of the Court of the Gentiles, back into the stoa. I went ahead and approached the Court of the Gentiles to see what was happening, while Jacob and my mother remained with the sheep at the entry to the stoa. When I entered the court of the Gentiles, I immediately saw Jesus.

He had a whip made of rope in His hand and was chasing the priests and the merchants out of the Court, driving their animals with them and turning over the tables and their stalls. I could hear Jesus shouting to the priests, *"Get these things out of here. Stop turning My Father's house into a marketplace!"* [3]

The priests retorted, "What are You doing? Who gave You authority to do this? If Your authority comes from God, then show us a miraculous sign to prove it!"

. . .

Jesus replied, *"All right. Destroy this Temple, and in three days I will raise it up."*

"What!" they exclaimed. *"It has taken forty-six years to build this Temple, and You can rebuild it in three days?"* [4]

Jesus did not respond, He simply stood there and stared. One by one the priests cleared the area and removed everything to the stoa. Jesus continued to watch them. I was amazed that though He showed a righteous indignation and displeasure toward the priests as He drove them away, He was never "out-of-control" with anger. Jesus had demonstrated He was very much in control. Even His anger was different from anything I had ever witnessed. And I pondered the statement Jesus had made – what did He mean when He said, *"Destroy this Temple, and in three days I will raise it up"*? [4]

After the priests cleared the area, Jesus stayed in the Court of the Gentiles and began to teach those gathered around Him from the Scriptures. The people marveled, and many turned their attention to Him, not only because of His teaching, but also because of the authority with which He had driven the merchants from the court.

As the turmoil calmed down, I saw Andrew, John, and several of the other men who had chosen to follow Jesus. I was also pleased to see my fellow zealot, Simon, was now among them. I walked over to greet these good friends. Andrew invited me to join them for their Passover meal, and to bring my mother and brother. I thanked Andrew for the invitation and went off to find Jacob and my mother.

When I caught up with them at the stoa, I found Jacob in a foul temper. The merchants had all become angry over what Jesus had done. His actions, they said, had caused their trade to suffer, which would cause their prices to drop. As a result, what they were willing to pay shepherds like Jacob for their sheep must also be reduced. Jacob had been faced with the choice of leading his sheep back home or selling them to the merchants for a greatly reduced price.

He needed the money to provide for his family through the summer months, so he was left with little choice but to accept the lower offer. This had not been a profitable trip for Jacob. He and his family would be able to get by until the Festival of the Tabernacles in the fall, but with little leftover. All because of "my friend" Jesus. If "this Jesus" was really the Messiah, He wasn't doing anything to make Jacob's life better. He had just made it worse!

When I shared the invitation to join Jesus and His followers for their Passover meal, Jacob declined. As much as I tried to convince him to the contrary, Jacob felt Jesus was responsible for this financial loss and had no interest in spending time with Him. He would head back home. However, my mother decided she would remain with me and join the group for the Passover meal.

After I located overnight lodgings for my mother and me, we joined Jesus and His followers at the Temple. The crowd around Jesus had continued to grow as He taught:

"Turn from your sins and turn to God, because the Kingdom of Heaven is near. God blesses those who are poor and realize their need for Him, for the Kingdom of Heaven is theirs. God blesses those who mourn, for they will be comforted. God blesses those who are humble, for they will inherit the whole earth. God blesses those who hunger and thirst for justice, for they will be satisfied. God blesses those who are merciful, for they will be shown mercy. God blesses those whose hearts are pure, for they will see God. God blesses those who work for peace, for they will be called the children of God. God

blesses those who are persecuted for doing right, for the Kingdom of Heaven is theirs. God blesses you when people mock you and persecute you and lie about you and say all sorts of evil things against you because you are My followers. Be happy about it! Be very glad! For a great reward awaits you in heaven. And remember, the ancient prophets were persecuted in the same way. You have heard the law that says, 'Love your neighbor and hate your enemy.' But I say, love your enemies! Pray for those who persecute you! In that way, you will be acting as true children of your Father in heaven. For He gives His sunlight to both the evil and the good, and He sends rain on the just and the unjust alike. If you love only those who love you, what reward is there for that? Even corrupt tax collectors do that much. If you are kind only to your friends, how are you different from anyone else? Even pagans do that. But you are to be perfect, even as your Father in heaven is perfect." [5]

Darkness was setting in, so Jesus released the crowd to go to their homes or their lodgings to partake in their Passover meal, and He and His followers did the same.

When we arrived at the room where the meal would take place, my mother immediately joined the other two women who were busily working to prepare the meal. My mother quickly learned that one of the women was Salome. She was the mother of John, the fisherman. Her husband, Zebedee, had given her leave to travel with her son John, while her older son James remained with Zebedee to keep their fishing enterprise going.

Zebedee had provided her with the funds to help support Jesus and the others in their travels and the cost of preparing this meal. Salome was short of stature but long on energy. She was a "take-charge" woman, and she was obviously leading in the preparations that evening.

. . .

The other woman's name was Mary. As it turned out, she was Jesus' aunt. Her husband was a man by the name of Clopas, who was the younger brother of Joseph, the earthly father of Jesus. Clopas and his sons were carpenters from the village of Nazareth, just like Joseph and Jesus. Two of his sons – James and Thaddeus – were also part of the group following Jesus. Clopas, like Zebedee, was helping to financially support their travels and had remained in Nazareth to carry on his trade. Mary was younger than Salome, so out of respect, she had graciously allowed Salome to take charge of their efforts.

My mother, as the unmarried widow, was younger than Salome, but older than Mary. She quickly stepped in to assist the other two women in whatever way she could with the preparation and serving of the meal. The meal consisted of roast lamb with bitter herbs and bread made without yeast, just like the meal eaten in the homes on that first night of Passover in Egypt over 1,500 years earlier. After the meal was served, while the men continued to recline around one table, and the women were eating at another, Jesus began to teach.

He reminded us of that night long ago when the lamb was sacrificed so its shed blood could enable the firstborn son of that household to escape death. And it was a reminder that as a result, the Jews had been set free from the bondage of slavery. But the meal was also a reminder of the promise that was still to come – the promise of the One whose blood would be shed to set them free of the bondage of sin. He quoted the prophet Isaiah:

"But He was pierced for our rebellion, crushed for our sins. He was beaten so we could be whole. He was whipped so we could be healed. All of us, like sheep, have strayed away. We have left God's paths to follow our own. Yet the Lord laid on Him the sins of us all."[6]

Then He went on to tell us:

"And as Moses lifted up the bronze snake on a pole in the wilderness, so the Son of Man must be lifted up, so that everyone who believes in Him will have eternal life. For this is how God loved the world: He gave His one and only Son, so that everyone who believes in Him will not perish but have eternal life. God sent His Son into the world not to judge the world, but to save the world through Him. There is no judgment against anyone who believes in Him. But anyone who does not believe in Him has already been judged for not believing in God's one and only Son. And the judgment is based on this fact: God's light came into the world, but people loved the darkness more than the light, for their actions were evil. All who do evil hate the light and refuse to go near it for fear their sins will be exposed. But those who do what is right come to the light so others can see that they are doing what God wants." [7]

As His followers in the room listened, we heard but didn't fully understand all Jesus was saying. What we did know was that our hearts affirmed that Jesus was speaking truth. And we knew we must continue to follow Him.

After the Passover, Jesus and His other followers left Jerusalem and traveled a short distance toward Jericho into the Judean countryside. There Jesus preached and His disciples baptized those who came. I accompanied my mother back to Bethlehem. As we walked, we discussed what we had heard from Jesus.

"Didn't our hearts feel strangely warm as He taught?" we asked each other. "He truly is the Lamb of God," mother said.

She believed in Him and knew that from that point forward, she would follow Him. For now, she needed to return to her home to bear witness of Jesus to her daughters, her daughter-in-law, her sons-in-law and Jacob. Jacob's heart had become hardened by the events at the Temple, but she knew God could soften it. He had already changed the hard heart of her eldest son!

I remained in Bethlehem for only two days, then I departed to rejoin Jesus and His followers near Jericho. News soon reached those near Jericho that John the Baptizer was baptizing in the Jordan River at Aenon, about thirty miles north of where Jesus and His disciples were.

We heard news that John's disciples went to him and complained. *"Teacher, the Man you ... identified as the Messiah is also baptizing people. And everybody is going to Him instead of coming to us."*

To which John replied, *"No one can receive anything unless God gives it from heaven. You know how plainly I have told you that I am not the Messiah. I am only here to prepare the way for Him. It is the bridegroom who marries the bride, and the bridegroom's friend is simply glad to stand with him and hear his vows. Therefore, I am filled with joy at His success. He must become greater and greater, and I must become less and less. For He is sent by God. He speaks God's words, for God gives Him the Spirit without limit. The Father loves His Son and has put everything into His hands. And anyone who believes in Him has eternal life."* [8]

John continued to prepare the way and bear witness to Jesus. And all of us knew we must do the same – follow Him and bear witness.

* * *

9

The woman said, "I know the Messiah is coming—the one who is called Christ. When He comes, He will explain everything to us." Then Jesus told her, "I am the Messiah!"[1]

E ach day the crowds grew as more and more people came to hear Jesus teach. He had chosen not to baptize the people Himself, but rather to have some of His followers do so. Jesus soon made a distinction among His followers, eventually selecting twelve to be part of an inner circle known as His apostles. On this day, Jesus chose the following to baptize those who were coming: the four fishermen, John, Andrew, Philip, and Bartholomew; the two carpenters who were the sons of Clopas, James and Thaddeus; and the zealot, Simon.

One day, Jesus received news that the Pharisees were saying He was baptizing and gathering more followers than John the Baptizer. Jesus knew the Pharisees were trying to incite a competition between Himself and John to divide the people. If the religious leaders could paint them as having competing ministries, they would discredit them both. Jesus would not allow that to happen, so He left Judea and returned to Capernaum in Galilee.

I knew there were three possible routes to Capernaum. One would be along the coast of the Mediterranean Sea, which would be a significantly longer journey. The second was to cross to the east side of the Jordan River and travel through Perea. The third possibility was to travel straight through Samaria.

The problem with this third option was that no self-respecting Orthodox Jew would travel through Samaria. When I was a boy my father had taught me there was a long-standing, deep-seated hatred between the Samaritans and the Jews that dated back several hundred years. As a result of the Assyrian captivity of the ten northern tribes of Israel in 722 B.C., the Jews of that region had intermarried with the Gentiles. Because of their mixed race, they were rejected by the Jews.

Because of this contention, the Samaritans established their own temple on Mount Gerizim, which only fanned the flames of prejudice. The hatred became so intense the Pharisees prayed that no Samaritan would be raised at the resurrection. As the centuries passed, the hatred and prejudice escalated on both sides. I learned at a young age if you wanted to insult someone, you would call that person a Samaritan.

Jesus surprised us all by announcing He "had" to travel through Samaria. It gave us all pause, but we knew He must have a reason. We had already come to realize Jesus never traveled anywhere by happenstance, and we would soon learn the Father had arranged for Him to have a divine encounter along the way.

. . .

After walking approximately twenty miles, we came to Jacob's well outside the Samaritan village of Sychar. All of us, including Jesus, were weary, and we needed food and refreshment. The well had been dug by the sons of Jacob over 1,800 years earlier. I had learned in Beth Sefer that after Jacob's brief reunion with his estranged brother Esau, he and his family had temporarily settled in this land, which was then called Canaan, near the city of Shechem. Jacob and his sons had been driving their animals hard through their travels, so they had dug this well soon after their arrival. Years later, this also had been the place where the Israelites buried the bones of Jacob's son, Joseph, after they settled in the Promised Land. The city of Shechem was now the Samaritan village of Sychar.

We arrived at the well at noon. Jesus decided to remain at the well and sent most of His followers into the village to find food. John and I stayed behind but stood at a distance so Jesus could be alone. A woman arrived at the well. We were surprised to see anyone there at this time of day. Typically, the women would come to the well early in the morning or late in the afternoon, so this was highly unusual.

As she approached the well to draw water, John and I watched as she eyed Jesus warily; she did not seem to pay much attention to us. When she began to draw from the well, Jesus said to her, *"Please give Me a drink."* [2]

The woman was surprised that a Jew would dare speak to her. *"You are a Jew,"* she said, *"and I am a Samaritan woman. Why are You asking me for a drink?"* [3]

Jesus answered, *"If you only knew the gift God has for you and who you are speaking to, you would ask Me, and I would give you living water."* [4]

· · ·

She looked at Jesus with great curiosity — and so did I. What was Jesus talking about?

The woman replied, *"But Sir, You don't have a rope or a bucket, and this well is very deep. Where would you get this living water? And besides, do You think You are greater than our ancestor Jacob, who gave us this well? How can You offer better water than he and his sons and his animals enjoyed?"* [5]

Jesus again replied, *"Anyone who drinks this water will soon become thirsty again. But those who drink the water I give will never be thirsty again. It becomes a fresh, bubbling spring within them, giving them eternal life."* [6]

As a shepherd, I had spent years looking for and leading my sheep to fresh water. I knew that left to their own devices, sheep could stand in the presence of water and still die of thirst. They needed to be led to drink. And as I watched and listened to Jesus, I realized He was leading this woman to drink from a spring that would never run out.

"Please Sir," the woman said, *"give me this water! Then I'll never be thirsty again, and I won't have to come to this well anymore."* [7]

But her tone made it obvious, even to me, that she did not understand what Jesus had said.

"Go get your husband," [8] Jesus said to her.

When she replied that she didn't have a husband, Jesus answered and said, *"You're right! You don't have a husband – for you have had five husbands, and you aren't even married to the man you are living with now."* (9)

But Jesus' tone was not condemning; it was obvious He knew her and her situation, but He did not belittle her. I knew exactly what it was like to have Jesus speak to you in that way. The Shepherd who was inviting her to drink His Living Water looked into her eyes and saw all she had ever been – and much more importantly, all that she would ever become.

He knew that she had come to the well at the noon hour to avoid the other women of the village. She was considered a woman of ill repute with whom none of the other village women would associate. They had scorned and belittled her. Her heart had been hurt so many times that it had become callous and hardened. She would no longer permit anyone to hurt her again. She avoided contact with other people – particularly other women – whenever possible.

"Sir, You must be a prophet," (10) she said. She could tell this Man was different – but still He was a Jew, so she asked, *"Why is it that you Jews insist that Jerusalem is the only place to worship, while we Samaritans claim it is here at Mount Gerizim, where our ancestors worshiped?"* (11)

To which Jesus replied, *"Woman, the time is coming when it will no longer matter whether you worship the Father on this mountain or in Jerusalem. Indeed, the time is here now – when true worshipers will worship the Father in spirit and in truth."* (12)

This time the woman looked into His eyes and said, *"I know the Messiah is coming – the One who is called Christ. When He comes, He will explain everything to us."* (13)

. . .

Then in response, Jesus said, *"I am He!"*[14]

But she had known that He was the Messiah, even before He said it. She had known it, just like I had known it, and just like my mother had known it. And immediately, without any thought for the water jar she had brought to the well, or the purpose for which she had come, she ran back to the village to tell everyone about the Man who *"told me everything I ever did!"*[15] The woman who had made it a practice to avoid everyone was now seeking out people to tell them about this Man. I knew exactly what that felt like!

As she was leaving, Jesus' other followers returned with the provisions they had purchased in the village. They were shocked to see that He had been talking to the Samaritan woman. Some of the men recognized her. They had passed her on the path when they were headed to the village. And being good Jews, they had known better than to talk to her. As a matter of fact, they had very carefully avoided her. So why had Jesus spoken to her? But none of them had the nerve to ask Him that question.

Instead, they urged Jesus to eat. He responded, *"I have a food that you know nothing about yet. My nourishment comes from doing the will of the Father who sent Me, and from finishing His work."*[16]

Then He went on to say, *"Wake up and look around. The fields are ripe for harvest. The harvesters are paid good wages, and the fruit they harvest is people brought to eternal life. What joy awaits the planter and the harvester! I am sending you to harvest where you didn't plant. Others have already done that work, and now you will get to gather the harvest."*[17]

. . .

And as Jesus said it, the disciples who had passed the woman on the path knew Jesus was rebuking and correcting them. They had missed the opportunity to gather the harvest. They had missed the opportunity to share the Good News of salvation. They had allowed their prejudice to stand in their way. And Jesus' words had pierced their hearts.

Soon, others from the village came to the well to see the One about whom the woman had told them. They begged Jesus to stay in their village. So, He agreed to do just that. Over the next two days, many more heard His teaching and His message of Living Water – and many believed. Jesus had found a village of unruly and disheveled sheep, and the Shepherd had led them to drink. They bore witness, *"We believe, not just because of what the woman told us, but because we have heard Him ourselves. Now we know that He is indeed the Savior of the world."*[18]

It was at that moment I and some of His other followers realized this was why Jesus "had" to travel through Samaria. I knew that every time I had led my sheep, I had led them with a purpose. I had led them to good grazing. I had led them to fresh water. I had led them to safe shelter. No portion of the trip was ever without purpose. And the same was true for Jesus. Every part of Jesus' journey had a purpose – the Father's purpose. That realization caused me to want to follow Him even more ... wherever He went!

At the end of the two days, we continued our journey into Galilee. As we passed through the village of Cana, Jesus was approached by an official of Herod's court, a man by the name of Chuza. Though he was short-statured, he conducted himself as one with royal authority. He enjoyed the trust of Herod and directed many as the manager of Herod's household. He was accustomed to giving a command and having it obeyed.

• • •

But today, he knew he was in no position to command. He was approaching Jesus as a beggar. He, and his wife Joanna, had a son who was extremely ill. The court physicians had told them the boy would soon die. The news of the miracles of healing Jesus had performed in Judea had already reached Galilee – even to the palace.

Chuza and Joanna had determined to take their son to this Miracle Healer. When they arrived in Capernaum, they learned Jesus had not yet returned home. He had been delayed in Samaria (of all places!) but was expected home within a matter of days. But Chuza knew his son did not have many days to live. So, he had set out for Cana in the hopes he could come upon Jesus along the way.

It was only one o'clock in the afternoon, but we had been traveling since early morning and were weary. Though Capernaum was our destination, it was still a full day's journey away. We would not be able to make it there by nightfall, and it was not considered safe for us to travel through the wilderness at night. Jesus had decided we would remain here and spend the night in Cana. But bear in mind, Jesus had another reason for staying in Cana that night and not traveling on to Capernaum. And that reason was about to unfold.

When Chuza approached Jesus, he begged Him to make haste and return with him that very hour to Capernaum to heal his son. We all could see the desperation in the father's eyes and hear it in his voice.

But instead of replying with compassion, Jesus directed a question to the crowd that was gathering around them: *"Will you never believe in Me unless you see miraculous signs and wonders?"* [19]

. . .

To which Chuza replied, *"Lord, please come now before my little boy dies."*[20]

Chuza's reply demonstrated two misunderstandings he had about Jesus; in reality, most of us gathered around Jesus had those same two misunderstandings. First, Chuza believed Jesus physically had to be in the presence of his son for his son to be healed. Second, he believed Jesus only had the power to heal and not to restore life.

Chuza, like the majority of the crowd, was looking at Jesus through the lens of his own understanding and not through the realization of who Jesus truly was. I, too, was only just beginning to see Jesus for who He truly was. At that moment, Jesus showed compassion on Chuza and told him, *"Go back to your son. He will live!"*[21]

I watched to see how the man would react. Would he continue to beg Jesus to return with him? Or would he attempt to use his position in Herod's court to command Jesus to come with him? But at that moment, Chuza demonstrated faith in who Jesus was, and in what He had said. Without any further hesitation, he turned and began his journey back to Capernaum.

After he walked away, Jesus turned to all of those standing around Him and commended Chuza for his faith. At that moment, I knew just as surely as I had seen Jesus transform water into wine in that very village, the boy had now been healed. Chuza had demonstrated the same faith by believing Jesus and going on his way that the servants had at the wedding feast by obeying Him without question.

The next day, while Chuza was still making his way to Capernaum, he was met by some of his servants bringing the good news that his son was well. He had been healed! After Chuza rejoiced in the news, he asked the servants when his son had begun to get better. *"Yesterday afternoon at one o'clock, his fever suddenly disappeared,"* [22] they replied. Before they had even answered, Chuza already knew that was the very moment Jesus had said, *"Your son will live."* [23]

On that day, Chuza believed in Jesus – not only for what He had done – but for who He was. When he told his wife Joanna, she too believed in Jesus – and so did their entire household. The next day, Chuza, his family, and his servants returned to Tiberias where he continued to perform his duties in the palace of Herod Antipas. God enabled him and his family to continue enjoying the favor of Herod and spend their days as witnesses to King Jesus among the household servants.

10

Then Jesus turned to the paralyzed man and said, "Stand up, take up your mat, and go on home, because you are healed!"[(1)]

* * *

A few days later, Jesus was preaching on the shore of the Sea of Galilee and the growing crowd began to press in on Him. There were two empty fishing boats at the water's edge. Simon Peter, Andrew, James, and John had fished throughout the previous night but hadn't caught any fish. They were now washing and mending their nets.

Andrew's older brother Simon, whom Jesus had renamed Peter, was a big man with the build and appearance of someone who had spent his life fishing the sea. He was a plain-spoken man without a hint of timidity in his demeanor. Peter was married, and he and his family lived in the village of Capernaum. He and Zebedee were partners in a fishing enterprise.

• • •

They had long ago determined they would be more successful together than apart. Zebedee was the older and the more levelheaded of the two. The two men's giftings complemented one another and God had blessed their efforts greatly. The two men, together with Peter's brother Andrew and Zebedee's sons, James and John, feared God and sought Him with their whole hearts.

Zebedee, Peter, and James never hesitated to release Andrew and John to go and follow John the Baptizer. And when the baptizer pointed Andrew and John to follow Jesus, the other three immediately supported their decision – not only with encouragement, but also with their finances. With Andrew and John's blessing, Zebedee and Peter hired two men to take their places working the nets.

As the crowd pressed in, Jesus asked Peter if he would push one of the boats offshore a little ways so Jesus could stand in it and address the crowd. Peter didn't hesitate and did exactly what Jesus asked. When Jesus was done speaking to the gathering, He turned to Peter and said, *"Now go out where it is deeper, and let down your nets to catch some fish."* [(2)]

Peter had been a fisherman all of his life. Jesus was a carpenter. There I stood as a shepherd listening to a carpenter tell a fisherman how to fish – and I couldn't help but smile. But then again, Jesus wasn't just any carpenter.

Peter replied, *"Master, we worked hard all night and didn't catch a thing. But at Your word, I'll let the nets down again."* [(3)]

As soon as the nets were in the water, the fish began practically jumping into the nets. Peter quickly called out to his partners to come out in the other boat and help him bring in the catch. Soon both boats were so full of fish they looked like they might sink. These men had grown up fishing on these waters and they had never experienced anything like this!

When Peter realized what had happened, he dropped to his knees before Jesus and cried out, *"Oh, Lord, please leave me, for I am a sinful man."* [(4)]

Peter had said it, but we all thought it. Even the fish of the sea obey His command!

And when they had brought their catch to shore, Jesus looked at Peter and James, and said, *"Do not fear! From now on you will be fishing for people!"* [(5)]

Immediately they knew they must leave their fishing boats to join their brothers as followers of Jesus. They never hesitated. And to Zebedee's credit, he never asked the men to consider what they were doing to him and the fate of their business partnership. He knew Jesus' call on their lives was also a call on his life to stay and maintain the business so they could go.

God would greatly bless Zebedee for his faithfulness to stay behind and financially provide for the ministry of Jesus and His disciples. Zebedee bid farewell to his sons, James and John, and his partners, Peter and Andrew, and even his wife Salome, as they and the others walked away to follow Jesus. It again reminded me of the price my brother Jacob was paying for me to follow Jesus.

Another man was in the crowd that day by the name of Judas Iscariot.

Judas came from the town of Kerioth, about ten miles south of Hebron in Judea. Like Simon and me, Judas had become a zealot. He, too, had become weary of living under the rule of Rome and their Herodian puppets, and he sought to be a part of the movement to cast off Roman oppression.

He was a clever man, perhaps too clever. He had joined the zealot group in Tiberias shortly before the failed raid at Caesarea. When he heard about its disastrous conclusion, he knew the current leadership of the zealot movement did not have the foresight or the leadership to defeat the tyranny of the Roman regime. He knew he needed to look elsewhere.

He had heard rumors of a baptizer at the Jordan River who was prophesying of the promised Messiah. After hearing John for himself, he was convinced he needed to seek out this Man called Jesus that John was talking about.

"If the baptizer is correct, then this is the Man I have been looking for," he thought to himself.

Judas had been told Jesus was in Aenon so he made his way there. Upon his arrival, he learned Jesus and His followers had recently departed for Galilee, so he departed with haste to catch up with Him. Judas had been standing on the shore as Jesus taught that day from the boat.

He sensed Jesus was unlike anyone he had ever seen or heard, as He spoke with such authority. Here was a Teacher! He had directed the fishermen to take their boats back out. The fishermen had obeyed without question. Here was a Leader of men! He had witnessed the miracle of the overwhelming catch, and he could not believe his eyes. Here was a Miracle Worker!

If the baptizer was right, here was a Man who could lead the Jewish people to overthrow the oppression of Rome. And if He was that Man, His closest followers would become leaders in His kingdom. Here was the Man whom Judas would follow!

Then and there, Judas made the decision to do whatever he needed to do in order to become one of Jesus' closest followers. As Jesus and His disciples began to walk along the shore, Judas joined the crowd.

In the days following, Judas looked for opportunities to make himself known to Jesus. He looked for ways to get close to Him and His closest followers. He knew in order to become a leader within this group, he must first be seen as a servant. So, he became the quintessential servant. He watched for a need to arise, then promptly went about meeting it. He quickly became known as one who could be relied upon if anything needed to be done.

Others in the group trusted him more than I did. I had met others like him when I was with the zealots. He struck me more as one seeking revolution than one seeking to be a fisher of men in a harvest of redemption. But others saw his willingness to serve. Even Peter, who was becoming the leader of the smaller group of apostles, was drawing Judas more into that inner circle.

I couldn't help but wonder if they were inviting a wolf into the sheep-fold – but I trusted that Jesus would know. He saw everything about everyone, so if Jesus wanted him to be one of His disciples, who was I to think anything to the contrary.

. . .

One day in a village near Galilee we came upon a man with an advanced case of leprosy, which was known as the "living death." Many believed that lepers were being punished by God for their sins. Those with the disease were considered to be unclean and couldn't come within six feet of another person. As a matter of fact, on a windy day they weren't permitted to be any closer than one hundred fifty feet.

The disfigurement of their bodies caused people to stay away. They were cast out of their homes and their villages to live solitary lives, or in some instances to live in community with other lepers – until they died or were somehow miraculously healed. Since lepers could not associate with others, they didn't work and had no way to provide for themselves. They depended on the kindness of family and the compassion of strangers. Sadly, many died of starvation rather than the disease itself. And leprosy was no respecter of persons or position. A diagnosis of leprosy immediately caused an individual to be swallowed into the abyss of hopelessness and desperation.

Such was the fate of a man named Simon, whom others called Lazarus. Lazarus and his sisters – one named Martha and a younger one named Mary – lived in Bethany. They lived comfortably thanks to the bountiful harvests of their family's vineyards. Dedicated servants maintained their business while the family enjoyed lives of ease in their large, well-appointed home in the heart of town.

But their charmed life was shattered one day when Lazarus was diagnosed by the priests with leprosy. He was immediately banished from town and went willingly to protect his sisters from the contagious disease. As the months passed, his condition deteriorated to the point he knew that death was near.

. . .

On this particular day, he saw a Man walking toward him surrounded by a large entourage. Lazarus had heard of a Man by the name of Jesus. He had heard this Man might be the promised Messiah and that He had the power to heal. Lazarus knew this was his only chance to get well.

So, he ran toward Jesus – not knowing that his healing was the reason Jesus had traveled there that day. I would soon realize every encounter we had on our journey was by the design of the Father and His Son.

As Lazarus approached Jesus, he bowed his face to the ground and begged to be healed, saying, *"Lord, if you are willing, You can heal me and make me clean."* [6]

Then Jesus did the unthinkable. He walked right up to him – not maintaining the six-foot barrier – and reached out and touched Lazarus! An audible gasp rippled through the crowd. What had Jesus done? He had now made Himself unclean! Why would Jesus do that?

Then Jesus said, in a voice loud enough for everyone to hear, *"I am willing. Be healed!"* [7]

Instantly, Lazarus' leprosy disappeared! I was standing just a few feet away and saw his skin miraculously transform in the blink of an eye. A hush fell over the crowd. I fell to my knees. I had seen Jesus perform miracles before, but I was overwhelmed by the sense we were standing on holy ground!

. . .

Jesus instructed Lazarus not to tell anyone what had happened. He told him, *"Go to the priest and let him examine you. Take the offering that is required in the law of Moses for those who have been healed of leprosy. And allow the priest to publicly declare that you have been cleansed."* [8]

There was another gasp as Lazarus reached out and embraced Jesus – and again as Jesus embraced him in return.

"After you have seen the priest, go and be restored to your sisters," Jesus told him. "They have prayed to the Father on your behalf. Tell them the Father has heard and answered their prayers. You and I will be together again soon, and you will see Me accomplish even greater things to the glory of the Father. Go and be declared clean, for what I have made clean can never again become unclean!"

Lazarus began his journey south to Bethany in order to tell his sisters about his miraculous healing. He also needed to arrange for the offerings he would need to go before the priest. Those of us following Jesus marveled at what we had witnessed.

As we continued our journey, we entered the nearby village, and Jesus, as usual, went straight to the synagogue to begin teaching. It seemed to me that every man from every village in all of Judea and Galilee was gathered in that place! Soon after Jesus began to teach, the people gathered around Him and there was no room to move. I decided to go up on the roof so I could get some air and still hear His teaching.

I was up there about thirty minutes when I was joined by a group of men carrying another man on a pallet. Apparently, the man was paralyzed, and his friends had traveled quite a distance to ask Jesus to heal him. When they arrived at the synagogue there was no way to get in because of the crowd. So, they had carried him to the roof.

In a few moments they began to remove some of the roof tiles. Initially no one seemed to notice. But as the opening grew larger everyone inside the synagogue began to look up – including Jesus. The men had attached ropes to the four corners of the pallet and were lowering their friend through the opening. Somehow the crowd parted as they lowered him to the ground right in front of Jesus.

As I watched these friends, I thought of the many times I had rescued sheep that had become stranded in the rocks. I would often need to make my way to the hill above where the sheep was stranded, and carefully climb down to the ledge. I would then tie a rope around the sheep's middle and lower it to another shepherd who was waiting below.

I couldn't help but think as these men lowered their friend, they were lowering him to the Shepherd – a Shepherd who could free him of all that bound him. I was struck by the compassion these men had for their friend and their confidence in Jesus to heal him.

As Jesus saw the faith of his friends, He said to the man, *"Young man, your sins are forgiven."* [9]

Immediately the Pharisees and religious leaders began to cackle like hens among themselves. *"Who does He think He is?"* they exclaimed. *"That's blasphemy! Only God can forgive sins!"* [10]

But Jesus looked at them and replied, *"Why do you question? Is it easier for Me to say, 'Your sins are forgiven,' or 'Stand up and walk'? So that you will know that I have authority to forgive sins, I now say to this man, stand up, pick up your mat, and go home!"* [(11)]

And immediately, the man jumped up, picked up his mat, and headed for home praising God!

As I watched the man's friends go to join him, I realized Jesus had not only touched the life of a paralytic that day, He had forever changed the lives of each one of those men.

As I looked down at Jesus through the roof opening, He smiled at me and His eyes seemed to say, "Another sheep has been rescued!" I realized the main reason Jesus had come to this village was to forgive the sins of that man and his friends – compelled by their faith. Once again, it confirmed to me that no action and no part of Jesus' journey was random. He had a purpose in it all!

When Jesus finished teaching, we left the village and passed a tax collector sitting in his collection booth on the side of the road. He was stationed there to collect taxes from anyone bringing goods to sell into the village, as well as from anyone who had made a purchase and was taking goods out of the village. He appeared to be having a very profitable day.

When we approached his booth, Jesus stopped directly in front of him, turned, and said, "Matthew, *follow Me and be My disciple!"* [(12)]

Some of His followers looked at one another and asked, "Doesn't Jesus know what this man does for a living? There isn't anyone lower than a tax collector! Why would Jesus invite him to be His follower?"

But they were even more surprised when Matthew immediately got up, left everything, and followed Jesus. Out of the corner of my eye I noticed an expression of disdain on Judas Iscariot's face. "What could be causing that reaction?" I wondered.

11

Then He walked over to the coffin and touched it, and the bearers
stopped. "Young man," He said, "I tell you, get up."[1]

* * *

Later that day, Jesus withdrew from us and went up onto a
mountain to pray. At daybreak the next morning, He returned
and called all of us together for an announcement. Though we were all
His disciples and followers, He had chosen twelve to be His apostles.
The group of twelve included:

The Fishermen
Simon, whom He named Peter
Andrew, the brother of Peter
James, the son of Zebedee
John, the brother of James
Philip
Bartholomew (also known as Nathanael)
Thomas

The Tax Collector
Matthew

The Carpenters
James ("the Less"), the son of Clopas
Thaddeus (also known as Judas), the brother of James

The Zealots
Simon
Judas Iscariot

Each man responded with an attitude of humility and meekness. That is, all except one. Judas Iscariot's countenance betrayed him as a smug look darted across his face as he tried to appear pious. As his look faded, I again reminded myself that Jesus knew what He was doing.

Judas had already demonstrated a fine attention to detail, so he was tasked with being the group's treasurer. I had wondered if that honor might go to Matthew, given his background, but Judas appeared to be pleased he had been chosen for that role. Watching over the treasury would be an important leadership role among this group, but it could become an even greater role when Jesus established His kingdom.

The crowd following Jesus continued to grow. On one particular day, Jesus decided to travel from Capernaum to Nain, about twenty-five miles away. We departed Capernaum at dawn and arrived at Nain late in the afternoon. As we approached the village, we encountered a large funeral procession headed for the burial ground. The funeral orator at the head of the procession was loudly proclaiming the good works of the deceased. Apparently, the deceased was the only son of his widowed mother whose name we later learned was Susanna.

· · ·

Overwrought with grief, she was walking immediately behind the orator surrounded by a group of mourning women. Her son's body was being carried behind on an open bier made of wicker wood. His face was uncovered, and his eyes were closed. His hands had been folded and carefully placed on his chest.

There were holes in the bier through which poles were inserted. The deceased man's friends and relatives, who were carrying the poles, walked barefoot so as not to lose their footing. Loud lamentations pierced the stillness; it was a tragic and hopeless scene.

My mind quickly raced back to the funeral procession for my father and baby brother. I could remember the cacophony of mourning as if it were yesterday. I remember my mother's unbearable grief. I remember my anger and hatred. But most of all, I remember the sense of hope-lessness – a hopelessness that had remained with me until the day Jesus took it away.

When Jesus saw the widow, He was visibly moved with compassion. She was not only grieving the loss of her only son, but she also was left alone with no one to care for her. She unfortunately lived in a society that did not have resources to assist widows with no family.

Jesus felt the pain and isolation that sin and death had brought into the world – and now He witnessed it in the life of this dear woman.

"Don't cry!" [2] He told her.

Then He walked past her and over to the wooden bier where her son's body had been carefully placed. He rested His hand on it to stop the procession. Jesus' followers and those in the funeral procession were all startled. What He had just done was a violation of Jewish law! Except for those who were preparing the body for burial, no one was permitted to touch a dead body or his coffin. To do so amounted to the worst kind of defilement. Not to mention He had just disrupted this very personal moment for this grieving mother.

As surprised as we all were, it was nothing compared to what we witnessed next. Jesus stood there for a brief moment looking at the body of the dead man and said, *"Young man, I tell you, get up!"* [3]

Immediately, the young man sat up and began to talk to those around him. I couldn't hear what he was saying, but the friends who were carrying him looked stunned. Gently, they set the wooden bier on the ground, and Jesus took his hand to help him stand up. Next, Jesus helped the young man walk over to his mother. There was absolute silence from the crowd as they embraced. Where there had been death and hopelessness, Jesus had restored life and hope!

A great and holy fear welled up within the hearts of everyone there – even those of us who were His closest followers. The testimony of the crowd quickly spread across the region – *"A mighty prophet has risen among us! Surely God has visited His people today!"* [4] A word from Jesus had changed everything.

Several days later we were traveling along the west shore of the Sea of Galilee, approaching the town of Magdala. We encountered a woman by the name of Mary. Her body was battered and bruised, and she was in complete agony. She was obviously under the control of evil spirits and appeared to have lost all control and dignity.

· · ·

We later learned she had lost everything she had known in her life. Her beauty and wealth had not spared her from the evil that assailed and attacked her relentlessly every day for as long as she could remember. She had become an outcast and her disheveled appearance masked the beauty she had once possessed.

Jesus looked at Mary's desperation and, unlike the rest of us, saw her for who she really was and who she would become. He saw the fear and hopelessness that resulted from her internal imprisonment. Then she began to convulse and fell on her knees in front of Jesus.

The demons from within cried out, "What do you want with us, Jesus, Son of the Most High God?"

Jesus declared, "Come out of this woman, you unclean spirits! I cast you into the prison of darkness to await the day of your judgment! Leave this woman and be gone!"

No sooner had Jesus spoken than the woman collapsed at His feet. He gently reached down and took her by the hand and said, "Mary, arise, for you have been set free!"

As Mary stood to her feet, she looked into the eyes of the One who had just given her back her life. She saw His compassion, but she also saw His authority. He was her Savior. She would forever follow Him.

Jesus quietly told her to return to her home and tell those she encountered that God had shown His mercy on her. He assured her that those who have been set free are free indeed! We all stood in amazement at the tenderness with which He spoke to this woman and the authority with which He had cast out the demons. He was more than a prophet! What was it the demons had called Him? Had they called Him the Son of the Most High God? Was Jesus the Son of God? I began to believe that He was!

We continued on our journey into the town of Magdala. One of the residents, a Pharisee by the name of Simon, greeted Jesus and invited Him and some of His followers to be his guests for dinner. Jesus told His apostles to follow Him, and then graciously turned around and invited me to join Him as well.

As we reclined at the table, Simon began to pepper Jesus with questions. Jesus graciously responded to each one with words from the Scriptures. But it soon became clear that the Pharisee wasn't seeking truth, but rather interrogating Jesus in an attempt to cause Him to misspeak.

While we were eating, Mary – the woman from whom Jesus had earlier cast out the demons – entered the room carrying a beautiful alabaster jar filled with expensive perfume. She walked over to where Jesus was reclining with His feet outstretched. She knelt at His feet and began to weep. Her tears fell on His feet and she wiped them off with her hair. She began to kiss His feet and anoint them with perfume. It was obvious to me the woman was expressing her love and gratitude to Jesus for all He had done for her. It was a demonstration of sincere worship.

Her compassionate gesture continued for several minutes. Though our host was well aware of what Jesus had done that day, he still looked upon her disapprovingly. Mary had a reputation among the villagers — not only for being demon-possessed, but also for her immorality. At this point, Jesus had not acknowledged Mary or her act of kindness.

. . .

But He looked at His host and said, *"Simon, I have something to say to you. A man loaned money to two people – five hundred pieces of silver to one and fifty pieces to the other. But neither of them could repay him, so he kindly forgave them both, canceling their debts. Who do you suppose loved him more after that?"* [5]

Simon replied, *"I suppose the one for whom he canceled the larger debt."* [6]

Jesus said, "You have answered rightly."

Then He turned toward Mary and said to Simon, *"Look at this woman kneeling here. When I entered your home, you didn't offer Me water to wash the dust off My feet, but she has washed them with her tears and wiped them with her hair. You didn't greet Me with a kiss, but from the time I first came in, she has not stopped kissing My feet. You neglected the courtesy of olive oil to anoint My head, but she has anointed My feet with rare perfume. I tell you that her sins – and they are many – have been forgiven, so she has shown Me much love. But a person who is forgiven little shows only little love."* [7]

Then looking at the woman, Jesus said, "Mary, *your sins are forgiven. Your faith has saved you. Go in peace."* [8]

As we walked to our lodgings later that evening, Jesus commented: "One was set free today and she has received eternal life. The other has chosen to remain in the bondage of the chains of his sin. The gateway to life is very narrow and the road is difficult. Only a few ever find it."

As we left the town of Magdala the next morning to continue our journey, Mary the Magdalene accompanied us. She joined Salome, the wife of Zebedee; and Mary, the wife of Clopas, who had both been with us from the beginning. Joanna, the wife of Chuza, whose son Jesus had recently healed, had also come to join our group of followers, as had Susanna, the widowed mother of the young man whom Jesus had raised from the dead. These women generously provided money from their own resources to Judas Iscariot to support Jesus and His apostles in their travels.

One afternoon two of John the Baptizer's disciples came to us with word for Jesus from John.

* * *

12

John's two disciples found Jesus and said to Him, "John the Baptist sent us to ask, 'Are You the Messiah we've been expecting, or should we keep looking for someone else?'"[1]

* * *

I knew firsthand that Herod the Great had no apprehension about executing people under his rule — whether it was little boys aged two and under or members of his own family. In fact, as his health was failing during his latter years, he even had two of his adult sons strangled on charges of treason.

One of those sons fathered his granddaughter, Herodias. Herod the Great favored his granddaughter Herodias, so he wanted to keep her future secure. So, he arranged for her to marry his son Herod II, her half uncle, whom he had designated to ascend to his throne as tetrarch upon his death. He thought the arrangement would be advantageous for both Herod II and Herodias.

. . .

If Herod the Great had died just a few days earlier than he did, history would have written the roles of Herod II and Herodias very differently. But, in his final days, Herod the Great was manipulated by other family members to change his will so that Herod II would no longer succeed him. When Herod the Great died, Herod II and Herodias did not ascend to the throne, but rather were destined to live out their lives as private citizens in Rome. They would have enjoyed a very comfortable life – but for Herodias it would have been an unfulfilled life because it was a life void of power.

When Herod the Great died, his rule passed to three of his other sons – Herod Archelaus, Herod Philip II, and Herod Antipas (the ruler of Galilee and Perea). Antipas was married to a princess of the Nabataean kingdom. Their marriage had been arranged by Herod the Great in order to solidify a political alliance. But as Rome's control of the entire region strengthened, such alliances became less important, or so Antipas thought. He later learned he was wrong. But for now, Antipas had become bored with his Nabataean bride.

Not long after Herod the Great's death, Herodias was seduced by Antipas' power and Antipas was seduced by the wiles and charms of his niece, Herodias. They plotted to escape their current unsatisfactory marriages so they would be free to marry one another. Normally such a divorce and remarriage wouldn't have made much of a ripple among the Galilean and Perean populace. However, there was one person who found great offense in their plan, and he was determined not to be silent about it.

John the Baptizer's condemnation of the union as adultery and incest caused the couple's planned nuptials to become the topic of conversation across the region. Though they didn't need popular support to divorce and remarry, they were still offended by the baptizer's accusations. In fact, they made Herodias livid. Antipas probably would have ignored the homeless prophet shouting in the wilderness, but Herodias was determined to get her revenge. She put her plan into action by talking her husband into arresting John the Baptizer.

One night, after the crowds had gone home, Herod's soldiers arrived at the Jordan River to arrest John. He and his followers had just settled in for a night's rest when the soldiers arrived without warning. Antipas wanted the arrest to occur at nighttime so as not to incite a riot among the crowd that gathered to hear John preach.

Herod's men arrested John without explanation and took him forty miles south to the hilltop fortress of Machaerus, east of the Dead Sea. Machaerus was far enough away from the day-to-day life of Galilee and Judea that Antipas felt John would eventually be forgotten. Antipas was content to have John live out the remainder of his days imprisoned in the fortress where he could do no harm.

But God had called John to be a prophet – a voice in the wilderness. And as the days in prison turned into weeks, he became discouraged. He was no longer able to do the very thing for which God had created him – to bear witness to the Messiah. Why had God permitted him to be imprisoned and his voice to be silenced?

Occasionally John was permitted to have visits from his disciples, but only two at a time. On one of those visits, when John was especially discouraged, he directed two of his disciples to go find Jesus and ask Him a question.

The two men found Jesus teaching a large crowd in the wilderness, just outside of Nain. As they approached, I recognized the men as being disciples of John. They came over and asked me if they could have a word with Jesus. They explained they had a message from John.

After Jesus finished speaking to the crowd, John's disciples said to Him, '*John sent us to ask, 'Are You the Messiah we've been expecting, or should we keep looking for someone else?'*'[(2)] Jesus replied to them, "*Go back to John and tell him what you have seen and heard — the blind see, the lame walk, those with leprosy are cured, the deaf hear, the dead are raised to life, and the Good News is being preached to the poor.*"[(3)]

John would know that Jesus was speaking in response to the prophecy of Isaiah: "*And when He comes, He will open the eyes of the blind and unplug the ears of the deaf. The lame will leap like a deer, and those who cannot speak will sing for joy. Sorrow and mourning will disappear, and they will be filled with joy and gladness.*"[(4)] And then He added, "tell him that I said, *God blesses those who do not fall away because of Me.*"[(5)]

After John's disciples had left, Jesus said to the crowd, "*I tell you, of all who have ever lived, none is greater than John. Yet even the least person in the Kingdom of God is greater than he is!*"[(6)]

Jesus knew that some in the crowd were asking, "If John is such a great prophet, why is he in prison?" Others, like me, were wondering why God had permitted John to be imprisoned and his ministry to be abruptly halted. John had been faithful. Why had God not allowed him to continue his ministry through which so many lives had been transformed? There were still so many people who had not heard! To some degree, even John was asking that question.

Jesus went on to teach not only the crowd but also many of us who followed Him an important truth that day. Even though many people, including those despised by the religious leaders, had repented of their sins and been baptized, there were still many more who had rejected the truth — like the religious leaders. Jesus made sure we realized that the truth of God John preached was not any less true because people rejected it.

The reality, He said, was that *"wisdom is shown to be right by what its followers do."*[7] Those who rejected truth had chosen to fall away, but as Jesus had reminded John, those who do not fall away will be blessed by God. And those who have accepted the truth will share that truth with others.

John's ministry had not been brought to a halt; rather, it soon would be greatly multiplied. Though John – and others who would follow – could be physically imprisoned, or worse, the message could never be imprisoned!

I realized something about myself at that moment. I originally sought out Jesus for what He could do for me. I wanted Him to exact revenge for the death of my father and brother. I wanted Him to overthrow a tyrannical regime. I wanted Him to take away the pain. And I had experienced His healing and transforming touch. I had experienced a peace and joy that so far surpassed anything I could imagine.

But it wasn't until now, when Jesus spoke of my friend John the Baptizer, that I realized the truth of God was not about me – it wasn't about John – it was about the glory of God and His Kingdom. Walls may imprison us. Our physical lives may be taken. But God's truth and His glory will endure – and the eyes, ears, and mouths of the blind, deaf, and dumb will continue to be opened. The lame will continue to be healed. And those who are spiritually dead will be raised to life. All for the glory of God!

. . .

Though Herod Antipas had imprisoned John, he considered it to be an act of protection – protecting John from his vindictive wife, Herodias. Herod knew that as long as John was imprisoned under his decree, she was powerless to harm him. Herod actually feared John, knowing that he was a good and holy man. On more than one occasion, Herod had John brought before him so they could talk. Herod was usually perplexed by what John said, but he knew John was speaking truth and he had a hunger to hear it. But all the while, Herodias continued to watch for an opportunity to exact her revenge.

Finally, her opportunity arrived. It was Herod's forty-eighth birthday and Herodias encouraged him to host a party for his high government officials, army officers, and the leading citizens of Galilee. She instructed their household manager, Chuza, to spare no expense in making this a most memorable celebration for her husband. It was to include only the finest food, the finest drink, and the finest music.

When the night arrived, the celebration was intoxicating for Herod. His every epicurean desire was met. Herodias had also made arrangements for her daughter, from her previous marriage to Herod II, to come in and perform a dance for Herod and his guests. At the instruction of her mother, the girl beguiled the drunken Herod through her dancing.

When it was complete, Herod said to her, *"Ask me for anything you like, and I will give it to you. I will give you whatever you ask, up to half my kingdom!"* [8]

The girl obviously did not know Herodias' plan, because she went out to ask her mother what she should ask for. At the direction of Herodias, the girl returned to the king and told him, *"I want the head of John the Baptizer, right now, on a tray!"*[9]

Immediately, Herod regretted what he had said. But because of the vow he had made in front of his guests, he could not refuse her. He dispatched a message to the executioner at the fortress to cut off John's head and bring it to him. Since the distance from the palace to the fortress was approximately fifty miles, it took several days before John's head was delivered to Herod.

When it arrived, Herod called for his household manager, Chuza, and told him to bring a tray to the throne room. Herod then had John's head placed on the tray and gave it to the girl, who in turn took it to her mother. Chuza was distraught to see John's head and to learn all that had transpired. Though he had never heard John teach, he knew of his ministry and he grieved his death. But even more, he grieved over the depravity and wickedness right there in the palace that had resulted in John's death. With a heart full of sorrow, Chuza sent out a messenger to tell Jesus what had happened.

Prior to his beheading, John's disciples had returned to him at the fortress with the message from Jesus. The message greatly encouraged him, providing John with a comfort, a peace, and a calm even in the midst of his imprisonment. That gracious gift remained with him as he laid down his head and took his last breath on this side of his executioner's blade and took his next in paradise. When they heard what had happened, his heartbroken disciples retrieved his body from the fortress and buried it in a tomb.

When Chuza's messenger arrived, Jesus was teaching the crowd. The messenger immediately sought out Joanna, Chuza's wife. Andrew, Philip, and I were standing together listening to Jesus when Joanna brought the messenger to us. He told us he had a message for Jesus from Chuza, but he needed to immediately return to Herod's palace. We told him we would convey the message to Jesus.

When he began to speak, I felt like someone had just hit me in my stomach with all of their might. My legs collapsed beneath me as I fell to the ground with a broken heart. Andrew fell to his knees as well. We could not believe the news about our friend! I had only ever felt that way once before – the day I saw my father's and my brother's dead bodies.

Wracked with grief, I looked at Jesus and He looked back at me. The sadness in His eyes told me He already knew. He had known the day He sent the message back to John – "tell him that I said, '*God blesses those who do not fall away because of Me.*'"[5] John was now experiencing those blessings to their fullest. He had not fallen away. He had remained faithful to the end, and the experience of those blessings would now last for eternity.

When Jesus was done speaking to the crowd, He took a boat to a remote area to be alone and talk to His Father about their servant John.

* * *

13

"If I can touch His robe, I will be healed."[1]

* * *

W hen Jesus was finished, He got back into the boat and we set sail for the other side of the lake, where a large crowd was waiting for Him on shore. Just as Jesus stepped out of the boat, a leader from the local synagogue arrived to meet Him. The man, whose name was Jairus, fell at Jesus' feet and pleaded with Him: *"My little daughter is dying. Please come, lay Your hands on her and heal her so she can live."*[2]

Without saying a word, Jesus reached down, helped Jairus stand to his feet, and the two began to walk toward the village, surrounded by the crowd.

In the midst of the crowd was a woman who had suffered for twelve years with constant bleeding. She had spent all the money she had and was no better; if anything, she had gotten worse. She had nowhere else to turn. No one had been able to solve her problem and much of what the physicians had tried had only made her worse.

The medical community had failed her. The religious community had labeled her as "unclean" and rejected her. Her friends had abandoned her. She was bankrupt financially, physically, and emotionally. Most of all, she had lost hope.

But then she heard about Jesus – how He made the blind to see and the lame to walk. There were even rumors His spoken word had calmed a storm and stilled the sea. She heard people in the village excitedly discussing Jesus as He arrived at the shore by boat. Everyone was scurrying in that direction to catch a glimpse of Him – and hopefully, to hear Him teach. Was this her opportunity to be healed? But surely, He wouldn't have time for her.

When the woman arrived at the shore, one of the leaders of the synagogue was kneeling before Jesus. She knew Jairus; she had previously sought his help. Jairus stood up, and he and Jesus walked toward the village. Jesus was obviously on important synagogue business. She wouldn't even be able to get close to Him. Plus, the crowd surrounding Jesus seemed impenetrable. How could she get near enough to speak to Jesus? Besides, she was a nobody. She was just one of the many nameless, faceless, desperate, people in the crowd.

She didn't know if it was faith or simple resignation, but she sensed Jesus was her last resort – and she knew she had to try to reach Him. So, she mustered what little strength she still had left, and began to press her way through the crowd. She covered herself so that no one would recognize her.

· · ·

She approached Him from behind to be as inconspicuous as possible. Fortunately, the crowd was also pressing in ahead of Jesus and slowing down His progress. It gave her just enough time to get near Him. If she could just touch His garment, she reasoned, that would be all she needed; He didn't even have to speak to her.

When she was within inches of Jesus, she carefully reached out her frail hand ... and touched His robe. Immediately she was healed. After twelve years of bondage to this disease, she had been set free. For a few moments the crowd pressed against her to move her forward, then they began to move around her. She stood still, silently rejoicing — her quest was over. She had experienced the healing she thought was beyond her grasp.

Then all of a sudden, Jesus stopped and turned around. As He turned, His eyes met hers, and He asked, *"Who touched My robe?"* [3]

I heard Peter lean in to Jesus and say, "Master, *look at the crowd pressing in on You. How can You ask, 'Who touched My robe?'"* [4]

But the woman knew that He knew! Trembling with fear, she fell down before Him. As she looked up into His eyes – those eyes that spoke volumes – she saw a kindness, a gentleness, and a compassion unlike anything she had ever witnessed. And she told Jesus what she had done and why.

As I listened to the woman speak, I knew Jesus already knew what she had done and why. He already knew who had touched His garment. He knew before the day began He would encounter her, and she would be healed by touching His robe. It was almost as if He had been waiting for her arrival. She may have thought she was just another face in the crowd, but she was one of the reasons Jesus had come to this village.

This was all part of the Father's plan for His Son – and for her – for this particular day. Her word of explanation was simply so the crowd would know what had just taken place. Her confession to Jesus was not for the purpose of enlightening Him; it was for the purpose of bringing glory to God.

And when Jesus said to her, *"Daughter, your faith has made you well – go in peace – your suffering is over,"*[5] she walked away with more than just physical healing. She walked away with peace. She reminded me of a sheep whose hoof had just been freed from a rocky crag who could now walk away joyfully. But even more than that, her expression was identical to that of the Samaritan woman at Jacob's well. Her life had been completely transformed in a single moment.

While Jesus was still speaking to the woman, messengers arrived from Jairus' home. Taking Jairus aside, they told him, *"Your daughter is dead. There's no use troubling the Teacher now."*[6] They believed it was too late for Jesus to do anything. Even though the crowd had just seen Jesus display His power by healing the sick woman, they – and the messengers – believed He had power over disease, but not over death. They thought His power was limited, and they weren't alone.

But Jesus overheard them and said to Jairus, *"Don't be afraid. Just have faith."*[7]

Then Jesus stopped the crowd and told them no one was to go any farther with Him and Jairus. He did not want to be surrounded by their unbelief. Then He turned to Peter, James, and John and told them to follow Him – and just before He walked on, He motioned for me to join them as well.

When we arrived at Jairus' home, there was much weeping and wailing. It reminded me of the day we had come upon the funeral procession of Susanna's dead son. As a matter of fact, I turned around to look for her and then remembered she was waiting with the crowd back on shore.

As we walked into the home, Jesus asked, *"Why all this commotion and weeping? The child isn't dead; she's only asleep."*[8]

Then the crowd in the home did something that clearly showed they did not know who Jesus was. They laughed at Him. I had heard people laugh when Jesus told a funny story, but this was different. I had never heard anyone laugh at Him in a way that demonstrated such disrespect, ignorance, and faithlessness. I knew that most in the crowd had not seen what His apostles and I had seen. But still, they had heard. The news of who Jesus was and what He had done had traveled near and far.

As Jesus looked at them, their laughter subsided and turned into an uncomfortable silence. They had not learned to look at situations through eyes of faith. And to be honest, I had not yet fully learned myself. Because of their faithlessness, Jesus made them all leave the home. I was mindful of what He had said on more than one occasion — that faithlessness displeases the Father. He had even gone so far as to say that *"without faith it is impossible to please God."*[9]

After the crowd left, Jesus took Jairus and his wife, together with those of us who had accompanied Him, into the room where the girl was lying. Then He took her hand in His, and said, *"Little girl, get up!"*[(10)]

Immediately, she sat up, stood, and began to walk around! I cannot begin to describe the emotions of her parents as well as the rest of us in the room. It was a combination of euphoria, elation, and amazement. Even those of us who had witnessed Jesus raise Susanna's son from the dead were overwhelmed to the point of trembling.

Jesus could not only heal the infirm, the blind, and the lame, He could also restore life to those who were dead. That was something I would never get used to seeing or consider "routine." Some detractors would say the little girl wasn't really dead; she was only asleep. I suggest they say that to those who initially laughed at Jesus and hear what they now have to say.

The girl's parents were filled with gratitude when Jesus told them to give their daughter something to eat. The crowd who had laughed was dumbfounded to see the girl walking about. When I learned the girl was twelve years old, it took me back to when I was twelve and the horrific death of my father and brother. These parents had seen their daughter restored to life. For a moment, I found myself wishing Jesus had been there that day to restore life to my father and brother.

But then I thought back to the promise and the hope Jesus gave me on the day we walked the road to Bethsaida – one day I *will* see them again! Yes, Jesus is the One who is able to restore life – in the past, in the present, and in the future, for all eternity. Only Jesus has the last word on death. Only Jesus can overcome death. Just ask this little girl and her parents!

. . .

Though Jesus gave the girl's parents "strict orders" not to tell anyone what had happened, there was no way they could keep this miracle a secret. Everyone in that village knew within the hour – and the news traveled throughout the entire region in the days that followed.

The next day we traveled to Nazareth, Jesus' hometown. Given the welcome He had received in the other villages throughout the region, we expected a large turnout to welcome Him home. But that didn't happen. Sabbath began at sundown, so the next morning Jesus went to the synagogue to teach, as usual. There were many who heard Him and were amazed. But the reception was much cooler than Jesus had experienced everywhere else.

While Jesus was speaking, the men who were gathered began to ask one another, *"Where did He get all this wisdom and the power to perform such miracles?"*[11] Then they scoffed, "After all, *He's just a carpenter*, the illegitimate son of Mary and Joseph. We know His brothers, and *His sisters live right here among us."*[12] As a result, the people of the town would not believe in Him.

I wanted to stand up and rebuke them. I couldn't believe that anyone could be so blind or deaf. I had seen and heard the angels announce His birth! How could they disparage Him in such a way? We had all seen Him perform one miracle after another. He had power over disease, illness and death! He had power over nature! He had power over the demons! Who were these people to question the One to whom all creation bore witness? How could they treat Him with such disrespect and disdain?

Then Jesus told them, *"A prophet is honored everywhere except in his hometown and among his relatives and his own family."*[13]

. . .

Because of their unbelief and lack of faith, Jesus was not able to perform any miracles among them, except to place His hands on a few sick people and heal them. This was one of the few times I ever saw Jesus look amazed. People, including me, were constantly being amazed by Him, His miracles, and His teaching. But on this day, it was Jesus who was amazed by the unbelief of the people of Nazareth. As a result, He never returned there.

I couldn't help but notice the sadness in His eyes. It wasn't a sadness for Himself. It was a sadness for the people – many of whom had been His neighbors for many years. Some of them were men and women whom He had grown up with ... gone to synagogue with ... done carpentry work for. And they rejected Him. How it must have broken His heart! How it must still break His heart when His own reject Him!

* * *

14

"Remember that I am sending you out as lambs among wolves."[1]

* * *

One day Jesus chose seventy-two of His followers and sent us in pairs throughout Galilee to all the towns and villages He planned to visit. I was paired with my friend and "fellow zealot" Simon. In some ways it reminded us of our times together under the leadership of Zadok and Judah, when we would be sent out to spy on the movement of Roman soldiers. However, this time we weren't going as spies of rebellion, but as ambassadors of peace!

Before we left, Jesus instructed us: *"The harvest is great, but the workers are few. Remember that I am sending you out as lambs among wolves. Don't take any money with you, nor a traveler's bag, nor an extra pair of sandals. Whenever you enter someone's home, first say, 'May God's peace be on this house.' Don't move around from home to home. Stay in one place, eating and drinking what they provide. Don't hesitate to accept hospitality. Heal the sick, and tell them, 'The Kingdom of God is near!'* And don't forget that *anyone who accepts your message is also accepting Me. And anyone who rejects you is rejecting Me. And anyone who rejects Me is rejecting God, who sent Me."*[2]

Jesus told Simon and me to go to the village of Chorazin. The villages of Chorazin, Capernaum, and Bethsaida formed a triangle on the north side of the Sea of Galilee. Jesus had already spent quite a bit of time in that region teaching and performing miracles. But, regrettably, the people had still not repented of their sins.

Before Simon and I started on our journey, Jesus told us this about Chorazin: *"What sorrow awaits you, Chorazin and Bethsaida! For if the miracles I did in you had been done in* the Gentile cities of *Tyre and Sidon, their people would have repented of their sins long ago, clothing themselves in burlap and throwing ashes on their heads to show their remorse."*[3]

As Simon and I headed to our destination, we talked about what we might encounter. Even Jesus had said it was a "hard" field. The people had not responded to Him! How would they ever respond to us? Jesus had compared us to lambs among wolves. I knew very well what wolves could do to lambs!

The village of Chorazin was the smallest of the three that formed the triangle and also farthest from the sea. It was only twenty-five acres in size and was home to about one hundred families. The village was subdivided into four quadrants with the synagogue being physically located at the center. The synagogue was also the social and religious center of daily life and rule in Chorazin, as it was in most villages.

Most of the buildings in the village were constructed of a black volcanic rock that was found nearby. It gave Chorazin a very distinctive appearance; everything was the color of ebony. The village was surrounded by groves of olive trees, which were believed to be between 1,500 and 2,000 years old. The olive trees were the mainstay of the local economy. The people of Chorazin traded their olives and olive oil with villages throughout the region.

As we entered the village and made our way toward the synagogue, we were surprised to encounter our former compatriot Barabbas. He was surprised to see us, too. After the failed raid outside of Caesarea, Barabbas had not stayed in any one place for long. One of his most frequented haunts was the road between Jerusalem and Jericho. The Jericho Road, as it was called, was a highly traveled trade route between the two cities. As a result, the winding, meandering path that was surrounded by hills also was known as the "Way of Blood," because of the blood that was often shed there by robbers.

Barabbas had initially chosen the road because it provided easy prey. He would target religious leaders, Jewish merchants who were profiting from the Roman occupation, tax collectors, and officials within the Herodian government. He favored raids that involved tax collectors because people didn't have much sympathy when they were robbed.

Though Barabbas initially began his raids under the ruse of the zealot cause, he soon dropped the pretense as the opportunity for personal profit grew. And while he never set out to murder his victims, Barabbas did not hesitate to shed their blood if they gave him cause. He was becoming somewhat notorious in that part of Judea. After the repeated pleas of victimized tax collectors to the Roman prefect, soldiers were dispatched to keep a more watchful eye. So, Barabbas decided to leave Judea for a while and traveled sixty miles north to this sleepy village of Chorazin in Galilee.

• • •

I wondered why Barabbas was telling us all of this until he made an attempt to recruit us to join his little band. He was certain the opportunity for revenge and profit would entice us. That is, until we told him about our journey since we had last seen him. We told him we had found the Messiah and His name is Jesus. He was the One who was promised to set us free from our bondage. We told him about the miracles we had seen Jesus perform with our own eyes. We explained the truths Jesus taught. We shared the change He had made in our lives, and that we had become His followers.

Barabbas told us he had heard that this Jesus was a worker of miracles. He also knew many of the villagers were talking about Him. But when we asked Barabbas if he would like to travel back with us and meet Jesus, he declined. He seemed sincere when he told us he was glad we had found who and what we were looking for. But he also made it clear that he, too, had found what he was looking for and didn't have any interest in this Jesus.

"But who knows," he said, "perhaps our paths will cross one day, and I will meet Him then!" He wished us well and we continued on to the synagogue, not knowing if we would see him again while we remained in the village.

As we entered the synagogue, the teacher was reading from the prophet Isaiah:

For a Child is born to us, a Son is given to us.
The government will rest on His shoulders.
And He will be called:
Wonderful Counselor, Mighty God, Everlasting Father, Prince of Peace.
His government and its peace will never end.
He will rule with fairness and justice from the throne of His ancestor David
for all eternity.

The passionate commitment of the Lord of Heaven's Armies will make this happen![4]

After the teacher read the passage, he sat down. At that moment, the Spirit of God came upon me and compelled me to speak.

"When I was ten years old, my father and I, as well as several other shepherds, were in the field outside of Bethlehem watching over our sheep. Suddenly an angel appeared in the sky and said, *'I bring you good news of great joy. The Savior – yes, the Messiah, the Lord – has been born tonight in Bethlehem, the city of David!'*"[5]

Then I went on to explain about the choir of angels that appeared in the sky announcing the birth of the Child. I told them how we had seen the baby in the manger who was the Prince of Peace. But then I told them about Jesus, and how He was that baby now grown into adulthood.

"You have seen Him perform many miracles," I said. "You have seen that the deaf now hear, the blind now see, and the lame can walk. You have heard that life has been restored to the dead. This same Jesus is the Child of whom Isaiah wrote. He is the Son who has been given to us. Follow Him this day, for the Kingdom of God is near!"

After I finished speaking, a few of the men came to ask questions and talk further, but most left without saying anything. One of the men invited Simon and me to come to his home. As we arrived, just as Jesus had instructed us, I said, "May God's peace be on this house." He and his wife fed us and provided us with lodging for the night.

· · ·

The next morning, one of their neighbors, a shepherd's wife, came to the door with her son Jonathan. The young mother explained that Jonathan was her third and only surviving child. Her first two sons had been stillborn. She and her husband had named him Jonathan because he was a gift to them from God. God had brought joy back into their lives through this precious gift.

But they soon realized Jonathan had been deaf since birth. Their son had never heard a bird sing, or the sound of the wind when it blows, or the sound of his mother's voice. The woman asked if we could heal her son. As I looked at this young shepherd boy, I was reminded of my brother Jacob when he was this age – full of life, with a tender heart.

I placed my hands over Jonathan's ears, and prayed, "Father, You know Simon and I have no power to heal this young lad, but we ask You to heal his ears and enable him to hear so that he and his parents, and others in this village, might believe on Your Son, Jesus Christ of Nazareth."

As I took my hands away, he immediately raised his hands up to his ears, because for the first time in his life he could hear! God had healed this precious young boy's hearing … for His glory and the glory of His Son! Jonathan's mother and our hosts began to rejoice. We thanked God for answering our prayer! And quickly the news of the boy's healing spread through the village!

We remained in Chorazin for two more days, and Jonathan remained close to our sides the entire time. Though he did not understand most of our words, he listened to us intently. I was impressed to pray that God would use this tenderhearted lad to bring great glory to His name. We continued to teach about the Kingdom of God, and some believed. Others, who were ill or diseased, were also healed.

. . .

The Father was gracious and the Good News was shared. We announced that Jesus would return to their village soon, and they would see and hear even greater things. There was no denying that God had done above and beyond anything that we ever imagined when we had entered the village three days earlier. Simon and I realized the biggest change we had seen the past few days was in us! We had experienced the power of God working through us for His glory! We couldn't wait to tell Jesus what had happened! As we left the village, we were watchful for Barabbas, but we did not see him. It would be many months before we would see him again.

The journey to Capernaum to reunite with Jesus and the other disciples was a short one – less than two hours. As we went to tell Jesus what had happened, we saw that everyone was clamoring to do the same. All of us had witnessed the power of God working through us! Many had seen people healed. Peter reported, "Lord, even the demons obey us when we use Your name!"

To which Jesus replied, *"I have given you authority over all the power of the enemy. But don't rejoice because evil spirits obey you; rejoice because your names are registered in heaven."* [6]

At the same time Jesus was filled with joy and He said, *"O Father, thank You for hiding these things from those who think themselves wise and clever, and for revealing them to these – the childlike. Yes, Father, it pleased You to do it this way."* [7] Then turning to us, Jesus said, *"Blessed are the eyes that see what you have seen. I tell you, many prophets and kings longed to see what you have seen, but they didn't see it. And they longed to hear what you have heard, but they didn't hear it."* [8]

. . .

The crowd was beginning to overtake us in Capernaum, and Jesus wanted to give us more time to tell Him about our experiences, so He led us to slip away quietly toward the town of Bethsaida. But the crowds quickly found out where we were going, and they followed us – to a spot out in the middle of nowhere.

15

He had compassion on them because they were like sheep without a shepherd.
(1)

* * *

As Jesus led us up a hill, we spotted a large crowd assembling in the valley. Jesus had compassion on them and began teaching. Meanwhile, a shepherd and his son led their flock toward us so they could hear what Jesus was saying.

As they got closer, I recognized the young boy was Jonathan. He must have spotted Simon and me about the same time because he began to wave at us wildly. He turned and began an animated conversation with his father. I speculated he was asking permission to join us. It wasn't long before he was there beside us with a grin from ear to ear. We waved to his father to signal that the boy was with us, then I invited him to join us as we listened to the Master teach.

. . .

Late in the afternoon, the apostles approached Jesus and said, *"Send the crowd away to the nearby villages and farms, so they can find food and lodging for the night. There is nothing to eat here in this remote place."* (2)

But the apostles were not ready for Jesus' answer. He said, *"That isn't necessary, you feed them."* (3)

Judas Iscariot had estimated the crowd was made up of five thousand men, plus women and children, for a total of approximately fifteen thousand people. Jesus turned to Philip and asked, *"Where can we buy bread to feed all these people?"* (4)

Judas had made it clear there was not enough money in the treasury to buy food. And even if there were, where could they possibly find that much food on such short notice?

So Philip replied, *"We'd have to work for months to earn enough money to buy food for all these people!"* (5)

Jesus immediately responded, "Don't look at what you don't have. Look to see what the Father has already provided. *How much bread do you have? Go and find out."* (6)

As we listened to this conversation, Jonathan tugged on my sleeve and showed me the food his mother had placed in his sack. Though he was still limited in his speech, his actions clearly showed he wanted to help by giving what he had. I turned to Andrew and showed him Jonathan's food.

. . .

Andrew called out to Jesus and said, *"There's a young boy here with five barley loaves and two fish. But what good is that with this huge crowd?"*[7]

In response, Jonathan walked over to Jesus and gave Him his small sack of food. Jesus watched Jonathan tenderly as he walked toward Him. For a moment, it was as if time stopped. As I watched Jonathan's unselfish act, I realized he had more faith than all of us combined. This little boy wasn't concerned with how Jesus could use his small offering of food. He just knew he needed to give Jesus all that he had. Holding anything back for himself never crossed his mind! One week ago, Jonathan had been deaf, but now he could hear. How could he give anything less than all he had to Jesus?

Jesus looked at us and said, *"Truly, I say to you, unless you turn and become like children, you will never enter the Kingdom of heaven. Whoever humbles himself like this child is the greatest in the Kingdom of heaven."*[8]

With Jonathan remaining at His side, Jesus said to us, *"Tell everyone to sit down."*[9]

We directed the crowd to sit down in groups. Then Jesus lifted the sack toward heaven and gave thanks to the Father for this young boy's faith. He then began to break the loaves into pieces, giving them to each of us to distribute to the people. We each had three groups of between fifty and one hundred people to serve.

We continued to carry the bread from Jesus to the people until everyone had received enough. Then, Jesus did the same with the fish. After everyone had eaten as much as they wanted and were full, He told us, *"Now gather the leftovers, so that nothing is wasted."*[10]

• • •

We filled twelve baskets to the brim with the leftover pieces of bread and fish. As the twelve baskets were set side by side, I looked over at Jonathan. His smile extended from one ear to the other. I bowed my head and thanked the Father for what He had allowed us to witness that day. And then I asked Him to grant me faith the size of Jonathan's.

We all had watched this miracle unfold. When the crowd saw the twelve baskets, they exclaimed, *"Surely He is the Prophet we have been expecting!"*[11] They had all come expecting Jesus to perform a miracle, and He had not disappointed them! The people began to clamor for Jesus to be their King so they would never have to work for food again!

But they had totally missed who Jesus was and, therefore, were unwilling to accept Him as their Savior and Lord. The clamor of the crowd increased and it became clear they were preparing to force Jesus to declare Himself as their King. Some of the disciples, most notably Judas Iscariot, seemed quite pleased with the reaction of the crowd. Now was the moment when Jesus would be raised to His rightful position as their Messiah.

Jesus knew His disciples were in danger of being caught up in the frenzy. He wanted to get us away from the harmful influence of the crowd. He took Peter aside and told him to gather the disciples into the boat and cross to the other side of the lake. Jesus then slipped away into the hills to be alone with the Father.

When the people saw that Jesus was gone, they began to disperse. Simon and I walked Jonathan back to his father on the hill with their flock. We carried two of the baskets of bread and fish for their family. The remaining baskets were taken by others in the crowd. Though Jonathan's father had seen the crowd being fed, he was still overwhelmed when he saw the baskets of food. I told him that Jesus' miracle had all begun with the unselfish act of his son. And I told him that all of us had learned from Jonathan that day. Then Simon and I returned to join the rest of the disciples.

As long as our boat remained onshore, many in the crowd continued to wait around for Jesus to return. Peter directed us to take the boat farther from shore so the crowd would return to their homes. There we would wait for Jesus to come back down from the hills.

But as darkness fell, Peter decided that Jesus must have walked back to Capernaum and intended for us to head across the lake without Him. So, we set out for our twenty-minute sail to Capernaum. Soon after we left, a gale swept down upon us and the waves became very rough. Peter instructed us to lower the sail and start rowing.

But even though we were rowing with all our might, we could not make any headway against the wind and the waves. We had been battling the storm for about five hours and were only halfway to our destination. Even experienced fishermen like Peter and Andrew determined that we were in serious trouble.

All of a sudden Simon called out that someone – or something – was walking toward us on the water. Thaddeus and his brother, James, cried out that it was a ghost. The closer the image came to the boat the more terrified we all became.

Then we heard a voice proclaim, *"Don't be afraid! I am is here!"* [(12)]

John looked at Peter and said, "That's Jesus!" That prompted Peter to call out, *"Lord, if it's really You, tell me to come to You, walking on the water."*[13]

Then, we heard Him say, *"Yes, come!"*[14]

To Peter's credit, he immediately jumped over the side of the boat and began to walk on the water toward Jesus! I can honestly say none of us had the faith to do what Peter did! Our minds were simply racing, trying to process what we were seeing. Peter had only taken a few steps when he started to look down at the waves. As he did, he began to sink. He cried out, *"Save me, Lord!"*[15]

Immediately Jesus reached out, pulled him back on top of the water and said, *"Why did you doubt Me?"*[16]

Jesus helped Peter back into the boat, and once they were both seated, the winds and the waves stopped! Looking at each of us, Jesus said, *"You have so little faith.*[16] Believe, with the faith like that of the young boy you witnessed today!" As He spoke, I thought of my prayer earlier that day. Where was my faith?

By this time, we had arrived at the shore of Capernaum — the hometown of Peter, Andrew, James, John, and Matthew. Capernaum was also the center of Jesus' activities whenever He returned to Galilee. He taught in the local synagogue, so the locals considered it His hometown. As a Jew living in Capernaum, He was expected to pay the temple tax here. The temple tax was a law of God instituted through Moses.[17] It was a required annual offering from each person twenty years of age and over for purification. Each person was to give half a shekel regardless of whether he was rich or poor. The offering was then used to care for the tabernacle, and later the temple.

. . .

One day, while Peter and I were walking together, the tax collectors approached Peter and asked why Jesus had not paid the fee. We both sensed they were trying to find another "infraction" with which to accuse Jesus. Peter, who had been paying the tax since he had turned twenty, hastily told them that Jesus would be paying the tax soon. He wanted to defend Him against yet another slanderous accusation by the religious leaders.

Later in the day, when we encountered Jesus, Peter approached Jesus about the tax. Jesus already knew what he was going to ask. I noticed that Jesus often knew the questions people planned to ask before they spoke.

Jesus explained an important truth to Peter and me that day about the notion of "purification." We were to give the offering of purification in order to enter into the presence of a holy God. But as Jesus explained, He did not have to pay the temple tax. He is the Son of the King – and most definitely did not need purification. And we were children of the King by virtue of our faith in the Son.

But as the Son of Man, Jesus did not want to offend the people. Being a Jew, He did not want the people to perceive He was violating God's law. Jesus had no reluctance to challenge the traditions of men when they placed unfair burdens on the people. But this was the Father's law. Though He knew it did not apply to Him, Jesus also knew those around Him did not fully comprehend that truth ... including Peter and me.

So, Jesus sent Peter and me to get the silver coin needed to pay the tax. But we were surprised when He told us where to go to get the coin!

. . .

"Go down to the lake and throw in a line," He said. *"Open the mouth of the first fish you catch, and you will find a coin. Take the coin and pay the tax."*[(18)]

He could have used anything to provide the silver coin. And He chose a fish! Peter had been fishing all his life. He had probably harvested hundreds, if not thousands, of fish. And I would venture not one of them ever had a silver coin in its mouth. But today, Jesus was sending him out to catch a fish with a coin in its mouth. What's more, the coin would be the exact amount needed to pay the tax! After Peter's experience of walking on the water, we were not about to question Jesus!

I recalled the day Jesus told Peter to *"Follow Me."* He had been fishing all night and hadn't caught a thing. But then Jesus told him to let down his nets in the deep water. And Peter caught so many fish his nets began to tear! So, we knew firsthand that Jesus had dominion over all of creation. If Jesus said the silver coin would be in the mouth of the fish – that's exactly where it would be!

I often wondered how the Master orchestrated for that fish to have a coin in its mouth. And how He arranged for that particular fish to be the one Peter caught that day. We would never learn the details. But what we did learn was that the Master is always able to accomplish His purpose and His plan. And He accomplishes them through whatever means He chooses – whether it's a little boy's simple sack lunch, an unexpected storm, or an unsuspecting fish.

* * *

16

"And who is my neighbor?"[1]

* * *

It seemed like the religious leaders were attempting to outsmart Jesus daily and trap Him into saying something contrary to Scripture. Or they would make some outlandish accusation about Him. But in every instance, Jesus would respond with wisdom beyond all of them, and truth that was unwavering.

Today was no exception. The leaders had sent another one of their experts – a scribe who was experienced in debating the finer details of the law. He was well versed in the six hundred thirteen precepts and commands recorded in the Torah. He could categorize them into the three hundred sixty-five negative commands – the "thou shalt nots" – as well as the two hundred forty-eight positive commands – the "thou shalts."

. . .

As a boy, I had been taught there was one negative command for every day of the year, and one positive command for every bone and organ in my body. And that is just in the Torah! That doesn't include the exhaustive code of conduct practiced as part of our Jewish rituals, our worship practices, and interpersonal relationships that make up the Talmud. There was a lot to keep track of! No wonder the religious leaders surrounded themselves with a team of lawyers to keep a close eye!

One of the favorite pastimes of the scribes was discussing which of these divine commandments was the greatest. These men, considered to be the greatest religious minds in the land, were known to spend countless hours debating the answer to that question. They had never come to a resolution. So, apparently at the behest of the Sanhedrin in their effort to entrap Jesus, a scribe was sent to pose this question to Jesus: *"Of all the commandments, which is the most important?"* [2]

Jesus replied, *"The most important one is this: 'Hear, O Israel: The Lord our God, the Lord is one. Love the Lord your God with all your heart and with all your soul and with all your mind and with all your strength.' The second is this: 'Love your neighbor as yourself.' There is no commandment greater than these."* [3]

As Jesus was speaking, I thought back to my days as a young boy when each night my father and mother led us to recite that command-ment as a part of the Shema.

"And who is my neighbor?" [4] the scribe responded.

Jesus knew this man was not a sincere seeker but a so-called "expert" in religious law who was attempting to test Him. There was nothing honorable about the scribe's motives. But Jesus answered his question masterfully, turning it into one of His greatest lessons.

"A Jewish man was traveling from Jerusalem down to Jericho, and he was attacked by bandits. They stripped him of his clothes, beat him up, and left him half dead beside the road. By chance a priest came along. But when he saw the man lying there, he crossed to the other side of the road and passed him by. A Levite walked over and looked at him lying there, but he also passed by on the other side. Then a despised Samaritan came along, and when he saw the man, he felt compassion for him. Going over to him, the Samaritan soothed his wounds with olive oil and wine and bandaged them. Then he put the man on his own donkey and took him to an inn, where he took care of him. The next day he handed the innkeeper two silver coins, telling him, 'Take care of this man. If his bill runs higher than this, I'll pay you the next time I'm here.'" [5]

When Jesus finished, He asked His inquisitor, *"Now which of these three would you say was a neighbor to the man who was attacked by bandits?"* [6]

The man replied, *"The one who showed him mercy."* [7]

Then Jesus said, *"Yes, now go and do the same."* [8]

The scribe's countenance swiftly changed from brash and confident to one of discomfort. He quickly left and went on his way. Jesus announced He wanted us to be in Bethany by nightfall, so we began the journey.

Though many people thought the story Jesus told that day was just another parable, I knew better. On the walk to Bethany, I asked Jesus about it and He confirmed that this story was true! He then shared more details.

The one person He did not disclose to us was the victim – the man who was traveling from Jerusalem to Jericho. We surmised the man was one of the countless tradesmen who traveled that road, probably on a regular basis. He was transporting his goods to Jericho to sell. Unfortunately, he ran up on a group of bandits who beat him, robbed him, and left him for dead. And then Jesus' words struck my heart; apparently, the ringleader of the bandits was my old "friend" Barabbas.

I was greatly saddened to hear how low Barabbas had sunk. He was now nothing more than a common criminal. I couldn't help but think back to our days together in Jerusalem. But maybe I didn't know him as well, even back then, as I thought I did.

The priest who came along and saw the injured man on the side of the road was none other than the former high priest Annas. He was traveling on important Temple business and could not be inconvenienced. Besides, he was an important person and his time was valuable. It would be much more appropriate for someone else to attend to the man, so Annas and the entourage traveling with him continued to pass by on the other side of the road.

Barabbas and his friends were accountable for the harm that had come to this man, but Annas and his companions were equally accountable for their failure to help him. Though Barabbas and Annas never collaborated, they were both to blame for this man's misfortune. Something told me this wouldn't be the last time those two men would be complicit in an ill-fated effort.

· · ·

Next to pass was a young Levite. He was frequently called upon by the Sanhedrin to investigate important matters and was becoming a recognized expert in the law of Moses. As a matter of fact, today he had been chosen by the Sanhedrin to come and question Jesus.

Yes, the scribe who tested Jesus was the same Levite who had passed by the man in need! The scribe quickly realized Jesus knew what he had done when Jesus was telling the story. But he couldn't figure out how Jesus knew; there hadn't been anyone else in sight that day.

As he looked into Jesus' eyes, he realized Jesus did in fact know! And from that point forward, the scribe averted his eyes and no longer looked directly at Jesus. As a matter of fact, he wanted Jesus to hurry up and finish the story so that he could get away from there – and Him – as quickly as possible.

The next person to come along was the Samaritan. He was from the village of Sychar and had previously met Jesus. The woman who had been living with him at the time had met Jesus at Jacob's well. She had told him, and almost everyone else in the village, about Jesus – and then he had met Jesus for himself!

From that day forward, his life had been changed as he sought to honor God through his every thought, word, and action. As he came upon the man on the road, he quickly realized that the man was a Jew. His first thought had been to pass him by. But quickly the question had come to his mind, "What would Jesus have me do?" He didn't need to think twice. He immediately stopped to care for the man.

The fact that the "hero" of the story was a Samaritan made it more poignant to the scribe and the other Jews who had been listening. It would have been one thing if the story had been about a Jew stopping to help a Samaritan; but, the fact that a Samaritan stopped to help a Jew, combined with the fact that two other Jews had already passed by, was a stirring indictment.

The Samaritan had shown love to someone who hated him. He was risking his own life and spending his own money. And he wasn't seeking any credit or honor for what he was doing. Instead, he felt compassion and showed the man mercy. There was no earthly reason for him to do what he did – giving of his time and his resources – without expecting anything in return. His only motivation was that of "loving his neighbor" as Jesus had taught him.

The scribe had intended to debate Jesus about *"who is my neighbor."* Instead, Jesus forced him to consider the man he had ignored. Ministering to the Jewish man on the side of the road had cost the Samaritan two silver coins and some time, but not helping the man had cost Annas and the scribe much more. It revealed their hearts and their lack of compassion. It revealed a carelessness and indifference toward their fellow man. How could they truly be shepherds of the people if they were unwilling to help someone directly in their path who was lost and hurting?

As we continued our journey to Bethany, Jesus turned to me and said, "Shimon, you're a shepherd. Tell us – do sheep ever go astray?"

"Yes, Teacher," I replied, "all of the time!"

"Why do they stray?" He asked.

· · ·

"Because they are foolish and easily distracted from the flock," I answered. "It is their tendency to stray. That is why we must constantly be watching them."

Jesus then asked me, "If you have a hundred sheep and one of them gets lost, what do you do?"

This was an easy question to answer because I had done it many times. I replied, "I will leave the ninety-nine others with the other shepherds and go to search for the one that is lost until I find it."

"Why will you search for the one that is lost?" Jesus asked.

"Because every sheep is dear to me," I responded. "I know the ninety-nine are safe. But the one sheep left alone will place itself in danger. I will search near and far. I do not want to lose any sheep no matter how foolish they are. A lost sheep means money out of my pocket. And an unrecovered sheep means I have been careless. They are my sheep, and they are under my care."

Jesus continued, "Have you ever taken great personal risk to recover a lost sheep?"

"Yes, Master," I said. "I have climbed to very dangerous heights to rescue a sheep that was trapped on the ledge of a mountain."

"What do you do when you have rescued the sheep?" Jesus asked.

. . .

That, too, was easy to answer because I had done this many times before. "I will place the sheep over my shoulders," I replied, "and carry it back to the rest of the flock – for all to see and rejoice with me!"

Jesus said, *"In the same way, there is rejoicing in heaven over one lost sinner who repents and returns to God!"* [9]

He went on to explain to us that the prophets had made it clear all of us have sinned and gone astray. Then He said, *"I came to seek and to save those who are lost."* [10] And He made sure we understood that if we were truly His followers, we must show the same compassion for His lost sheep.

When we arrived in Bethany, we immediately went to the home of Lazarus and his sisters, Martha and Mary. By this point, Lazarus, Martha, and Mary had become good friends of Jesus, and every time we traveled through Bethany, Jesus would lodge and dine with them. Tonight was no exception. However, on this occasion, Lazarus was away on business, so Martha and Mary were not only serving, they were also the hosts.

The entourage that traveled with Jesus now numbered about eighty people. You can imagine Martha's consternation when she learned she had eighty unexpected guests arriving for dinner! Martha wanted everything to be perfect for Jesus – the food, the accommodations, and the hospitality. Jesus had healed her brother of leprosy. There was no way her family could ever repay Him. Attending to all of the details to make Jesus' stay comfortable was a lot for Martha to balance!

From the moment Jesus arrived and sat down, Mary had knelt at His feet. This was her act of gratitude, servitude, and affection. Mary's heart was also overflowing with gratitude to Jesus for healing her brother. But Martha and Mary expressed their love and gratitude in different ways. They reminded me of my own sisters, Hannah and Rachel. Hannah had always expressed her affection through acts of service, and Rachel through her desire to give of her time in conversation and companionship. Being here with Martha and Mary made me ache to see my own family.

As the evening progressed, Martha approached Jesus and said to Him, *"Lord, doesn't it seem unfair to You that my sister just sits here while I do all the work? Tell her to come and help me."*[11]

But Martha was surprised by Jesus' response: *"My dear Martha, you are worried and upset over all these details! There is only one thing worth being concerned about. Mary has discovered it, and it will not be taken away from her."*[12]

I will confess that at first I was taken aback by Jesus' response to Martha. It sounded as if Jesus were belittling Martha's hard work and the love she was expressing for Him through her service that night. She clearly wanted the experience of her honored Guest to be the best it could possibly be. And I was mindful that I, too, always wanted to do my absolute best for Jesus. But as I thought about His response, I realized He wasn't belittling her effort; rather, He was reminding her our work on His behalf must never become a substitute for spending time with Him. Our work must always flow *out* of our time with Him.

I thought back to the conversation earlier that day with the scribe. We had been taught from birth that our relationship with God was built around the do's and don'ts of our works. But Jesus was teaching us our actions must flow out of a love relationship with Him – a relationship of mercy and grace, not one earned out of work or obedience. As always, the words Jesus directed to one person – in this case, Martha – were not just intended for her, they were intended for all of us. Just as I had heard Jesus say many times before: *"Anyone with ears to hear should listen and understand!"*[13]

* * *

"There is still one thing you lack."[1]

* * *

One day we encountered ten lepers as we approached a village between Galilee and Samaria. Most of the lepers we had met lived in complete solitude, isolated from friends and family, like Lazarus had been before Jesus healed him. But these men were living in community with one another.

Leprosy had become the great equalizer. Some of the men were from Galilee, some were from Judea, and some were from Samaria. Some were fishermen, some were farmers, some were even landowners. Normally these men would have had nothing to do with one another. As a matter of fact, normally they would have had great disdain for each other.

But leprosy had changed all of that. They had discovered a companionship with one another through their disease. They were a group of different cultures, different beliefs, different races, but they had been brought together by one common circumstance – they were all considered outcasts and unclean.

They remained together "at a distance" from the village and weren't permitted to have contact with anyone outside of their group. They would be stoned to death if they dared to try. If an outsider attempted to talk with them, that person would be deemed unclean and would also be banished from the village. These men led a lonely, miserable life with nothing to look forward to but death.

But even in their isolation, these men had heard about the miracles Jesus had performed. They knew He had the power to heal them. As they saw Him approaching, they recognized Him and cried out, *"Jesus, have mercy on us!"* [2] Unlike Lazarus, these men did not attempt to approach Jesus. They remained a safe distance away.

This time, Jesus did not reach out to touch any of the men. Rather, He simply said to them, *"Go, show yourselves to the priests."* [3]

The men did not ask anything more of Jesus. I could not see any visible change in their appearance, as we had when Lazarus was healed. These men still showed all the signs of leprosy. And yet, they immediately turned, in obedience to Jesus, and headed to the village to show themselves to the priests.

Though we had all seen Jesus heal people many times, we stood there wondering what would happen when these leprous men walked into the village. Previously when Jesus healed someone, the results had been immediate. But nothing visible had occurred with these men!

. . .

As the lepers got closer to the village, I fully expected to hear screams coming from the townspeople. But we didn't hear any screams! Rather, we watched as the men jumped up and down excitedly and embraced one another. One of the men turned and ran back toward us.

As he got closer, we could see his leprosy had disappeared. The only indication he had ever been diseased was the appearance of his clothes. His skin was as clear as mine. As he approached Jesus, he shouted, *"Praise God!"* He explained that when the men were a short distance from the village, they looked at each other and realized they had been healed! The former leper fell to the ground at Jesus' feet, giving Him thanks and praise for what He had done.

After a moment, Jesus asked him, *"Didn't I heal ten men? Where are the other nine? Has no one returned to give glory to God except for this one* Samaritan?"[4] Then Jesus looked down on the man with compassion and said, *"Stand up and go. Your faith has healed you."*[5]

All of the lepers were men of faith, but all of them – except the Samaritan – lacked one thing. Though the other nine had also received the gift of healing, they had failed to thank the Giver. As a result, they did not receive all the Master wanted to do in, through, and for them. Their spirit of thanklessness left them with their sins unforgiven. Ten lepers had been healed physically, but only one left that day with his sins forgiven.

I had seen many people come to Jesus out of curiosity or out of need during my time with Him. Most followed Him from a distance, seeking what Jesus could do for them – a miracle, a meal, money, or position. Some of us followed Him closely and intimately because we believed, and we surrendered our lives to Him.

There were those who followed but eventually turned away, rejecting His declarations that He came from heaven, and that He is the son of God. They ultimately rejected Him. Some refused to believe because He threatened their power and position – like the religious leaders. Some, like this leper, came to the very feet of Jesus, and their lives were forever changed. They experienced physical and spiritual healing through the love and the touch of the Master.

But one day, a man came running up to Jesus, just as the healed leper had done. Though he was young, he was a religious leader and enjoyed a position of authority. He appeared to be very wealthy and seemed to have everything going for him. As he approached Jesus, he knelt down.

Unlike most of the religious leaders who questioned Jesus, this man did not appear to have ulterior motives. He didn't act like he was trying to entrap Jesus with his questions. He seemed to seek Jesus with an attitude similar to what I had seen in Nicodemus and Joseph of Arimathea. He was obviously a student of the law – most likely a teacher himself.

I had noticed him in the crowd following Jesus for some time now. He listened as Jesus taught and watched as Jesus performed miracles. He seemed to genuinely respect Jesus as a teacher. I could tell there was something on his mind … something he obviously wanted to ask Jesus. Apparently, he didn't feel comfortable asking the Pharisees and priests but believed Jesus could help him. I watched as he worked up the nerve to approach Jesus: *"Good Teacher, what must I do to inherit eternal life?"* [6]

. . .

Addressing Jesus as "Good Teacher" was a sign of respect. The young man had probably used that title for other mentors and teachers whom he greatly admired. It took him – and to be honest, all of us – by surprise when Jesus responded by saying, *"Why do you call Me good? Only God is truly good."*[7]

But then Jesus went on to say, *"But to answer your question, you know the commandments. You must not murder. You must not commit adultery. You must not steal. You must not testify falsely. You must not cheat anyone. Honor your father and mother."*[8]

The young man looked relieved when he replied that he had obeyed all of these commandments since his youth. His view was consistent with what the religious leaders were teaching – that a person could do something to merit eternal life. But he failed to notice that Jesus had only listed the fifth through tenth commandments. These commandments speak to how we are to relate to others. But the first four commandments, which Jesus had not listed, speak to how we relate to God.

When Jesus prefaced His response to the man by asking, *"Why do you call me good? Only God is truly good."*[7] Jesus was, in fact, pointing him back to those very first commandments – that eternal life is the result of our relationship with God and not what we have done (or not done) for others.

And then Jesus put the young man's relationship with God to the test: *"Go and sell all your possessions and give the money to the poor, and you will have treasure in heaven. Then come, follow Me."*[9]

. . .

The issue was not the man's riches; the issue was that he valued his riches over his relationship with God. And he did not see himself as a condemned sinner before a holy God. He thought his superficial good works were sufficient to merit favor with God.

Time and again, many others have stumbled on this very point. They value riches, possessions, position, or other relationships over their relationship with God. Jesus had felt a genuine love for this young man, just as He had demonstrated His love for each one of us. The reality is He loved us long before we ever loved Him.

And if we refuse to love Him with our whole heart, soul, and mind and refuse to surrender everything else in our lives to Him, then we will walk away empty, incomplete, and unfulfilled. No matter what else we possess, there will always be a void in our lives that cannot be filled apart from one thing – a loving relationship with the heavenly Father.

Jesus looked at the man, waiting for him to respond. He didn't plead with him. He spoke the truth in love. Now it was up to the young man to decide.

The man hung his head and walked away from Jesus without saying a word. As he left, Jesus looked at us and said, *"How hard it is for the rich to enter the Kingdom of God! In fact, it is easier for a camel to go through the eye of a needle than for a rich person to enter the Kingdom of God!"* [(10)]

We were all astounded by Jesus' statement, and several in our group asked, *"Then who in the world can be saved?"* [(11)]

.   .   .

Jesus looked at us intently and said, *"Humanly speaking, it is impossible. But not with God. Everything is possible with God."*[(12)]

Then Peter spoke up and said, *"Master, we've given up everything to follow You."*[(13)]

"Yes," Jesus replied, *"and I assure you that everyone who has given up house or brothers or sisters or mother or father or children or property, for My sake and for the Good News, will receive now in return a hundred times as many houses, brothers, sisters, mothers, children, and property – along with persecution. And in the world to come that person will have eternal life. But many who are the greatest now will be least important then, and those who seem least important now will be the greatest then."*[(14)]

Jesus then told us this story: *"There was a certain rich man who was splendidly clothed in purple and fine linen and who lived each day in luxury. At his gate lay a poor man named Lazarus who was covered with sores. As Lazarus lay there longing for scraps from the rich man's table, the dogs would come and lick his open sores. Finally, the poor man died and was carried by the angels to sit beside Abraham at the heavenly banquet.*

"The rich man also died and was buried, and he went to the place of the dead. There, in torment, he saw Abraham in the far distance with Lazarus at his side. The rich man shouted, 'Father Abraham, have some pity! Send Lazarus over here to dip the tip of his finger in water and cool my tongue. I am in anguish in these flames.' But Abraham said to him, 'Son, remember that during your lifetime you had everything you wanted, and Lazarus had nothing. So now he is here being comforted, and you are in anguish. And besides, there is a great chasm separating us. No one can cross over to you from here, and no one can cross over to us from there.'

. . .

"Then the rich man said, 'Please, Father Abraham, at least send him to my father's home. For I have five brothers, and I want him to warn them so they don't end up in this place of torment.' But Abraham said, 'Moses and the prophets have warned them. Your brothers can read what they wrote.' The rich man replied, 'No, Father Abraham! But if someone is sent to them from the dead, then they will repent of their sins and turn to God.' But Abraham said, 'If they won't listen to Moses and the prophets, they won't be persuaded even if someone rises from the dead.'" [15]

Jesus then explained He was telling us what would happen to that young man in the future. The rich young man was in fact the rich man clothed in purple and fine linen in His story, Jesus declared. One day, he would find himself in the place of the dead. In his lifetime he would think he was doing good by allowing the sick and the poor to eat scraps from his table. He would attempt to earn his way to heaven through his wealth and his good works. But his good works would never be good enough.

He could never do enough to inherit eternal life, because it is humanly impossible. But the one whom Jesus called Lazarus – though he had nothing – would enter into eternal life because he had believed in and trusted Jesus. The Master concluded by saying, "Eternal life is a gift from God by His grace, which will never be earned or deserved. It can only be received by believing in Me by faith."

After hearing Jesus' teaching that day, a number of those who had been traveling with us turned away. They had followed Jesus in order to see what they could get from Him – not what they needed to surrender to Him. They were sheep who thought they knew better than the Shepherd. I saw the sadness in the Shepherd's eyes – because He knew the condition of their hearts.

* * *

18

"Where are your accusers? Didn't even one of them condemn you?"
"No, Lord," she said. And Jesus said, "Neither do I. Go and sin no more."[1]

* * *

Six months had passed since Jesus fed the five thousand. It was now October. We had been traveling throughout Galilee as Jesus continued to teach and perform miracles in the villages. Though we did not fully comprehend all that was taking place, Jesus knew the religious leaders in Jerusalem were plotting to kill Him. So, He decided to stay out of Judea. His decision was not out of fear of the religious leaders; rather, He knew His time had not yet come.

The annual Festival of Tabernacles was approaching. This was a time when we as Jews looked back at God's provision for His people in the wilderness and looked forward to the coming of the Messiah. Since the Israelites lived in tents during the wilderness journey, the feast is characterized by tents, or shelters. During the festival, the inner court of the Temple is illuminated with torches. These torches represent the pillar of fire that guided the Israelites by night. And according to the prophet Malachi, it is a reminder that when the Messiah comes as the Light, He will take up residence in His Temple.[2]

Jesus' half brothers – James, Joseph, Simon, and Jude – were headed to the festival in Jerusalem, as was the practice of all Jewish men. At this point, His brothers were not following Jesus because they did not believe Him to be the Son of God. They admitted He had a special anointing and a gift to perform miracles, but that was the extent of their belief. So, any advice they gave Him was influenced by their doubt.

They counseled Jesus to go to Jerusalem and prove Himself to the world by putting His miracles on display for everyone to see! Jerusalem would be crowded with religious pilgrims, and this would give Jesus an opportunity to enlist more disciples and gain the approval of the crowd. His brothers knew many of His disciples had recently abandoned Him. They were aware the religious leaders were plotting against Jesus, and they did not want any harm to come to Him.

Rather, they wanted Jesus to be honored by the people in a way that would keep the religious leaders from doing Him any harm. They reasoned He couldn't be honored if He stayed in Galilee. And while they truly did want Him to be honored, they also were aware His notoriety and success would bring them gain as well. After all, brothers of the Messiah surely would hold positions of prestige in His kingdom!

Many in our party thought this was wise advice. Judas Iscariot in particular encouraged Jesus to heed His brothers' guidance. They all thought it was time for Jesus to declare Himself as Messiah and assume His role as leader of the nation. Just like Jesus' brothers, Judas and others were certain they would benefit, too. Jesus knew what they were thinking, and He knew their counsel was anything but wise. It was contrary to His wisdom and the will of the Father.

Once His half brothers left, Jesus told us we would all be attending the festival. However, He planned to stay out of public view and arrive midway through the festivities.

As the festival began, the religious leaders were surprised – and disappointed – when Jesus did not arrive. They kept asking people in the crowd if anyone had seen Him, and they continued to spread lies that Jesus was a fraud and a deceiver. As two days passed, they decided He was not coming and their plan to capture Him would have to wait. Imagine their surprise when halfway through the festival Jesus showed up in the Temple and began to teach!

Jesus knew what the leaders had been saying about Him so He told the crowd as they began to gather, *"Anyone who wants to do the will of God will know whether My teaching is from God or is merely My own. Those who speak for themselves want glory only for themselves, but a person who seeks to honor the One who sent Him speaks truth, not lies."* [3]

Some in the crowd began to ask each other, *"Isn't this the man they are trying to kill? But here He is, speaking in public, and they say nothing to Him. Could our leaders possibly believe that He is the Messiah? But how could He be? For we know where this man comes from. When the Messiah comes, He will simply appear; no one will know where He comes from."* [4]

Jesus heard their questions and called out, *"Yes, you know Me, and you know where I come from. But I'm not here on My own. The one who sent Me is true, and you don't know Him. But I know Him because I come from Him, and He sent Me to you."*[5]

Many in the crowd at the Temple believed in Him. *"After all,"* they said, *"would you expect the Messiah to do more miraculous signs than this Man has done?"*[6] When the Pharisees heard what people were saying, they sent the Temple guards to arrest Jesus.

By the climax of the festival, the crowd was divided over who Jesus was. Some of them declared, *"Surely this man is the Prophet we've been expecting."*[7] Others said, *"He is the Messiah."*[8] But some argued, *"But He can't be! Will the Messiah come from Galilee? For the Scriptures clearly state that the Messiah will be born of the royal line of David, in Bethlehem, the village where King David was born."*[9]

I wanted to shout at them that Jesus *had* been born in the village of Bethlehem, and that He had been born of the royal line of King David. I wanted to cry out that I had been there when the angels announced His birth. I had seen Him as a baby that night in the manger. But Jesus stopped me. "You will never lead them into the Kingdom by winning a debate. Only those who are drawn by the Father will believe. And as they believe, they will enter into the Kingdom of God."

When the Temple guards returned to the religious leaders without arresting Jesus, the leading priests and Pharisees demanded, *"Why didn't you bring Him in?"*[10]

"We have never heard anyone speak like this!"[11] the guards responded.

"Have you been led astray, too?"[12] the Pharisees mocked. *"Is there a*

single one of us rulers or Pharisees who believes in Him? This foolish crowd follows Him, but they are ignorant of the law. God's curse is on them!" [13]

Then Nicodemus, the Pharisee, stood up among them and said, *"Is it legal to convict a man before He is given a hearing?"* [14]

But the leaders abruptly belittled him as one of Jesus' fellow Galileans, and pointedly reminded everyone that no one of importance could possibly come from Galilee. At that point the meeting broke up, and everyone went home for the night.

Early the next morning Jesus was back teaching in the Temple – and the crowd had formed again. At a time when they could create the greatest possible spectacle, the scribes and Pharisees brought a woman before Jesus. They had caught the woman in the act of adultery.

"Teacher, this woman was caught in the act of adultery," her accusers said smugly. *"The law of Moses says to stone her. What do You say?"* [15]

The woman stood there – disheveled and in disarray – as a mixture of defiance, embarrassment, fear, and regret flashed across her face. The religious leaders who accused her lined up behind her, waiting with an air of superiority and contempt for Jesus to reply.

As I watched, it became obvious this spectacle was being orchestrated to ensnare Jesus. Where was the man who was caught in the act with her? The law required both the adulterer and the adulteress be put to death. [16] Since the man had not been brought before the crowd, it was clear the accusers were not trying to enforce the law; rather, they were seeking to trap Jesus so they could accuse Him.

. . .

The adulterous man was probably just a puppet in the religious leaders' plot. Their goal was not to stone the woman as the law required; instead, their goal was to stone Jesus.

The crowd pressed in, leering at the woman and craning their necks to watch Jesus. In the midst of them all, Jesus stooped to write in the sand, ignoring all the commotion around Him. Talk about peace in the midst of a storm! That time on the boat when Jesus stilled the storm didn't even begin to compare with this!

I strained to see what Jesus was writing in the sand. He was listing names, with a sin recorded beside each one. By one He wrote "adultery;" by another He wrote "blasphemy;" by yet another He wrote "thievery." He must have listed twenty different names and sins.

I soon realized Jesus was entering the names of the woman's accusers – in the form of a ledger detailing their specific sins. These were "secret" sins the religious leaders believed no one else knew about. Sins, that if they were made public, would not only cause great embarrassment but would also cost them their positions of influence. They could even cost some of them their lives.

As the religious leaders again pressed the question, Jesus replied, *"All right, but let the one who has never sinned throw the first stone!"* [17]

One by one, as each looked more closely at what Jesus had written, he realized that Jesus knew his secret sin! It wasn't repentance that overtook the men, it was fear! Scowling, they turned and left, pretending to have some pressing business that required their attention. But they didn't leave out of remorse over conviction of their sin; they left out of fear and hatred. Now they had more motivation than ever to destroy Jesus ... who knew everything they had ever done.

The woman whom the religious leaders had used as a ploy was still waiting for Jesus to pass judgment. Though she was guilty of adultery, Jesus had not come that day to judge her. He had come to save her.

Jesus looked at her and said, *"Woman, where are your accusers? Didn't even one of them condemn you?"* [18]

"No, Lord," [19] she said.

To which Jesus replied, *"Neither do I. Go and sin no more."* [20]

After bringing to light the sins of the religious leaders, Jesus turned back to the crowd and said, *"I am the light of the world. If you follow Me, you won't have to walk in darkness, because you will have the light that leads to life."* [21]

He explained how darkness and light cannot co-exist because darkness is the absence of light. Darkness cannot extinguish light, for it is light that erases the darkness. Unholiness and unjustness cannot survive in the light, as we had all just witnessed with the religious leaders. Jesus is absolute holiness and justness because He is the Light.

There is no beauty or color without light. However, Jesus has made everything beautiful in its time, [22] because He alone is the Light.

Those who follow Him have the Light, but those who do not follow Him walk in darkness. The Light leads to life; darkness leads to death.

As I reflected over the events that happened during the Feast of Tabernacles, I thought about how the torches placed in the inner court of the Temple were a reminder that God had led the children of Israel by the light of a pillar of fire. Whenever and wherever the pillar of fire led, the Israelites followed. It was not coincidental Jesus used this analogy of light in the midst of this celebration. And it wasn't lost on the Pharisees, either! Jesus was again declaring to them Who He is.

It occurred to me that when Jesus wrote in the sand, He literally and figuratively had drawn a line. The line divided light from darkness, truth from fabrication, and righteousness from sin. There is no "in between" place. There is no "almost good enough." There is law, and there is grace. There is only One who will ever measure up under the law. It is by Him and through Him that God's grace is extended.

The words of the prophet Isaiah came to mind: All of us, like sheep, have strayed away. And all of us have turned to go our own way. But God is preparing to lay on Him the sins of us all.[23] And I began to get a hint of where this journey was heading.

* * *

19

"Who is He, Sir? I want to believe in Him."[1]

* * *

It seemed to me that everyone came to Jesus expecting something. We all looked at Him through our own personal lens. Those looking for a Messiah who would establish His government and break the bonds of Roman rule saw Jesus as their pathway to freedom. Those who sought position and prestige in His new government saw Him as their pathway to power. Those who sought healing or relief saw Him as their pathway to deliverance.

The religious leaders who were seeking to hold on to their own positions and power saw Him as a threat. In our eyes, He was a Teacher, a Prophet, a Miracle Worker, a Judge, the Messiah, or even a threat. But none of us had fully grasped the truth He was the Son of God come to earth to be our Savior. Though some of us had been with Jesus for almost three years and listened to His teachings, we were still somewhat blinded.

. . .

That was even true of His twelve apostles. One day as we were all walking, Jesus turned to us and asked, *"Who do people say I am?"* [2]

Andrew answered, *"Some say You are John the Baptizer."*

Thaddeus said, *"Some say Elijah."*

Thomas spoke up and said, *"Others say you are one of the prophets."* [3]

Then Jesus asked, *"Who do you say I am?"* [4]

Peter was the first to reply: *"You are the Messiah."* [5]

As Peter's answer hung in the air for a few moments in silence, a number of us looked at one another and nodded in agreement – first Judas Iscariot, then John, followed by the other son of Zebedee, and so on, until everyone agreed. Jesus then told us not to tell anyone else who He was. I didn't understand His warning at the time. We were His followers. We had credibility as the ones who knew Him best. Why wouldn't He want us to bear witness to who He was?

Judas Iscariot was probably the most incredulous about His warning. He, like others, could not understand why Jesus wanted to keep this a secret. It was several months later before I realized why He had cautioned us to remain silent. The truth was we still had much to learn about Him and who He truly was.

. . .

As we were walking along the trade road, just south of Jerusalem, we passed a blind man begging alongside the road, near the Pool of Siloam. Jesus pointed to him, so that one of His disciples would give him something to eat. Philip quickly walked over to speak with the man and shared a piece of bread with him from his sack. He learned the man had been born blind, and each day someone helped him come to this place so he might receive coins or food from the merchants and travelers who passed by. As Philip stood there with the man, he called out to Jesus and asked, *"Teacher, why was this man born blind? Was it because of his own sins or his parents' sins?"* [6]

Jesus answered, *"It was not because of his sins or his parents' sins. This happened so the power of God could be seen in him."* [7]

As I looked around at our group, it was obvious everyone was puzzled by Jesus' statement. How was the power of God being displayed through the life of this blind man as he sat beside the road begging? We couldn't see anything either powerful or very God-like about this man.

Jesus could see our lack of understanding, so He said, *"We must quickly carry out the tasks assigned us by the One who sent us.* [8] *The time is quickly coming when we will no longer be able to do any work. But the Father has placed Me here in the world for just such a moment. I am the light of the world.* [9] And where there is light there can be no darkness."

Then Jesus walked over to the man. Without saying a word, He spat on the ground, made mud with His saliva and spread the mud over the blind man's eyes. Then He told him, *"Go wash yourself in the pool."* [10] Immediately, the man stood to his feet. He had no idea who Jesus was.

But He had spoken with authority, and the man's heart compelled him to do exactly what Jesus had said.

I walked up to the man and placed his hand on my shoulder so I could lead him to the pool. Once there, the man knelt and washed the mud from his eyes. He squinted at first and then fully opened his eyes. For the first time in his life, he saw light. He couldn't believe the brightness! He shielded the light from his eyes as he began to blink rapidly, adjusting to this new sensation. After a few minutes, his senses were bombarded with the new stimuli of light and color.

I stood there in amazement as he took my face in his hands and stared at me. He had never seen another person. He had never seen anything! All of a sudden, joy began to spread across his face, and he could not contain his excitement. He asked me who had applied the mud to his eyes, and I pointed to Jesus. Immediately, the man ran back to Jesus, knelt at His feet, and thanked Him profusely. Jesus told him to get up, go back to his village, and find his family.

As the man walked away, I was reminded of Jesus' miracle in Cana. Did the water turn to wine when the servants filled the water pots? Or did it become wine when they drew it out in obedience and took it to the host? Was this man healed of his blindness when Jesus applied the mud? Or was he healed when he walked in obedience to the pool?

I believed it was the latter case in both instances. Jesus responded to the faith of the servants and the faith of this man and, as a result, miracles occurred. In both instances, as with all miracles Jesus performed, God was glorified. Just as Jesus had said when we first saw the blind man, the power of God had been displayed through the life of this man born blind.

· · ·

When the man entered his village, his neighbors began to point at him saying, *"Isn't this the man who used to sit and beg?"* [11] Some said he was, but others said he wasn't. But the man kept saying, *"Yes, I am the same one! The man they call Jesus made mud and spread it over my eyes and told me, 'Go to the pool of Siloam and wash yourself.' So I went and washed, and now I can see!"* [12]

As we entered the village, I saw that his neighbors were taking the man to the Pharisees. I decided to follow to see how everyone was responding to this miracle of God. When the man was brought before the Pharisees, he explained how Jesus had enabled him to see.

But instead of rejoicing in the miracle, some of the Pharisees denounced Jesus as not being sent by God because He had healed the man on the Sabbath. Still others argued, *"How could an ordinary sinner do such miraculous signs?"* [13] So they set out to disprove the miracle. They questioned the man again to see if there were inconsistencies in his story. Surely this man had not been blind from birth. His blindness must have been only a temporary condition that had somehow corrected itself.

The Pharisees decided to send for the man's parents so they could question them. When his parents entered the synagogue, the man ran to them and they embraced. He was seeing his parents for the first time in his life! The Pharisees grew impatient and interrupted the family reunion with their questions. His parents confirmed he had in fact been born blind, but they had no idea how he was now able to see ... short of a miracle.

The village was now aware the Pharisees were trying to denounce Jesus by discrediting the miracle. And it was obvious they would seek retribution against anyone who got in their way. But the parents' testimony left little doubt a miracle had taken place. So, the Pharisees continued to press on in an effort to dishonor Jesus while acknowledging the miracle had occurred. They announced, *"God should get the glory for this, but we know this man Jesus is a sinner."* (14)

"I don't know whether He is a sinner," the man who had been given sight replied. *"But I know this: I was blind, and now I can see!"* (15)

As the Pharisees continued to press him, the man became bolder in his response. The more they tried to discredit Jesus, the closer the man was drawn to Him. *"Look!"* the man exclaimed. *"I told you once. Didn't you listen? Why do you want to hear it again? Do you want to become His disciples, too?"* (16)

His last question made the Pharisees angry. *"You may be His disciple,"* they said, *"but we are disciples of Moses! We know God spoke to Moses, but we don't even know where this man comes from."* (17)

"Why, that's very strange!" the man replied. *"He healed my eyes, and yet you don't know where He comes from? We know that God doesn't listen to sinners, but He is ready to hear those who worship Him and do His will. Ever since the world began, no one has been able to open the eyes of someone born blind. If this man were not from God, He couldn't have done it."* (18)

The one whose eyes had been opened was now schooling the "teachers" whose eyes were blinded by unbelief. The Pharisees were furious.

"You were born a total sinner!" they scorned. *"Are you trying to teach us?"* (19)

· · ·

The irony of their statement wasn't lost on me. Here they were, accusing the man of being born a sinner – as if they themselves were not born sinners! And they insisted the man had been born blind either because of his own sin or his parents' sin. Jesus had told us he was born blind for the glory of God, but these men were too blind to see it.

In their rage, the Pharisees "excommunicated" the former blind man from the synagogue. An audible gasp went up from the crowd. The Pharisees were wielding their ultimate power on this man whose only offense was speaking the truth. The synagogue was the center of village life. Being thrown out was tantamount to having your citizenship revoked. Your family and neighbors could no longer have anything to do with you. The parents, with whom he had just been reunited in sight, were now no longer permitted to have anything to do with him.

I went straight away to tell Jesus what had happened. He immediately set out to find the man. When He saw him in the village, Jesus asked, *"Do you believe in the Son of Man?"* [20]

The man answered, *"Who is He, Sir? I want to believe in Him."* [21]

"You have seen Him," Jesus said, *"and He is speaking to you!"* [22]

"Yes, Lord, I believe!" [23] the man said. And he fell down at the feet of Jesus and worshipped Him! Ironically, God had used the Pharisees' arguments to convince the man that Jesus *is* the Son of God.

When the religious leaders excommunicated the man from the synagogue, he was presented with a choice between religion and Jesus. He chose Jesus. He chose well! The blind man could see more in his blindness than the Pharisees could see with their sight. He had received more than physical sight that day; he had received spiritual sight and his sins had been forgiven.

Jesus turned to the crowd and said, *"I entered this world to render judgment – to give sight to the blind and to show those who think they see that they are blind."*[(24)]

Some of the Pharisees who were standing nearby heard Him and asked, *"Are You saying we're blind?"*[(25)]

Jesus replied, *"If you were blind, you wouldn't be guilty. But you remain guilty because you claim you can see."*[(26)]

No longer welcome in his synagogue or village, the man decided to follow Jesus as one of His disciples. As we began to walk down the road, a man and woman ran to catch up with us. It was the man's parents. If their son could not remain in the village, neither would they. They wanted to be with their son and learn more about this One who had given him sight. Little did we know soon we would all be seeing things much more clearly!

* * *

20

"I am the Good Shepherd. The Good Shepherd lays down His life for the sheep."[1]

* * *

A s we continued walking, Jesus turned to me and said, "Shimon, the Father has business for me to attend to in Bethlehem. How long has it been since you last saw your mother and your family?"

"It's been over two years since I last visited," I replied.

"Then it's about time. Let's go," Jesus said. And with that, we journeyed the short distance to the village of Bethlehem.

But instead of stopping in the village, Jesus led us up into the fields where I had grown up tending sheep. The shepherds led their flocks to other areas to graze in the summer, but they had just returned to the

Bethlehem hills. As we approached, I saw my brother Jacob and my sister Hannah's husband tending to their sheep, along with other shepherds from the village.

It was late in the day and they were already leading their sheep toward the sheepfold for the night. The sheepfold was constructed using rocks on two sides abutting a rocky hill that had an indentation, creating a natural enclosure. The opening that was left between the two constructed walls served as the sheep gate.

I ran ahead to see my brother and brother-in-law, not knowing how they would receive me. When we were last together, Jacob had been angry over what Jesus had done at the Temple, and he had projected that anger toward me when I chose to leave and follow Jesus. But I was relieved they both received me with an embrace and a kiss. There was no hint of animosity. Rather, it was a demonstrative reunion of close brothers who had not seen each other in a long time.

The crowd that always appeared whenever Jesus stopped was beginning to assemble – some had been following us as we traveled throughout the day and others came from the village. Jesus sat on the ground at a high point on the hill as the people gathered around Him. Soon, He began to teach.

My brother-in-law continued leading the sheep to the sheepfold so that Jacob and I could catch up on family news. Jacob told me our mother was well. On several occasions she told Jacob she wanted to leave her home and join me in following Jesus. He had discouraged her from doing so because of her age, but that had not diminished her fervor for Jesus. Jacob was certain she would want to go with us when we left! His sons were now five and three. They reminded him of the two of us when we were growing up – the older son keeping a careful watch on his younger brother.

God had continued to bless the family sheep trade. The flock continued to multiply and each season there were more sheep to sell to the Temple merchants. The priests and merchants had not yet been allowed to move the animals and tables back into the Court of the Gentiles. Jacob wasn't sure if it was out of fear of Jesus' wrath or the watchfulness that He had awakened in the people themselves. Regardless, the merchants had figured out a way to make their businesses just as profitable, so Jacob's financial challenges had been short-lived.

The last time Jacob was at the Temple, he heard the former high priest Annas was starting to make noise about bringing the merchants back into the court for Passover, but that remained to be seen. Now that things had settled down on that front, Jacob did not appear to harbor any ill will toward Jesus.

I shared with him some of what I had seen and experienced as I followed Jesus. I told him Jesus was truly the Messiah – and that He is so much more than I ever imagined the Messiah would be. I told him about all of the people I had seen Jesus heal. I told him about little Jonathan from Chorazin and how Jesus had used the lad's lunch to feed the crowd of five thousand men. I told him about the young man and young woman whom I had seen Jesus raise from the dead. "But most of all," I said, "is the way He teaches us the Scriptures in a way that reveals the truths of God – not as an endless list of rules, but rather, as how we can have a relationship with our loving Creator and Father."

I explained how I had seen Jesus talking to the Father in ways similar to how Jacob and I had spoken with our own father. There was an intimacy and a relationship I had never known anyone else to have with God. I told Jacob I had come to believe that Jesus truly is the Son of God, and I would follow Him – "wherever He goes, all the days of my life," I told him. I could tell Jacob was pondering everything I said. "Let's draw closer to where Jesus is, so we can hear Him teach," I suggested. So, we walked over to join the crowd.

As we drew closer, we could see that Jesus was pointing toward the sheepfold as He was speaking. *"I tell you the truth,"* He said, *"anyone who sneaks over the wall of a sheepfold, rather than going through the gate, must surely be a thief and a robber! But the one who enters through the gate is the shepherd of the sheep. The gatekeeper opens the gate for him, and the sheep recognize his voice and come to him. He calls his own sheep by name and leads them out. After he has gathered his own flock, he walks ahead of them, and they follow him because they know his voice. They won't follow a stranger; they will run from him because they don't know his voice."* [2]

Many people in the crowd did not fully understand what Jesus was saying, but the shepherds did. We understood clearly; each one of us had lain down at the opening to the sheepfold many times. In doing so, we became the gate to the sheepfold. Most of the time there were several flocks gathered together in the sheepfold overnight. Whichever shepherd served as the "gate," or the "gatekeeper" at night, would know each shepherd who had placed a flock in the sheepfold.

The gatekeeper wouldn't let anyone else into the sheepfold. If someone was trying to rob the sheep, the thief would have to climb over the wall. But even if the thief got in, he wouldn't be able to get the sheep to follow him. In the morning, each shepherd would come to the gate and call out his own flock. The sheep of that respective flock would respond only to their own shepherd's voice.

. . .

Jesus went on to explain His illustration. *"I tell you the truth, I am the gate for the sheep. All who came before Me were thieves and robbers. But the true sheep did not listen to them. Yes, I am the gate. Those who come in through Me will be saved. They will come and go freely and will find good pastures. The thief's purpose is to steal and kill and destroy. My purpose is to give them a rich and satisfying life."* [3]

The only way in and out of the sheepfold is through the gate. Jesus was saying that only those who trust Him enter into His sheepfold and have the privilege of going "in and out" and finding pasture. As the gate, He is the only one who can deliver sinners from bondage and lead them into freedom.

Those who "came before" Him are like the religious leaders of our day. We had just seen the Pharisees excommunicate the man born blind out of the fold. They were not true gatekeepers. They did not have the best interest of the sheep at heart. They did not love the sheep, nor did they have the approval of the Father. They were exploiting the sheep and abusing them for their own purpose. They were only interested in providing for and protecting themselves. And behind these false gatekeepers was *the* "thief" – Satan.

Jesus continued by saying, *"I am the Good Shepherd. The Good Shepherd sacrifices His life for the sheep. A hired hand will run when he sees a wolf coming. He will abandon the sheep because they don't belong to him and he isn't their shepherd. And so the wolf attacks them and scatters the flock. The hired hand runs away because he's working only for the money and doesn't really care about the sheep. I am the Good Shepherd; I know My own sheep, and they know Me, just as My Father knows Me and I know the Father. So I sacrifice My life for the sheep. I have other sheep, too, that are not in this sheepfold. I must bring them also. They will listen to My voice, and there will be one flock with one shepherd."* [4]

· · ·

I wasn't quite sure what Jesus meant when He said He would willingly sacrifice His life for His sheep. I knew John the Baptizer had referred to Him as the Lamb of God, but I had yet to learn He had voluntarily taken on the form of a "sheep." He had come down from heaven and taken on flesh so He could identify with us. It was only as a sheep without blemish He could be the sacrifice for our sin. And it was only as a sheep following the Father He could show us how to follow Him.

As a sheep, He was the Son of Man, reflecting His humanity. But as the Good Shepherd, He was reflecting who He is as the Son of God. He is not merely a hireling who watches over the sheep only because He is paid to do so. When there is danger, a hired hand will run, but every shepherd knows the true shepherd will stay to protect and care for the flock. He will willingly risk his own life for his sheep.

Jesus was teaching us that He is our Good Shepherd because He knows each one of His sheep individually. He knows our nature. He knows our needs. He knows our quirks and our shortcomings. He knows our fears. He knows our secret thoughts. And He knows us better than anyone else – including ourselves. Just as He had called each of His disciples by name and already knew each of us before we first met Him, He knows the heart of each and every person.

He is our Good Shepherd because His sheep know His voice. How many times had His voice penetrated my own heart with truth that confirmed the reality of Who He is? Time and again, He showed me He knows me intimately. He speaks to me as no other can. He speaks in a voice no other can imitate or replicate. He speaks the truth I need to hear – though not necessarily always what I *want* to hear. He speaks His truth that is absolute, perfect, and unchanging. And He speaks it *when* I need to hear it.

· · ·

His sheep may not always want to hear His voice, but we know His voice. As His sheep spend more and more time with Him, we come to know Him more intimately. And as we follow Him more closely, we grow to love and trust Him more. He has "our best" in His heart. He knows better than we do what "our best" is, and He is able to bring it about.

He is our Good Shepherd because He follows the Father. He follows Him obediently ... perfectly ... lovingly. The true Shepherd was sent by the Father. The true Shepherd loves us as sheep perfectly and cares for us meticulously. The Father bears witness to the true Shepherd.

And because our Good Shepherd follows the Father, we, as His sheep, can follow Him with confidence, with hope, and with assurance.

Then Jesus added, *"The Father loves Me because I sacrifice My life so I may take it back again. No one can take My life from Me. I sacrifice it voluntarily. For I have the authority to lay it down when I want to and also to take it up again. For this is what My Father has commanded."*[5]

When Jesus said that, the people became divided in their opinions about Him. They could not understand why He was talking about sacrificing His own life. Nor could they understand why He thought anyone was trying to take His life, because they did not understand what the religious leaders were plotting. Some said, *"He's demon possessed and out of His mind."*[6] But others said, *"How can one who is demon possessed open the eyes of the blind?"*[7] The crowd then began to break up and go their separate ways.

Jesus called out for Jacob and me to come join Him. I sensed some apprehension from Jacob, but still he walked over to meet Jesus with me. As we drew near, Jesus asked my brother, "Jacob, do you allow thieves and robbers into your sheepfold?"

"No, Teacher," he replied.

"What about wolves?" Jesus asked.

"No," Jacob answered. "I will not allow anything or anyone in the sheepfold that could harm the sheep. My responsibility as their shepherd is to protect my sheep. I will protect them from anyone or anything that could harm them."

Jesus looked straight into Jacob's eyes and said, "Jacob, I will do whatever I can to protect My sheep as well. That includes cleansing the sheepfold when there are robbers and thieves inside."

Jacob knew Jesus was referring to the day He had cleansed the Temple. Jacob realized Jesus knew the resentment he still held in his heart. But now he saw Jesus' actions that day in a much different light. Jesus had not done anything to harm His "sheep," rather He was protecting His "sheep."

"That is why I am willing to lay down My life in order for My sheep to live," Jesus added.

As a shepherd, Jacob had on occasion risked his life to protect his sheep from harm, but he wasn't certain he was willing to lay down his life for his sheep. He would lay down his life for his family, but he wasn't so sure he would do the same for his sheep. But here was Jesus telling him He would willingly do so for His sheep – and Jacob knew he was one of those sheep.

At that moment, Jacob was flooded with an awareness of the love, mercy, and grace of God, unlike anything he had ever felt or known before. As He stared into the eyes of the Teacher, he knew Jesus was inviting him to believe – and the love of Jesus compelled him. As my brother fell to his knees before the Master, Jesus said, "Jacob, today salvation has come to you and to your household."

I could not contain my joy knowing my younger brother was now a follower of Jesus. I knelt beside Jacob and wrapped my arms around him as tears of joy cascaded down our faces. Silently, as we knelt there embracing, I turned and looked at Jesus. As I did, I instantly realized why Jesus had told me the Father had given Him business to attend to in Bethlehem. Jacob was that business! Jesus had come to Bethlehem for the redemption of Jacob, if for no one else! The Good Shepherd had left the ninety-nine to seek out the one!

As we stood up, Jacob invited Jesus to come to our family home for dinner. When we arrived, my mother met us at the door. She had been watching for us. My brother-in-law had alerted the family we were in the field, so dinner preparations were already well under way and the familiar, fragrant aroma of my mother's cooking wafted in the air as we arrived.

My mother and I lingered in our embrace, then she turned to Jesus and embraced Him, welcoming Him and all of His disciples into our home. Together we all enjoyed a delightful night of fellowship around the table. Even Thomas, who at times was somewhat gloomy, seemed to enjoy himself. Jacob and John instantly became good friends. Our home was filled with abundant joy! The Master had not only come to dine with us, He had transformed our lives. And in so doing, He had transformed our home. The memories of that night together are forever etched in my mind.

The next morning, as we prepared to go, my mother informed us she was coming with us. And no one tried to talk her out of it. We all knew she was supposed to join us. God was ordering all of our steps, including hers, even though none of us, except Jesus, knew where those steps would lead.

Before we left that morning, Jesus took Jacob aside and reminded him of the psalm written by a shepherd, who also had grown up near our village:

> *The Lord is my Shepherd; I have all that I need. He lets me rest in green meadows; He leads me beside peaceful streams. He renews my strength. He guides me along right paths, bringing honor to His name. Even when I walk through the darkest valley, I will not be afraid, for You are close beside me. Your rod and Your staff protect and comfort me. You prepare a feast for me in the presence of my enemies. You honor me by anointing my head with oil. My cup overflows with blessings. Surely Your goodness and unfailing love will pursue me all the days of my life, and I will live in the house of the Lord forever.* [8]

Jacob had heard the psalm many times before, but this morning he was hearing it with new ears and receiving it with a new heart, all as a result of the Good Shepherd Himself.

* * *

21

Then Jesus shouted, "Lazarus, come out!"[1]

* * *

The Feast of Dedication, which some people call Hanukkah or the Festival of Lights, had just concluded. Once called the Feast of the Maccabees, it is an annual celebration that lasts for eight days to commemorate the cleansing of the Temple in Jerusalem after it had been desecrated by the Syrians under Antiochus Epiphanes. Antiochus massacred numerous Jews, outlawed Judaism, and looted the Temple. He even went so far as to erect an idolatrous altar on top of the altar of burnt offering, where he defiled it by sacrificing pigs. Judas Maccabaeus led a revolt in 165 B.C. to overthrow Syrian rule and restore the worship of God in the Temple.

When the Temple was recaptured, Judas Maccabaeus ordered it to be cleansed, a new altar to be built, and new holy vessels to be made. After these steps, the Temple was rededicated to the Lord. However, unadulterated, undefiled, pure olive oil with the seal of the high priest was needed for the lampstand in the Temple, which was required to burn throughout the night every night. But they could only locate one flask of oil, which would burn only one day.

It took eight days to prepare a fresh supply of pure oil for the lampstand. And, yet, that one day's supply of oil kept the lampstand burning for eight days until the new oil was ready. This miracle is commemorated during the Feast of Dedication. The festival is characterized by the illumination of synagogues and homes. It is a time of celebration, and no public mourning is permitted during the feast.

One day during the festival, Jesus had been walking through Solomon's Portico on the east side of the Temple's outer court, when the religious leaders surrounded Him and asked, *"How long are You going to keep us in suspense? If You are the Messiah, tell us plainly."*[2] How ironic! The true light – the Light of the world – was walking through the Temple in the midst of the Festival of Lights and the religious leaders were too blind to see it.

"I have already told you, and you don't believe Me," Jesus responded. *"The proof is the work I do in My Father's name. But you don't believe Me because you are not My sheep. My sheep listen to My voice; I know them, and they follow Me. I give them eternal life, and they will never perish. No one can snatch them away from Me, for My Father has given them to Me, and He is more powerful than anyone else. No one can snatch them from the Father's hand. The Father and I are one."*[3]

Not only were the religious leaders blind to the Light, they were also deaf to the Shepherd's voice. Though they possessed the Scriptures, there was no truth in them, and they sought to stone Jesus.

· · ·

Jesus told us it wasn't yet His time. We really weren't sure what He meant, but we knew His travels were with purpose. So, we thought nothing of it when He led us out of Jerusalem to travel north to Bethabara in Perea on the east side of the Jordan River.

It was winter, which is our rainy season. We pray for winter rains so our water supplies can be replenished to carry us through the arid summers. As a shepherd, I would often pray for "rains of blessing," which were particularly torrential rains to fill the water table. Very few of us ever complained about a rainy day.

The two months following the Feast of Dedication are the coldest of the year. On rare occasions, we had even seen a light snowfall. Because of the rain and the cold, we rarely traveled much this time of year, opting to stay in each village a longer period of time. Some of Jesus' disciples even returned to their own homes so they wouldn't become a burden on our hosts. The men and women traveling with Jesus now numbered over one hundred people. But for the winter, there were only about thirty of us. We remained in Bethabara for much of that winter.

A messenger arrived from Bethany one day with a message for Jesus from Martha and Mary. The women's brother, Lazarus, was seriously ill – an illness they believed could lead to his death. The sisters' message said, *"Lord, Your dear friend is very sick."*[(4)] They believed Jesus would come to Bethany to heal His friend, just as He had healed him of his leprosy.

There was no doubt in their minds if Jesus could get there, their brother would be well again. Unfortunately, Lazarus had died soon after the messenger left Bethany. By the time he arrived with the message for Jesus, Lazarus' body was already being placed in a tomb.

. . .

When Jesus received the message, He told us, *"Lazarus' sickness will not end in death. It has happened for the glory of God so that the Son of God will receive glory from this."* [5]

We mistakenly assumed Lazarus was healed as Jesus spoke those words, just as Chuza and Joanna's son had been healed. The messenger would return to Bethany the next morning to find all was well with Lazarus – or so we thought.

Jesus, however, knew better. And though He loved Lazarus, Martha, and Mary, and did not want the sisters to grieve, He decided to remain in Bethabara for two more days. We thought we were remaining there because Lazarus was already healed. We later discovered that we remained there so even greater glory would be given to the Father and the Son.

On the third day after Lazarus' body had been placed in the tomb, Jesus announced early that morning, *"Let's go back to Judea."* [6]

Immediately Peter and James spoke up. "Rabbi, only a short while ago the religious leaders in Judea were trying to stone You. Surely You don't want to go back there!"

Jesus looked at them and said, *"Our friend Lazarus has fallen asleep, but now I will go and wake him up."* [7]

Bartholomew, the apostle "without guile," replied, *"Lord, if he is sleeping, he will soon get better!"* [8]

. . .

Remember, we all thought Jesus had already healed Lazarus, until He clearly announced, "*Lazarus is dead. And for your sakes, I'm glad I wasn't there, for now you will really believe. Come, let's go see him.*"[9]

Jesus' last statement took us by surprise! Lazarus was Jesus' friend. Why had He allowed Lazarus to become ill? Didn't Jesus' friends have special privileges over illness and the like? If Lazarus didn't have special privileges, what about us? And the sisters were Jesus' friends, as well. If He had not already healed Lazarus, why had He quietly waited two more days before announcing His plans to go to Bethany?

On the other hand, the religious leaders were trying to kill Jesus. Why go back? Why risk being killed to see a dead man? Why did He not just heal him from here? He had done that before! And now Lazarus was dead! We had seen Jesus restore life before, but how long had Lazarus been dead? Was Jesus too late?

This did not make any sense to any of us. And why did He say, "For your sakes, I'm glad I wasn't there?" Thomas was the next one to speak up. He tended to look at everything with a sense of gloom and doom. But this time, he was speaking for all of us when he said, "*Let's go, too – and die with Jesus.*"[10]

Soon we set out on the journey and arrived in Bethany near the end of the day. We were told that this was now the fourth day Lazarus' body had been in the grave. As we approached, we saw people gathered around the home of Martha and Mary to console the sisters. Someone got word to the sisters that Jesus was approaching, so Martha came outside the village to meet Him. But Mary stayed in the house.

. . .

Martha's demeanor not only conveyed her grief, but also her disappointment in Jesus. Though she knew Lazarus had died before Jesus received the message, she couldn't understand why He had waited so long to come see them. The messenger she had sent to tell Jesus had already been back for two days. Also, Jesus seemed to know all things. Why hadn't He known Lazarus was sick even before He received the message? He could have come and healed Lazarus while he was still alive.

Martha knew, as did the rest of us, that no one had ever died in Jesus' presence – at least for the almost three years I had been following Him. Jesus had let her down. If He had been there, her brother would not have died. Apparently, Mary felt much the same way, because the woman who was always kneeling at the feet of Jesus hadn't even come outside to greet Him.

Martha politely, but somewhat strained, said, *"Lord, if only You had been here, my brother would not have died. But even now I know that God will give You whatever You ask."*[11]

"Your brother will rise again,"[12] Jesus told her.

Martha responded, *"Yes, he will rise when everyone else rises at the last day."*[13]

Martha believed firmly the teaching in Scripture that the dead would be resurrected at the last day. But she did not believe – and in fairness to her, none of us believed – Lazarus would rise from the grave this very day!

· · ·

Jesus told her, "Martha, *I am the resurrection and the life. Anyone who believes in Me will live, even after dying. Everyone who lives in Me and believes in Me will never ever die. Do you believe this, Martha?"* (14)

"*Yes, Lord,*" she told Him. "*I have always believed you are the Messiah, the Son of God, the One who has come into the world from God.*" (15)

Martha believed Jesus was the Messiah. But given that, why had He permitted her brother to die?

When Martha returned to the house she called Mary aside and told her, "*The Teacher is here and wants to see you.*" (16)

When the mourners at the house saw Mary leave so hastily, they assumed she was going to Lazarus' grave to weep so they followed her. Mary found Jesus at the place where Martha had left Him. Her heart compelled her to fall at His feet and cry out, "*Lord, if only You had been here, my brother would not have died.*" (17)

When Jesus saw her weeping and the other people wailing with her, a deep anger welled up within Him, and He became deeply troubled. I had only seen Jesus angry once before – the day He cleansed the Temple. I was puzzled by His anger. I knew He was not angry with Martha and Mary. I didn't even think He was angry with the people who were wailing with her.

Several days later I had an opportunity to ask Jesus about His reaction. He said He was angry at Satan and the ravages of sin and death upon His creation. He was angry at the enemy for sowing the lies of fear and hopelessness. And He had wept over the fact that the One who is "the

Resurrection and the Life" was standing right there in the midst of all of us, and none of us – Mary, Martha, the crowd, not even those of us who were His disciples – had the faith to see Him for who He truly is. None of us believed He could raise Lazarus from the grave. The enemy had blinded all of us with his lies.

As Jesus explained all of this to me, I felt like such a failure. The crowd had simply mirrored the responses and reactions of those of us who were close followers of Jesus. They mirrored our lack of faith. At a time when our words and actions could have helped build their faith, we led them astray from seeing Jesus for who He truly is.

"Where have you put him?" [18] Jesus asked the crowd that had followed Mary. They told Him, *"Lord, come and see."* [19]

When they arrived at the tomb, a stone was rolled across its entrance. *"Roll the stone aside,"* [20] Jesus told them.

He asked the crowd to show Him where the body was buried – not because He didn't know – but because He wanted them to be drawn in closer to what He was about to do. He could also have removed the stone, but He didn't so that they – and all of us – would be participants in the miracle that was about to take place.

Martha spoke up, protesting, *"Lord, he has been dead for four days. The smell will be terrible."* [21]

Jesus responded, *"Didn't I tell you that you would see God's glory if you believe?"* [22]

· · ·

So they rolled the stone aside. Jesus looked up to heaven and said, *"Father, thank You for hearing Me. I know that You always hear Me, but I said it out loud for the sake of all these people standing here, so that they will believe You sent Me."*[(23)]

Then Jesus shouted, *"Lazarus, come out!"*[(24)]

The crowd was silent as all eyes focused on the entrance of the tomb. We could not imagine what was about to happen. I'm not sure if we stood there in faith believing Lazarus was about to walk out of that tomb, or in disbelief Jesus would say something so outlandish. But I can tell you, no one looked away from that entrance!

Time stood still, but suddenly someone – or something – came hopping out of the entrance of that tomb. His hands and feet were bound in grave clothes, preventing him from walking. His face was wrapped in a headcloth, so we weren't totally sure if it was Lazarus. Jesus told those closest to him, *"Unwrap him and let him go!"*[(25)]

At first, no one moved. Was this a ghost? Would they be defiling them-selves by touching whomever or whatever this was? Then one man stepped forward and began to unwrap the grave clothes. Soon another joined him, and then another. In a couple of minutes, they had unwrapped his arms and his legs, and removed the head covering. There standing in front of everyone was Lazarus!

Martha ran toward her brother. Mary at first was conflicted whether to fall at Jesus' feet or run to her brother. She finally chose the latter. The crowd stood in stunned silence but then began shouting "Hosanna!" One by one, everyone present knelt at His feet. We knew we were on holy ground. As I knelt there looking up at Jesus, I saw movement out of the corner of my eye. It was Martha and Mary, together with the one who had been dead but was now alive, as they all, too, knelt to worship their Savior. Death had been defeated!

Yes, I had seen Jesus restore the life of Susanna's son and Jairus' daughter. But I had not seen Him raise someone who had been in the grave for four days – and neither had anyone else. Jesus truly is the Son of the Living God!

As I continued to reflect on what I had just witnessed, two thoughts came to mind. First, Jesus had called Lazarus by name. I am convinced, if He had not, there would have been a parade of every dead body within the sound of His voice coming out of their graves. When He shouts, all obey!

Second, and I have never had the opportunity to ask Lazarus about this, but I am certain when he heard Jesus call out to him, he knew he must obey. He was stepping from paradise back into a corrupt world, and someday he would have to go through the experience of death all over again. Yet, still he obeyed his Master. He stepped back into those binding grave clothes and "came out" in order to bring glory to God! I truly believe it was Lazarus who demonstrated the greatest faith that day – and maybe one of the greatest faiths of all time.

Jesus taught us all many truths through that miracle. Three were especially significant to me. First, I learned the Master's timing is absolutely perfect! His delays are purposeful. He sees the big picture – and I don't. I must always trust His timing.

Second, Lazarus wasn't immune to death or disease as a follower – or as a dear friend – and neither am I. But I can be confident Jesus will always work everything, no matter what it is, in such a way that it brings glory to God.

Third, the only thing that stands between the spoken promise of God and my realization of that promise is my faith. I must guard against the enemy trying to limit my faith. Jesus is trustworthy! I can and must trust His Word. I can and must trust His promise. I can and must trust Him!

Yes, many believed in Jesus that day. But there were also a few who slipped off to the Temple to bring a report to the Pharisees about what Jesus had done. None of us realized that day that Jesus' ministry on earth was soon coming to an end.

22

"Zacchaeus," He said, "quick, come down! For I must be a guest in your home today."[1]

* * *

Passover was again approaching, and Jesus planned to go to Jerusalem despite the threat of the religious leaders. We had learned from our recent trip to Bethany that it would be futile to try to dissuade Him. His face was set like flint on the journey before Him. We knew that nothing ever happened that caught Jesus off guard. We also knew that every journey and every act had its purpose. Nothing was ever random with Jesus. He was being led by the Father. He was following the Father. And we would follow Him.

Our journey led us to Jericho and Jesus' encounter with a tax collector by the name of Zacchaeus. But before I tell you about their encounter, I want to tell you what Zacchaeus later shared with me.

• • •

Zacchaeus hadn't always wanted to be a tax collector. He was the second son of a merchant by the name of Hiram and his wife Lydia, who lived in Jerusalem. Zacchaeus was always small for his age. His mother had been very ill throughout her pregnancy. Some attributed his small stature to her illness.

In many respects, he had been a miracle baby. The midwife had warned Lydia that her baby might not survive birth. But he and his mother did survive childbirth; Lydia, however, died soon afterward. Zacchaeus was sickly as a baby and required constant care, so Hiram arranged for a nurse to care for him. Even as a young child, he continued to be chronically ill, which caused him to be feeble and stunted his growth.

His older brother, Joshua, five years his senior, was healthy and athletic. He grew to be a handsome young man with physical strength and confidence. He was quite popular, and more favored than the younger, sickly Zacchaeus. But Joshua was also a kind brother who was always attentive and protective of his little brother. As Zacchaeus grew, the other boys would often belittle him and torment him. But they never did it when Joshua was around.

Hiram favored his oldest son. Though he would never admit it, it was obvious in the different ways he treated his two sons. He hoped both boys would become successful merchants like himself, helping him with his trade, and one day taking over the business. But he held out greater hope for Joshua's success than he did for Zacchaeus. As a result, he invested more time and effort in his older son.

Though Zacchaeus had always been viewed as less likely to succeed, he was keenly intelligent and inventive. He had persevered through a life of physical limitations with a strong mind and a determined will.

As he grew into a young man, what he lacked in brawn he made up for through his wit. Zacchaeus loved and appreciated his older brother, but he did not want to live in his shadow. He knew he needed to find his own way.

He also knew it would not be as a merchant. He realized others would always try to take advantage of him due to his slight stature. And he recognized he needed to pursue a trade that did not require great physical strength, but rather, a quick wit. He didn't particularly care what others thought of him. He had developed a pretty tough skin growing up.

Zacchaeus had carefully studied tax collectors as his father dealt with them over the years. He watched as they extracted their duty for goods his father transported out of Jerusalem. And he had watched their fellow tax collectors extract their portion as he brought his goods into Jericho. As long as goods were being bought and sold, the tax collectors appeared to be in a good position to accumulate their own wealth.

The Romans had grown accustomed to having the rest of the world pay for their comforts and amenities. The citizens of Rome knew the more their empire expanded, the less tax needed to be extracted from their own pockets. The motivation for growing their empire was more power and more riches. The strategy for achieving this was more soldiers and more taxes.

Rome did not conquer the Judean provinces out of a love for the Jewish people. They despised us and thought our notion of worshipping one God was unnatural and primitive. They had conquered our lands in order to enlarge their tax base. They then divided their conquests into taxing districts from which they extracted an assessment they believed the population could support. Those taxes were considered a tribute to Rome for the support and protection the empire provided, albeit unsolicited.

Tax collectors were required to pay the amount of that assessment to Rome up front, and then recover their money by collecting taxes from the local citizens. The tax collector would charge extra to provide for his own living and welfare. As you can imagine, the system lent itself to the practice of extortion and usury. Rome received her taxes. The tax collectors became wealthy. And the whole system was protected by the Roman soldiers.

Towns like Jerusalem and Jericho contained multiple districts with multiple tax collectors. In each of those towns, there was a chief tax collector, who not only collected taxes from his own district, but also collected a portion from the other tax collectors in his town. Every tax collector aspired to be a chief tax collector.

When he became an adult, Zacchaeus set his sights on that goal. He announced his intentions to his father and brother and walked away from his portion of the family business. To be honest, neither Hiram nor Joshua believed Zacchaeus would be successful. Tax collectors were hated and despised by everyone. Despite their wealth, they were viewed as the lowest form of sinner – right there with prostitutes and thieves.

His father and brother doubted Zacchaeus could endure the treatment he would receive. But they forgot how thick-skinned he had become over the years.

Zacchaeus began his career working as an apprentice to a tax collector so he could learn and become successful. He caught on quickly and became highly valued by his mentor. He was able to accumulate a modest savings due to his unpretentious lifestyle, which enabled him to acquire the tax rights for a small district in Jericho. Over time, through his cleverness, he was able to leverage his profits in order to acquire the rights for a more lucrative district. Zacchaeus was beginning to enjoy financial success, but with it came the ever-increasing disdain of the local townspeople. Now in his mid-forties, Zacchaeus had become the chief tax collector for the town of Jericho.

Jericho had become the winter resort for Jerusalem aristocracy. Under Roman rule, a hippodrome stadium was constructed for horse and chariot racing, as well as numerous aqueducts for irrigation, which enabled the city to display rich vegetation. It was considered to be a beautiful "city of palms" and was the site of one of Herod the Great's palaces. As a result, it was a thriving city, frequented by the "rich and famous" of Roman, Herodian, and even Jewish society. Though I knew Jesus didn't come to Jericho that day to see the rich and famous, I was still surprised when He turned His attention to one diminutive tax collector.

Zacchaeus, like everyone else, had heard about Jesus. When he saw the commotion as Jesus walked into town, he wanted to get a better look so he climbed a sycamore tree. Imagine his surprise – and ours – when Jesus looked up at him and said, *"Zacchaeus, quick, come down! I must be a guest in your home today."* [2] Jesus hadn't come to visit the leading citizens, or the chief Pharisee – He had come to spend time with a deceitful tax collector!

Zacchaeus quickly climbed down to lead Jesus and the rest of us to his home. He was beside himself with excitement as he greeted Jesus. Immediately we could hear the grumbling coming from the crowd around us: "Doesn't He realize He is going to be the guest of that notorious sinner?"

. . .

When we arrived at his home, Zacchaeus directed his servants to bring fruit and bread as we reclined at the table. He sat immediately across from his guest of honor. Zacchaeus knew he was a sinner. He had been taught the Scriptures when he was a lad. He knew the truth, but he had chosen to disregard it in order to pursue his success. He had never entertained a religious leader in his home, let alone a prophet and a miracle worker like Jesus.

When Jesus addressed him, it reminded me of the way He spoke to the rich young man.

"Sell your possessions and give the money to the poor, and you will have treasure in heaven. Then come, follow Me," Jesus commanded Zacchaeus. Unlike the young man who had valued his riches more than a relationship with God, Zacchaeus immediately believed in Jesus and let go of all that he had.

He said to Jesus, *"I will give half my wealth to the poor, Lord, and if I have cheated anyone on their taxes, I will give them back four times as much!"* [3]

He knew without any further word from Jesus he needed to make public restitution for his sin. He knew where he had cheated others, he must give back to them according to the Mosaic Law. [4]

His neighbors were astonished when Zacchaeus began to return four-fold all he had taken from them. They had heard about Jesus performing miracles, but they never imagined He could change the heart of a "crook" like Zacchaeus! It made me sad, though, to think how most of them were so overjoyed by their unexpected financial windfall but were unwilling to consider the life-changing miracle Jesus could bring about in their own lives.

Zacchaeus was an example that you can't stay where you are – or how you are – and follow the Master. He could no longer cheat and extort. He now had a heart to give instead of take. And there weren't too many opportunities to do that as a tax collector! A change in his heart required a complete change in his life. Jesus had come to Zacchaeus to seek and save him. And on that day, Zacchaeus began his own walk with the Master.

We left Jericho and began our journey to Bethany along our way to Jerusalem. The Master's work in Jericho that day was done. Zacchaeus quickly made restitution to people he had wronged. Then he left Jericho and caught up with us. He was determined to follow Jesus wherever He led. Though he may have been a man who was short physically, that day he became a giant of a man in the Kingdom of God.

* * *

23

"I assure you, wherever the Good News is preached throughout the world, this woman's deed will be talked about in her memory."[1]

* * *

What a difference seven weeks can make! Seven weeks ago, we had come to Bethany for an entirely different reason. Seven weeks ago, Lazarus was dead, and his body was lying in a tomb. Seven weeks ago, the house was filled and surrounded with mourners. Seven weeks ago, Martha and Mary couldn't understand why Jesus had delayed in responding to their request to heal their brother. Seven weeks ago, their home was filled with grief.

And then, seven weeks ago, Jesus arrived! Seven weeks ago, He told the people to roll away the stone. Seven weeks ago, with a shout, He told Lazarus to come out! Seven weeks ago, Lazarus came out of that grave – and he who had been dead was now alive. Seven weeks ago, Jesus upended all of our worlds. And nothing had been the same since!

. . .

Seven weeks ago, any doubt I still had was taken away, and once and for all I knew that Jesus – the One whose birth was announced that night by angels over the shepherds' fields – *is* the Son of the Living God who came to seek and to save those who are lost!

Seven weeks ago, Peter, James, and John lifted their outstretched arms in praise and worship as tears streamed down their cheeks, as they knelt in adoration and praise before their Lord.

Seven weeks ago, Andrew and Phillip removed their sandals as they fell prostrate before Jesus, because they knew they were standing on holy ground.

Seven weeks ago, the rest of the apostles, except Judas Iscariot, lifted their voices and began to sing "Holy, Holy, Holy" as they fell to their knees before the One who is holy.

Seven weeks ago, Martha and Mary ran toward their brother to embrace him, then together with their brother they turned and knelt at the feet of Jesus with hearts overflowing with thanksgiving.

Seven weeks ago, the crowd stood there as silent lambs trying to comprehend all they had just witnessed.

Seven weeks ago, I had seen Judas Iscariot smile while, as I would later learn, he said to himself, "Finally, Jesus will take His rightful place on the throne. All I have waited for will finally occur. Having performed this miracle, Jesus will now establish His kingdom!"

· · ·

And seven weeks ago, the council of the Sanhedrin began to plot how they might kill Jesus and Lazarus before things got further out of control. Too many people had already deserted the religious leaders and turned to Jesus. He had to be stopped!

Now, Jesus had returned. A dinner had been prepared in His honor. Martha had been preparing the meal for days. The women who traveled with us, including my mother, assisted Martha in the final preparations. It was the finest food, prepared with the greatest of care. No expense had been spared. No detail was overlooked. Only the best would be served to Jesus. He had raised their brother from the dead! How could anything ever be enough to thank Him?

Martha had learned her lesson. Though she would be serving tonight, she wouldn't be distracted by the details. She had arranged everything well in advance, so that she could now be attentive to only One – her guest of honor!

Lazarus greeted his guest of honor with a kiss on the cheek. He anointed Jesus' head with sweet-smelling olive oil and provided Him with water to wash His feet. He pulled out his finest robe and placed it across Jesus' shoulders. Then he showed Him to the seat of honor at the table.

Lazarus invited the rest of us to make ourselves comfortable around the table, as he positioned himself directly across from his guest. He wanted to be close in order to attend to any need Jesus might have. Jesus was his friend. But He was more than that, He was the Messiah. But He was even more than that, He was the One who had power over death.

. . .

One person was noticeably absent when we arrived, and she was still missing when dinner began. Jesus was reclining at the table, as was the custom, with His feet outstretched. As He began to eat, she quietly came into the room. She approached Jesus from behind, carrying a beautiful alabaster jar. Quietly, she knelt beside Jesus' feet and opened the jar. Suddenly the room was filled with the sweet, spicy, and musky aroma of an expensive perfume made from the essence of nard. It is considered to be the most precious of oils.

First, she poured a small portion of the oil over His head. In so doing, she was acknowledging Jesus as the Messiah – the "anointed one." Next, she began to anoint His feet and then wiped them with her hair. She was quietly expressing her love and thanksgiving to Jesus as the One who held power over death. Jesus continued to eat and did not acknowledge Mary. The rest of us were silent. We just watched her.

Then Judas Iscariot broke the silence and said, *"That perfume was worth a year's wages. It should have been sold and the money given to the poor."*[2]

A few of the other disciples nodded their head in agreement. I doubted Judas really cared about the poor. I had never seen him make any effort to minister to the poor and needy. I couldn't help but wonder if he was more interested in using the money for himself, and would have liked the price of this perfume added to the disciples' treasury. The other disciples who had agreed with him began to scold Mary.

Then Jesus spoke up and said, *"Leave her alone. Why would you criticize her for doing such a good thing to Me?"*[3]

"Yes," I thought, "it had only been seven weeks, but how quickly we forget!"

· · ·

Silence again fell over the room. Then Jesus said, *"You will always have the poor among you, but you will not always have Me. She has poured this perfume on Me to prepare My body for burial. I tell you the truth, wherever the Good News is preached throughout the world, this woman's deed will be remembered and discussed."*[4]

Mary was taking the same care that would typically be reserved for the burial of a loved one. At the time, only Jesus knew that was exactly what Mary was doing. None of us knew that in just a matter of days, Jesus' body would be buried in a tomb. And here was Mary expressing her worship to her Lord the best way she knew how, overflowing with love and adoration.

I could see Judas was seething following Jesus' rebuke. Judas resented looking foolish in front of the others. As I studied his face, I felt a sense of foreboding. His dark eyes looked black and I could tell he was plotting something. I looked at Jesus. He was looking at Judas. And I could tell from His expression He knew exactly what Judas was thinking.

Judas was so deep in thought he didn't realize Jesus was staring at him. It had been seven weeks since Jesus raised Lazarus from the dead. But He still had not declared Himself to be the Messiah. Judas had faithfully followed Him for almost three years. If he helped himself to a few coins in the meantime, what difference did that make?

They were nothing compared to the big treasure that awaited him when Jesus established His government. Why was Jesus wasting His time sitting at this table when He could be sitting on His rightful throne in Jerusalem? This young woman's expression was nothing compared to what the masses would do if Jesus stepped up and assumed His rightful position as king.

Judas resolved he could no longer rely on Jesus to do what needed to be done. Someone needed to force His hand. Perhaps that was exactly what Jesus was waiting for. Perhaps He was waiting for one of His disciples to step forward and take the initiative. Jesus had specifically selected each one of His apostles. Had He selected Judas for just this purpose? Had nothing yet occurred because Judas hadn't taken action?

Judas decided what he needed to do. He must help Jesus take the steps He needed to become king. Jesus would be grateful to Judas! Perhaps that was why Jesus had rebuked him tonight – not because of what Judas said, but because Jesus was frustrated Judas had not done anything yet.

Judas knew the High Priest and the rest of the High Council were plotting to kill Jesus. For some reason they seemed incapable of executing a plan. Jesus had probably frustrated their plans while He waited on Judas to take action. That made perfect sense! No one was able to take the next step until Judas did.

After they arrived in Jerusalem tomorrow, he would find time to slip away from the rest of the disciples and talk to the High Priest. Jesus would know what he was doing. Jesus would be counting on him to work out the details. Judas would help the religious leaders arrest Jesus. He would arrange the best time and place so the crowd wouldn't interfere. Then when the religious leaders made their move, Jesus could declare Himself and call out the crowd to follow Him as their promised King. He would establish His government and Judas would ascend into his rightful role. Victory was in sight!

· · ·

Judas turned from his thoughts and looked at Jesus. Jesus was looking at him. Their eyes met. Judas smiled and nodded at Jesus. He would take care of this for Jesus. All was forgiven. Jesus hadn't really meant to rebuke him. Jesus was just getting his attention. It had worked. Judas now knew what to do. He was sorry he hadn't realized it sooner. After all, it had been seven weeks since Jesus had raised a man from the grave!

I was the only one in the room who saw Jesus and Judas exchange looks. The Master's eyes were filled with sadness, while in Judas' eyes I saw smug satisfaction. Some of the disciples were laughing at something someone had said. Lazarus and Martha were still hovering over their guest of honor, attending to His needs. Mary continued to kneel at Jesus' feet, the aroma of her perfume permeating the air.

No one had any idea that one week from tonight Jesus' body would be lying in a tomb. Well, One Person knew. The same One who had called another to come out of a tomb just seven weeks ago.

24

"I tell you that if these should keep silent, the stones would immediately cry out."[1]

* * *

The next morning, we departed from Bethany and made our way toward Jerusalem. When we arrived at the Mount of Olives, Jesus called out to Andrew and me, saying, *"Go into the village over there. As soon as you enter it, you will see a donkey tied there, with its colt beside it. Untie them and bring them to Me. If anyone asks what you are doing, just say, 'The Lord needs them,' and he will immediately let you take them."*[2]

Jesus went to a secluded area of the mount to be alone and pray to the Father, while He and the others waited for us to return.

Andrew and I were puzzled by Jesus' request. We had entered Jerusalem many times before without the need of any animals. But we knew Jesus always had a reason for whatever He did, so we went in search of a donkey.

As soon as we entered the village of Bethphage, we came upon a donkey and colt tied to a post, just as Jesus said. As we untied them, a man walked out of the stable and asked what we were doing. We responded just as Jesus had told us: *The Lord needs them.*[3]

The man replied, "They are ready for the Master's use, just as I promised Him."

He must have sensed our surprise by his response.

"Jesus asked me to have them ready for Him a few months ago when He was here for the Feast of Dedication," he explained. "He told me He would send two of His disciples to retrieve them when it was time. He even pointed the two of you out to me so I would know what you look like."

This was all news to us and we weren't sure if we were supposed to pay the man. We asked him, "Do we owe you anything for the use of your animals?"

"No," he replied. "Three years ago, Jesus healed my son. I owe Him a debt I can never repay. This is just a small way for me to show Him my gratitude. You can return them when you come back by here later this afternoon.

. . .

"Have you heard about the crowd gathering in Jerusalem?" he continued.

We knew a large crowd of pilgrims from all over gathered in Jerusalem every year for Passover, but this man seemed to be talking about something else.

"Is the crowd greater than in the past?" we asked.

"People have been arriving for days," he said. "Many who would not have chosen to come to Jerusalem to observe the Passover have come to see Jesus! They have heard He raised a man from the dead who had been in the grave for four days. Close to two million people have gathered in Jerusalem – and many for the express purpose of seeing Jesus. There has never been such a crowd!"

As we returned to the mount with the animals in tow, we pondered what Jesus was going to do with the donkey and its colt. Whatever it was, He had been planning it for a while! We had no idea the planning for His entry hadn't begun just a few months ago ... the planning had begun before creation.

When we got to the mount, Jesus was there waiting for us. We asked Him what we should do with the animals. "I will ride the colt alongside of its mother from here to the Temple," He replied.

Again, we were surprised! Jesus had never ridden an animal in any of our travels! He had always walked. Why was He choosing to ride the colt? We were full of questions, but we didn't ask them. We knew Jesus would reveal the answers when it was time. Zechariah's prophecy never crossed our minds:

Look, your King is coming to you. He is righteous and victorious, yet He is humble, riding on a donkey ... riding on a donkey's colt.[(4)]

Several of us placed our garments over the colt in order to make it more comfortable for Jesus as He rode.

We began to make our way toward the Sheep Gate, the one Jesus most often used so He could quietly enter the city. However, Jesus redirected us: "Today we will enter the city through the Eastern Gate." It appeared today we were not going to make a quiet, inconspicuous entry into the city!

As we continued on our journey, news spread quickly that Jesus would soon arrive. People poured out of the city to join in the procession. Many began to spread their garments on the road ahead of Him. Others laid down palm branches they had cut in the nearby fields.

I happened to glance over and see Judas Iscariot nearby. He seemed quite happy with all the attention Jesus was receiving today. "The donkey's colt was the animal used by all of our ancient kings as they processed among the people," he commented to me. "Jesus is presenting Himself as king today. The Messiah has arrived! Today will be the day!" Honestly, I did not know what he meant by that last statement. And neither of us knew what Jesus would do next.

A multitude soon surrounded Jesus so that He was in the center of the procession. Then spontaneously and continuously, the crowd sang and shouted with one voice, *"Praise God for the Son of David! Blessings on the One who comes in the name of the Lord! Praise God in highest heaven!"*[(5)]

. . .

The shout grew louder and louder as more people joined the procession. The entire city seemed to be in an uproar as Jesus entered. Some of the Pharisees even came out to see what all the commotion was about.

When they saw Jesus, they indignantly called out to Him, *"Teacher, rebuke Your followers for saying things like that!"* [(6)]

To which Jesus replied, *"If they kept quiet, the stones along the road would burst into cheers!"* [(7)]

The few who were unaware asked, *"Who is this?"* [(8)] The crowd replied, almost in unison, *"It's Jesus, the prophet from Nazareth in Galilee."* [(9)]

When we arrived at the entrance to the Temple, Jesus dismounted from the colt and the crowd parted the way so He could enter. As He walked through the Court of the Gentiles, He saw the tables and stalls had not been returned to the courtyard. He then entered through the Beautiful Gate into the outer Court of the Women. It was in this court Jesus most often taught when He was at the Temple. Today, however, He did not stop to teach.

The religious leaders watched Jesus very carefully as he walked through the Temple. We knew the spontaneous demonstration of praise and accolades from the people agitated the leaders, but we did not know it prompted a decision that they must destroy Jesus now or be destroyed themselves.

. . .

We did not realize Jesus was forcing the religious leaders to act now, in the time and way He and the Father had chosen. The priests did not attempt to engage Him right then. They seemed to be waiting for Him to do something or say something – which He did not. Off in a corner, I saw Annas standing with his son-in-law Caiaphas, the current High Priest. They were watching Jesus' every move. Annas was speaking to the younger man in hushed tones. Caiaphas nodded his head in agreement.

This was the calm before the storm, and little did we know the extent of the coming storm. Only Jesus and His Father knew about the battle that would rage over the next few days. In fact, I suspect they were discussing it even as Jesus walked throughout the Temple.

And, though I did not know what the priests were saying, I knew they were plotting against Jesus. The others who were gathered in the Temple kept watching Jesus, as well. They wondered if He planned to teach or perform any miracles. But they would have to wait until tomorrow. Jesus motioned to us it was time to return to Bethany for the night.

As we were leaving the city, we encountered my brother Jacob and his helper arriving with a drove of sheep they were delivering to the Temple merchants. He planned to stay in the city for the night, so I arranged to meet up with him when we returned in the morning. We continued on our journey to the home of Lazarus, and Jacob made his way to the merchants' stalls.

When Jacob arrived at the stoa, it was bustling with activity. Annas had just directed the merchants to set up their stalls in the outer Court of the Gentiles so they would be ready for the morning. He said the large attendance of pilgrims this year would require additional stalls – and those stalls needed to be inside the Temple's Court.

But everyone sensed there must be some other reason for such a sudden change. It had been three years since Jesus had driven them all out of the Temple. Everyone clearly remembered that day and how the Priests had backed down from Jesus. They knew the Priests had not attempted to bring the stalls and tables back into the Temple since. They had also heard that Jesus had just left the city. How would He react when He returned in the morning? But they were not in a position to question Annas. If this is what he wanted done, this is what they would do.

Jacob was directed to wait with his flock while the stalls in the court were being set in place. Once they were completed, he was to lead his sheep to the newly assembled area. While Jacob waited, he also prayed. He knew the thieves and false shepherds were attempting to make their way back into "the sheepfold," as Jesus had taught. He knew the Good Shepherd would protect "His sheep." But He also knew that Jesus knew all things and nothing could occur that wasn't permitted by the Father. The Father had a purpose in all things – including this. Perhaps that would be made clear in the morning. In the meantime, he continued to feel uneasy.

While Jacob was waiting, a full cohort of Roman soldiers passed by him. They were surrounding a man who clearly had been beaten. But he did not look like a man filled with remorse over his plight. Rather, he looked like someone with deep hatred for his captors. He was not broken. He was belligerent. The soldiers had bound him with chains and heavy rope, and they were leading him to the prison.

Jacob was surprised one prisoner required so many soldiers. The show of force meant he must be a notorious prisoner. But he did not appear to be putting up any resistance. It all seemed very calm. As they passed Jacob, one of the soldiers shouted at the prisoner: "Pick up your feet, Barabbas! Your cross is waiting for you!" Jacob sensed this man was dangerous, even bound in his chains. Something told him this wouldn't be the last time he would see this prisoner. He had a feeling trouble followed this man.

On our way out of the city, I saw Judas again. This time his smile was gone. Now he appeared to be brooding.

"Wasn't today exciting as the people welcomed Jesus as the Son of David into Jerusalem! Don't you agree, Judas?" I asked.

"It would have been a much more exciting day if Jesus had allowed them to crown Him king," Judas replied. And I could see there was a storm brewing behind those brooding eyes.

While Jesus and the rest of the disciples continued on to Bethany, Andrew and I stopped in Bethphage and returned the donkey and its colt to the stable with the Master's thanks. Our trip out of the city had been much quieter than our entry earlier in the day. The sun was beginning to set. It would be a beautiful spring night. There wasn't a cloud in the sky. But a storm was coming!

* * *

25

"By what authority are You doing all these things? Who gave You the right to do them?"[1]

* * *

I t was Monday morning when we left Bethany and Jesus told us He was hungry. He saw a fig tree in full leaf nearby, so He walked over to it to see if He could find any fruit. But there were only leaves because it was too early in the season for it to bear figs. Then we heard Jesus say to the tree, *"May no one ever eat your fruit again!"*[2]

I must confess I thought this was a strange thing for Jesus to say. Since it was not yet fig season, why had He expected the tree to have figs? And why did He curse the tree for not having figs at this time of year? It seemed unfair. So, as we continued in our journey, I asked Him why He had cursed the tree.

Fig trees produce leaves in March and April, then bear mature fruit twice each year – the first, smaller crop at the beginning of June, and the second, larger crop from August through October. During this time of year as fig trees were becoming fully leafed, they would produce a crop of small knobs, called "taqsh" (pronounced "tuhk-wAAsh"). These are forerunners to the mature figs and drop off the tree before the "real" fruit is formed. If, however, there are no taqsh, it is an indication there will be no figs. Seeing no taqsh, Jesus knew there would be no figs when the time came.

The tree gave the outward appearance it was healthy and growing. It was pleasing to the eye, and looked as if it would produce a bountiful harvest. But Jesus knew, and explained to us, the tree was not healthy. God created the tree with one purpose – His purpose – to bear fruit. He didn't create it to be a fruitless tree. And though harvest time had not yet arrived, it was obvious by the condition of the tree it would be barren.

As Jerusalem came into view, Jesus interrupted His explanation and began to weep. Eventually, He continued His explanation by telling us the fruitless fig tree was a picture of Jerusalem. The Father had created and called His people, Israel, to bear fruit to His glory – to bear witness to His Majesty and to worship Him through their very lives. And yet, they had rejected Him. They had turned their focus upon themselves to the point they no longer even recognized Him – when He stood in their presence.

Though Jerusalem appeared to be bountiful and growing, signs of its fruitlessness were already present. One day soon it would be destroyed just like that fig tree. Jesus wept because He was grieved over its imminent destruction. He grieved over the people's lostness. He grieved over their fruitlessness. He grieved as the Good Shepherd over the sheep that were lost and would never be found.

•   •   •

As Jesus finished His explanation, we quietly entered the city through the Sheep Gate. Today we would not repeat the pageantry of yesterday's entry through the Golden Gate. Jesus had other plans for this day.

As we approached the Temple, Jesus saw the tables and stalls had been returned to the outer court. He saw the brisk trade again taking place at the money changers' tables, the dove sellers' tables, and the animal stalls. Immediately upon entering the Temple, Jesus declared, *"It is written: 'My house will be a house of prayer.' But you have made it 'a den of robbers.'"* [3]

He turned over the tables and chairs, and drove the merchants from the Temple, just as He had done three years earlier. This time the merchants were not caught off guard; they expected Jesus to act this way. They exited the court quickly and without any resistance, and returned to their stalls and tables in the stoa. They knew they were being used as pawns in a battle between the priests and Jesus. Even the crowd seemed to be expecting Jesus' reaction.

I again saw Annas and Caiaphas standing in a corner watching it all. I was a little surprised by their expressions. Instead of shock and dismay, they looked smug, as if everything was going according to their plan. The priests were obviously arranging something!

After Jesus cleared the Temple, He entered the Court of the Women. The blind and lame came to Him and He healed them. The teachers and priests watched as those who were healed and even the children began to shout, *"Praise God for the Son of David!"* [4]

As the children continued to shout, the leaders became more and more indignant. *"Do You hear what these children are saying?"*[5] they asked Jesus.

"Yes," He replied. *"Haven't you ever read the Scriptures? For they say, 'You have taught children and infants to give You praise.'"*[6]

My brother Jacob arrived at the Temple as Jesus was healing those who were coming to Him. He told me what had happened the night before – how Annas had arranged for the merchants to set their tables and stalls inside the Temple. Everyone knew Jesus would clear the Temple this morning, even Annas and Caiaphas. It was obvious there was something treacherous being planned. Everyone sensed it, but none of the merchants knew what it was.

Jacob had overheard another conversation between Annas and Caiaphas – and this one struck even closer to home. Annas reminded his son-in-law that in his younger days, Annas had been one of the leading priests and teachers whom King Herod the Great had consulted to ascertain the birthplace of the Messiah when a group of magi from the east had arrived seeking Him thirty or so years earlier.[7] Annas and the other priests had not shown any interest in seeking after the promised Messiah themselves. Apparently, the magi were supposed to report back to King Herod after they found the newborn Messiah, but they never did.

Herod had flown into a rage and ordered the murder of all little boys under age two who lived in and around Bethlehem in an attempt to murder the newborn King. This decree is what had resulted in our brother and father being massacred. But last night Jacob had heard Annas bragging to Caiaphas that where "the great Herod" had failed, they would now succeed. They would eliminate Jesus as a threat once and for all!

. . .

Jacob also told me about the prisoner he had seen. When he told me his name, I knew it was my "old friend." Justice had finally caught up with him! If there were ever a man who deserved Roman justice, it was Barabbas.

But still, in my heart I grieved for him. I could have ended up just like him. I was on that path. And on the day of the failed raid outside Caesarea, Barabbas had actually saved Simon's and my lives. I owed him a debt of gratitude that now I would probably be unable to repay. Though I knew what he had done to so many, I also knew no one was beyond forgiveness if he truly believed in Jesus. I considered trying to talk to him one more time.

The people continued to flock into the Temple throughout the day to be healed by Jesus. He received them all, one by one. But as the afternoon drew to an end, He announced it was time for us to return to Bethany for the night. Once more we returned to the home of Lazarus.

As we returned to Jerusalem the next morning, Peter pointed out the fig tree Jesus had cursed the day before. It was completely withered. We all marveled that it had happened so quickly. In one day, a tree full of leaves that had given the outward appearance of health and growth had now completely shriveled up and died. A process that should have taken weeks, or maybe months, had occurred overnight. It appeared as if it had been completely cut-off from its source of water at its roots, but also all of the moisture that had existed within the tree had completely evaporated.

After Peter pointed out the dead tree, Jesus began to teach us about faith. Yesterday Jesus had used this tree to teach us about the spiritual health of the people of Israel and the truth God has created us all to be fruitful. Today, He began to teach us fruit will not occur apart from faith. He told us we must live in total dependence on Him – acting and asking in alignment with His Word. When Jesus speaks His Word, and His Word "remains" in us, it will require a response from us – and the response will either be faith or faithlessness. Even no response is faithlessness.

He told us if a mountain is standing between us and what God has told us to do, we must step out in faith, trusting and asking God to move the mountain. The prophet Zechariah wrote of Zerubbabel when he was chosen to lead the Jews back to Jerusalem, *"Nothing, not even a mighty mountain, will stand in Zerubbabel's way; it will become a level plain before him!*(8)

Why couldn't a mighty mountain stand in his way? Because he was walking in obedience to God on His mission – nothing could stand in His way! Jesus said no mountain can stand in our way if we are walking in obedience to God's Word and His will. If we ask according to His will and His way, we will see God take those mountains and "throw them into the sea!"

Then Jesus spoke to us about forgiveness. We are to walk – not only in the Word of God and according to the will of God – but also abiding in the love of God. We can't allow anything to stand between us and God, or ourselves and another person. If we hold a grudge, or fail to forgive, we are sinning and inhibiting our abiding relationship with God.

Jesus told us before we pray, we are to make sure we are not holding on to grievances. We are to forgive an individual and, if possible, make amends. But He added our forgiveness does not obligate God to act, it simply clears the pathway between us and Him.

. . .

When we arrived at the Temple, the priests, teachers, and elders were waiting for Jesus. They were indignant and combative. As far as they were concerned, Jesus' actions yesterday had completely undermined their authority. He had demonstrated a flagrant disregard for their position. He failed to seek their approval before He acted. They had never delegated Him any authority. He had been disrespecting them for far too long. Of all the things Jesus had said and done, that was their major offense against Him.

As Jesus was walking through the Temple, they demanded to know, *"By what authority are You doing all these things? Who gave You the right to do them?"*(9)

But Jesus knew this was part of their plot. They were not seeking truth. They were looking for evidence to use to destroy Him. The merchants had been brought back into the Temple yesterday to set up this charge. There was nothing sincere about what these men were asking. So, Jesus very deftly countered their question with another question. In so doing, He exposed their hypocrisy and their hard heartedness.

He asked them, *"Did John's authority to baptize come from heaven, or was it merely human?"*(10)

I knew the religious leaders now had another dilemma. How should they respond to Jesus' question? I was with John the Baptizer when the Pharisees disrespected and accused him. As they now stood before Jesus, they weren't considering "What is true?" or "What is right?" but rather, "What is safe?"

. . .

They knew whichever way they answered, the crowd would turn on them, and their authority, position, and prestige would be lost. So, they refused to answer His question by pleading ignorance. Which then prompted Jesus to respond, *"Then I won't tell you by what authority I do these things."*[11]

Throughout the day, Jesus used parables to confront the religious leaders and teach the crowds. Eventually the religious leaders withdrew from the courtyard to escape the light Jesus was shining on them and their sinful motives. They sequestered themselves behind closed doors – and away from piercing eyes – so they could discuss their evil plans. They needed to catch Jesus saying something so egregious the Roman authorities and the crowd would side with them. So, throughout the day they sent their representatives to question Him.

The first were the Herodians. They began their questioning by flattering Jesus in an attempt to disarm Him. *"Teacher, we know that You speak and teach what is right and are not influenced by what others think. You teach the way of God truthfully."*[12]

But Jesus knew their hearts. He knew their motivation. He wasn't drawn in by their feeble attempt to manipulate Him through flattery.

Next came their big question. *"Is it right for us to pay taxes to Caesar or not?"*[13]

They were confident they had just trapped Jesus. We were an occupied nation required to pay taxes to our Roman oppressors. Every tax payment was another expression of the Roman boot pressing down on our necks. If Jesus spoke in favor of paying the tax, the crowd would rise up against Him. If Jesus opposed the tax, He would be in trouble with Rome. Regardless, the Herodians thought they had Jesus right where they wanted Him.

Jesus had a choice. He could call out the Herodians and the Pharisees for their evil intent and their hypocrisy and refuse to answer them. Or He could use this moment as an opportunity to silence His enemies and teach the people an important truth. Naturally, Jesus chose the latter.

He asked His questioners to produce a coin. As they did, He asked, *"Whose picture and title are stamped on it?"* [14]

The fact the coins they offered bore the image of Caesar meant they accepted his authority. At that point, Jesus differentiated between that which belongs to Caesar and that which belongs to God. He taught us all a couple of important lessons. First, if we honor God, we must honor and obey the rulers whom God has placed, or allowed to be placed, in authority over us – and that included Roman rule.

Second, we must honor and obey God. He is our Creator. He has stamped each one of us with His image. All we have – and all we are – is from Him. Our honor to Him is not through simple coinage; our honor to Him is through the total submission of our lives in worship of Him. This was the primary truth Jesus was teaching all of us that day.

The religious leaders wanted to elevate the issue of money and taxes to entrap Him because they failed to live out this important truth. Honoring and obeying is not simply a matter of money; instead, it is the act of surrendering and completely submitting our lives to God.

• • •

The parade of questioners continued throughout the day, and in every instance, Jesus turned their treacherous questions into an opportunity to teach the crowd and rebuke the religious leaders. I was exhausted by the end of the day and I hadn't been the one who was being questioned! I was amazed by Jesus every day I walked with Him. I saw Him perform countless miracles. I heard Him teach countless truths. But if I had to pick one day when I was the most amazed by Jesus to this point, it would be this day. Even more than the days He fed the multitudes, or stilled the storm, or raised Lazarus from the grave.

Today He had responded with truth and authority to every question intended to entrap Him. The religious leaders had attacked Him with everything they had, and they had been resoundingly defeated. It wasn't surprising the Son of God had prevailed, but the day gave me a confidence my Lord could defeat anything the enemy would ever send His way! And I would be able to walk in the confidence He would defeat anything the enemy would ever send my way!

Earlier that afternoon, I had noticed Judas Iscariot slip away. It was obvious he did not want to be seen. A little later in the day, I saw he had returned. I wouldn't know until later what Judas had been up to. He had witnessed the failed attempts by the religious leaders to entrap Jesus. Time and again, he had seen Jesus outsmart them, outmaneuver them, and outwit them.

The religious leaders were the pawns Judas required for his plan to force Jesus to show His hand. The leaders wanted to arrest Jesus, so if he could help them do that, Jesus would have to declare His authority and establish His kingdom. He had disappeared to go find his unlikely allies and try to convince them to go along with his plan.

The religious leaders were afraid of the reaction of the crowd. They knew they could not take action in the light. Whatever they did, it had to be done clandestinely and in the cover of darkness. So, they were delighted when one of Jesus' own disciples approached them to discuss the best way for Jesus to be arrested.

These unwitting allies all delighted in their own craftiness. To seal the deal, the religious leaders agreed to pay Judas thirty pieces of silver – which was not a lot of money. Judas was too ambitious to betray Jesus for such a paltry sum. And the religious leaders were too self-aggrandizing to stoop to paying a high bounty for One they disdained so greatly. The thirty pieces of silver merely sealed their agreement. Judas had his sights on much more.

As we left the Temple at the end of the day, Jesus told us we were going to spend the night on the Mount of Olives. We would not be returning to Bethany. Jesus knew the religious leaders had not abandoned the notion of arresting and killing Lazarus. And Jesus did not want to put Lazarus in harm's way by being arrested at his home in Bethany. So, Jesus started spending His nights on the mount so Judas would know where to find Him when it came time to arrest Him.

* * *

26

"I tell you the truth, slaves are not greater than their master. Nor is the messenger more important than the one who sends the message."[(1)]

* * *

Jesus announced on Wednesday He would not be going to the Temple to teach that day. Tuesday had been a full day and night and He needed to spend time away from the crowds with His Father before the arrival of the Festival of Unleavened Bread. So, He found a secluded area there on the Mount of Olives where He could be alone in prayer.

I decided this was a good opportunity to find out if I could visit Barabbas in prison. I didn't know if the officials would allow it, but I felt like it was something I was supposed to do. I had never visited a prison, so I wasn't sure what to expect. I found out Barabbas was to be crucified on Friday, so this could be my last opportunity.

.   .   .

Barabbas had become notorious throughout the province. He was seen as a murderous zealot in the eyes of the Roman rulers, and he was viewed as a dangerous criminal in the eyes of the Jewish populace. Barabbas' crimes along the Jericho Road had become well-known, particularly for the viciousness of his attacks.

Merchants and travelers were afraid to make that journey without the protection of a Roman guard, but the prefect did not have enough manpower to accommodate all of those requests. The Jews and the Romans were divided on most things, but they were united on their view of Barabbas. He was a threat that needed to be eliminated.

The prison was located within the Antonia Fortress in Jerusalem. The prison was used only as a holding place for those who were condemned to die by crucifixion. Prisoners who were to be held for an extended time were taken to the prisons in Caesarea Maritima or Machaerus (where John the Baptizer had been held).

The fortress also housed the Praetorium. This was the residence for the Roman prefect when he was in Jerusalem. Normally the prefect resided in Caesarea in the palace King Herod the Great had built, but on certain occasions he stayed in Jerusalem.

Passover was always one of those occasions. Since Passover celebrated the deliverance of the Israelites from their Egyptian rulers, it was a time that often stirred revolt and rebellion in the hearts of the zealots. Since Jerusalem was flooded with people this time of year, it was considered the most likely spot for trouble. The prefect wanted to be nearby to maintain order and quickly extinguish any sparks of revolution that might occur.

· · ·

The current prefect was Pontius Pilate. He had succeeded Valerius Gratus three years earlier and was now the fifth prefect to govern the Iudaean province. The prefect was assigned a small auxiliary force of three thousand soldiers (approximately half a legion) scattered across the region to maintain order throughout the province. Most of the soldiers were recruited from within the province. The commanders were typically dispatched from Rome. Normally one cohort of eighty soldiers was assigned to the Antonia Fortress, with eight of the soldiers assigned to guard the prisoners.

During the Passover Festival, more soldiers were brought to Jerusalem so that a larger force of fifteen hundred soldiers was in the city to maintain order among the two million people in attendance. The prison guard had also been enlarged to half of a cohort. The soldiers assigned to the fortress were under the command of a centurion by the name of Gaius Marius, named after a famous Roman general.

When I arrived at the fortress, I was told I would need permission from the centurion before I could visit Barabbas. I wasn't certain what to give as an explanation for wanting to see him. Anyone who admitted knowing Barabbas would certainly be a suspected criminal. I most definitely wanted to avoid that possibility!

As I made my way from the Mount of Olives to the fortress, I continued to pray: "Father, I believe You have led me to come speak with Barabbas. I am taking this step in obedience to You. Grant me favor in the eyes of the Roman soldiers that I might be permitted to see Barabbas. And grant me the words You would have me say to him."

By God's grace, I was granted an audience to speak to the centurion. I explained to him I was a shepherd from Bethlehem who was now a disciple of Jesus. I told him when I was a younger man, Barabbas had saved my life, and I believed my God would have me thank him before he died. I asked the centurion to grant me just a few minutes to speak to him. Then I waited in silence as he considered my request.

He asked me a few questions about my family and then about Jesus. He told me he had heard of Jesus and the miracles He had performed. He told me he had seen Jesus riding on the donkey's colt on Sunday as He entered Jerusalem. And he said he remembered seeing me with Jesus.

Then he turned to one of his soldiers and told him to allow me to speak with Barabbas through the gate for five minutes. I thanked him for his kindness. Just before I turned to follow his soldier, he said, "Tell your Teacher, Jesus, the religious leaders are plotting against Him. He needs to be careful. I would not want to see any harm come to this Miracle Worker."

The prison was really more of a dungeon. The soldier led me to a small room with a hole in the floor. The hole was secured by an iron gate. When the gate was opened, He told me to climb down the ladder approximately twelve feet to the floor below. As I climbed down, he secured the gate above me. The only light coming into the space was from the opening through which I had just entered.

As my eyes adjusted to the darkness, I realized I was standing in front of another gate that led into a disgusting and vile room. The stench and filth were overwhelming and caused my eyes to water. It was difficult to see, but the room appeared to be about thirty feet long by twenty feet wide, and slightly more than six feet high. The walls and ceiling were made of stone, and the floor was dirt. There was nothing in the room other than the six figures that were beginning to come into focus.

. . .

I had heard that three men were to be crucified on Thursday and three, including Barabbas, on Friday. Each of them had staked out his own area against one of the walls. One of the men had claimed a corner for himself. The rest of the men were keeping their distance from him. I started to call out to the men, but the stench took my breath and caused me to start coughing uncontrollably. It took a minute before I was able to call out, "Barabbas, it's Shimon!"

The man in the corner turned to face me. His clothing was dirty and blood stained. His body was obviously bruised and beaten. Because of the height of the ceiling, he remained hunched over and wasn't able to stand up straight. Slowly, he made his way toward me at the gate. When he was about two feet away, he stopped and looked at me. It had been slightly more than two years since I had last seen him in Chorazin.

The years had not been kind. He bore the scars and appearance of one who had been enslaved by his choices, as well as the bruises and lacerations from his Roman captors. He asked me what I was doing there.

"I have come for two reasons," I explained. "First, to again thank you for saving my life that day outside of Caesarea Maritima. If you had not stopped us, both Simon and I would have been cut down by the Roman soldiers. I know in the years since then you may have taken the lives of others, but on that day, you saved ours. So, I thank you."

Second, I told him though he had saved my physical life, it was Jesus who had truly saved me. He had set me free from the bondage of sin and my past. He had taken away my pain and brokenness and replaced it with healing and purpose. I reminded him when we had last seen one another, he had said, "Perhaps our paths will again cross one day and I will meet Jesus then."

"This may be the closest our paths come together before you are placed on a cross in two days," I continued. "But Barabbas, I want you to know you can believe in Him today. Whatever you have done, He can and will forgive you, if you will only believe in Him. Turn to Him before it's too late!"

I can't say for sure, because it is so outside of his character, but I think there was a tear in Barabbas' eye when he thanked me for coming to see him. He made no other response except, "You're welcome. Saving your life was probably one of the few good choices I ever made." And with that, he walked back to his corner in the prison. The soldier above me called out and told me to climb the ladder.

My time was over. My errand was accomplished. I had been faithful to what God directed me to do. My heart was filled with sadness for Barabbas. I prayed before he took his last breath he would believe in Jesus. But as I made my way out of the fortress and back to the Mount of Olives, I was also grateful to God. I realized I could have gone down the same path as Barabbas. But God had rescued me through His Son. He had forgiven me. He had made me a new person. I continued to pray that would happen for Barabbas before it was too late.

The next day was the fifth day of the week – Thursday. The Passover Festival would begin at dusk with the Passover Seder and continue for seven days. In preparation for the festival, all of the leaven was removed from Jewish households. Leaven symbolized corruption, or sin, so for the seven days of Passover we were to eat only unleavened bread.[2] Any leaven remaining in the households on this day was removed and burned. This morning the pungent odor of burning leaven permeated the air in and around the city. Every household was busy completing their preparations.

The preparations were so important to Jesus that He sent Peter and John to make the arrangements. They invited me to join them. Peter wisely asked Jesus for His specific instructions. All of us knew what preparations were required under the law. And we had all traveled to Jerusalem many times before for the observance of Passover. It would have been easy for us to do what we believed was the right thing. But we had learned Jesus was always very specific in what He required of us. As usual, Jesus had all the details already worked out.

Just as Jesus had arranged for the donkey and its colt to be available for His entry into the city, He had also made prior arrangements for the Passover meal, down to the slightest detail. Here were His instructions: *"As soon as you enter Jerusalem, a man carrying a pitcher of water will meet you. Follow him. At the house he enters, say to the owner, 'The Teacher asks: Where is the guest room where I can eat the Passover meal with My disciples?' He will take you upstairs to a large room that is already set up. That is where you should prepare our meal."*[3]

When we arrived in Jerusalem, we found everything exactly as Jesus told us it would be.

As was custom, the women traveling with us came to prepare the meal. The group now included Jesus' mother Mary, Mary Magdalene, Salome (the wife of Zebedee), Mary (the wife of Clopas), Joanna (the wife of Chuza), Suzanna (the widow whose son Jesus raised from the dead), and my mother (Ayda). They busily began to make everything ready for that evening.

.   .   .

Later in the day, Jesus and the rest of the disciples arrived. Before the meal began, Jesus reclined at the table. Looking back, I cannot believe how calm He was. Jesus knew what was about to unfold; and yet, there He was looking completely relaxed. I would have at least been anxious, if not outright panicked. But, as the Son of God, He knew that everything was going to happen according to His Father's plan. So, He rested and renewed His strength for what was coming.

Jesus knew the very foundation of our belief in Him was about to be shaken. He knew the tragedy and despair we would experience. He began pouring into us, nurturing us, and encouraging us once again. He knew exactly what we needed. But He also knew the victory we would witness and experience on the other side of our pain. He made every minute with us count, preparing us to walk through the hours ahead.

Then Jesus did something that took us off guard. He got up from the table and kneeled before each one of us and washed our dirty feet before drying them with the towel He wore around His waist. The Son of the Almighty God was washing our feet! We sat there in shock not knowing what to say. This was our Lord and our Master serving us in such a menial way.

I looked around the room – there was John (the beloved), Thomas (the skeptic), Judas Iscariot (the one with questionable motives), and a group of fishermen, carpenters, zealots, and tax collectors. And there I was – a lowly shepherd – all of us sinners, and none of us deserving His grace, let alone having Him wash our feet. A silence fell over the room as Jesus knelt before one man and then the next.

Then Jesus came to Peter, who protested saying, *"Lord, are You going to wash my feet?"* [4]

. . .

Jesus replied, *"You don't understand now what I am doing, but someday you will."*[5]

"No," Peter protested, *"You will never ever wash my feet!"*[6]

"Unless I wash you, you won't belong to Me,"[7] Jesus replied.

Then in typical Peter fashion, he exclaimed, *"Then wash my hands and head as well, Lord, not just my feet!"*[8]

To which Jesus responded, *"A person who has bathed all over does not need to wash, except for the feet, to be entirely clean. And you disciples are clean, but not all of you."*[9]

I was curious what Jesus meant by His last statement. But before the sun rose again, I would be painfully aware.

When Jesus finished washing our feet, He put His robe back on and returned to His place at the table. *"Do you understand what I was doing?"* He asked. *"You call Me 'Teacher' and 'Lord,' and you are right, because that's what I am. And since I, your Lord and Teacher, have washed your feet, you ought to wash each other's feet. I have given you an example to follow. Do as I have done to you. I tell you the truth, slaves are not greater than their master. Nor is the messenger more important than the one who sends the message. Now that you know these things, God will bless you for doing them."*[10]

As we ate our Passover meal, I thought about what Jesus had just said, and His message became clear. Jesus is our Master; we are His slaves. He is our King; we are His messengers. As He has done, we are to do likewise. If He served, we are to serve. If He humbled Himself for the sake of the Kingdom, we are to humble ourselves for the sake of the Kingdom. If He gave all for us, we are to give all for Him.

My thoughts were interrupted when Jesus said, *"Here at this table, sitting among us as a friend, is the man who will betray Me. For it has been determined that the Son of Man must die. But what sorrow awaits the one who betrays Him."*[11]

The disciples began to look at each other around the table. John was sitting next to Jesus and Peter motioned to him to ask, *"Who's He talking about?"*[12]

Jesus responded, *"It is the one to whom I give the bread I dip in the bowl."*[13]

Then Jesus dipped the bread and gave it to Judas. We all observed it. Peter and John looked at one another with a quizzical expression as if to say, "What does Jesus mean? What is Judas going to do?"

Most of the other disciples thought Jesus was honoring Judas by giving him the first portion of the bread He had dipped. In their minds, Jesus was acknowledging the important role Judas always played in His ministry. A couple of the disciples even thought that through this honor Jesus was making up to Judas for having publicly rebuked him the other night at the home of Lazarus.

Judas looked at Jesus and thought, "Jesus knows what I am about to do. He knows this has to be done so He can establish His kingdom. He has led me to do all of this. And now is the time. But why is there sadness in Jesus' eyes? Why did He say someone was betraying Him? And why did Jesus say He was going to die? Of course, He won't die. The crowd will come to His aid. The Father may even send a host of angels to protect Him. In a day or so, we'll all be in our places in the palace. I'm helping Him! My plan will work. Surely He sees that. Surely He knows that!"

Then Jesus said, *"Hurry and do what you're going to do."* [14]

Judas got up from the table and walked out of the room. Most of the disciples thought Jesus had sent him out on business.

As I sat there beside John watching and listening to what had just happened, my heart grew heavy as I realized Judas was preparing to betray Jesus. For the first time since I started following Him, I was overwhelmed with sadness and fear. I didn't know how or why, but for some reason Judas had become so blinded to his sin and so twisted in his thinking, that he, too, thought Jesus was sending him out on business. But he wasn't going out on Jesus' business or the Father's business. He was going out on Satan's business.

After Judas had departed, Jesus took some bread and gave thanks to God for it. Then He broke it in pieces and gave it to us, saying, *"This is My body, which is given for you. Do this in remembrance of Me."* [15]

After supper He took another cup of wine and said, *"This cup is the new covenant between God and His people – an agreement confirmed with My blood, which is poured out as a sacrifice for you. Take this and share it among yourselves. For I will not drink wine again until the Kingdom of God has come."* [16]

Now as I think back, I understand what Jesus meant when He told us to remember His broken body and His shed blood. But at the time, all I really knew was my heart was heavy. This had not been like any other Passover meal we had celebrated together. Jesus was pointing us more to what was to come, rather than to what had already passed.

We sang a song together, and then departed for the Mount of Olives. As we walked in the night air, I looked up at the sky. Storm clouds were starting to roll in. A storm was drawing near!

* * *

"I am the way, the truth, and the life.
No one can come to the Father except through Me."[1]

* * *

As we made our way back to the Mount of Olives for the night, some of the apostles again struck up a discussion about who was the greatest among them. This wasn't the first time that question had been raised. They all truly believed Jesus was the Messiah, and most still believed He would soon declare Himself and establish His kingdom. Their concern was where they stood positionally when that occurred. They had served Him faithfully these past three years. They had all given up their homes and their careers to follow Jesus. So, where would they rank once He established His kingdom?

The conversation started in response to Jesus' statement one of them was going to betray Him. All of them – except one – could not imagine one among them would be disloyal to Jesus. Then someone mentioned the seating arrangements around the table at supper. Jesus had just given Judas the piece of bread dipped in sauce befitting the guest of honor. Jesus then had apparently sent him off on an important mission. Perhaps Judas would have the greatest position in the kingdom.

But Peter was the more likely choice. He often spoke on behalf of all of the apostles, and Jesus had renamed him "the rock." Another possibility was one of the sons of Zebedee. James and John, together with Peter, often accompanied Jesus to places where the rest of them were not invited. Perhaps the three of them would have the greatest positions.

Jesus heard this argument taking place, and He interrupted them saying, *"In this world the kings and great men lord it over their people, yet they are called 'friends of the people.' But among you it will be different. Those who are the greatest among you should take the lowest rank, and the leader should be like a servant. Who is more important, the one who sits at the table or the one who serves? The one who sits at the table, of course. But not here! For I am among you as One who serves. You have stayed with Me in My time of trial. And just as My Father has granted Me a Kingdom, I now grant you the right to eat and drink at My table in My Kingdom. And you will sit on thrones, judging the twelve tribes of Israel."*[2]

The apostles had been arguing from a worldly point of view instead of a Kingdom point of view. Jesus brought us all back to the reality that in the Kingdom, *"those who are the greatest among you should take the lowest rank, and the leader should be like a servant."*[3] He had said, *"like a servant."* That meant we are not just to serve, but we are to serve in the humble posture of a servant and with the selflessness of a servant. Instead of the greatest being the one sitting in the seat of honor, it is the servant humbly serving all those in the room. Jesus was redefining "greatness." He wasn't telling us not to be great or that we wouldn't have positions of greatness in the kingdom; He was redefining what that meant!

. . .

We define greatness in the context of position, power, influence, wealth, and recognition. But Jesus was saying those characteristics reflect selfish ambition – and selfish ambition is the enemy of servant-hood. It is the exact opposite of greatness in the Kingdom.

Jesus said, *"I am among you as One who serves."* [4] He is our model for servanthood. He deserves the best the world has to offer ... He is worthy of all accolades and honor ... He merits all comfort and adora-tion ... yet, He served. And anyone who would be honored in the Kingdom must likewise be a servant of all.

Jesus was not rebuking the apostles for having the discussion, He was only rebuking them for their worldly perspective. He extended grace and affirmed each one for having stayed with Him until the end (though none of us realized the "end" was upon us). Jesus knew He was entrusting His apostles and the rest of us as His disciples with the "keys of the Kingdom." He was charging us with His mandate and commission to make disciples of all peoples. We were to be bridges through whom His Holy Spirit would work to draw all the people of the world unto Himself. We would have a significant role in the Kingdom.

Earlier Jesus had told us the story of a man who had entrusted three of his servants with talents of his wealth that they might further his busi-ness. Two of the servants had wisely invested their talents and brought an equal return to their master. The third had foolishly buried his talent out of fear and therefore had nothing to give to the master for his investment. The returning master had affirmed his first two servants for their faithfulness. Jesus was doing likewise with us. He assured us – that just like the returning master had said to his faithful servants – if we were faithful with what He entrusted to us, we would receive positions of honor in the Kingdom. As a matter of fact, He told the apostles they would have seats at His table and *"sit on thrones, judging the twelve tribes of Israel."*[5]

Then Jesus referred to us as His children and said, *"Dear children, I will be with you only a little longer. And as I told the Jewish leaders, you will search for Me, but you can't come where I am going. So now I am giving you a new commandment: Love each other. Just as I have loved you, you should love each other. Your love for one another will prove to the world that you are My disciples."*[6]

Two days earlier, while Jesus was teaching in the Temple, we had heard Him say the greatest commandment is to *"love the Lord your God with all your heart, all your soul, and all your mind,"*[7] and the second greatest is to *"love your neighbor as yourself."*[8] Now He was telling us that He was giving us a new commandment to *"love each other."*[9] Love God. Love your neighbor. Love each other. Why had Jesus felt it was important to add that third statement? Isn't loving each other a part of loving your neighbor?

A few years earlier, Jesus' mother Mary and His half brothers had come looking for Him, and He said to us, *"Whoever does the will of God, he is My brother and sister and mother."*[10] Jesus was teaching us that His followers were not only family to Him, but also to one another. When He said, "Love God, love your neighbor, and love each other," He was saying, "Yes, love your neighbor, and make sure you don't leave out loving your family of brothers and sisters in Me."

Jesus knew that sometimes we can be more loving and giving to our neighbors than we are to our immediate family. The argument some of the disciples had been having earlier was an example of this. He knew that sometimes we can be loving neighbors and still be a feuding family. Sometimes we can be more forgiving of others than we can be of our immediate family members.

We are to love each other like He has loved us. That sentence seemed so simple, but I don't think any of us fully understood how much Jesus loved us. We had, however, learned His love is patient, kind, not jealous, or boastful, or proud, or rude. It is a love that does not demand its own way. It is not irritable, and it keeps no record of being wronged. It does not rejoice about injustice but rejoices whenever the truth wins out. It is a love that never gives up, never loses faith, is always hopeful, and endures through every circumstance.[11] His love is selfless. It is a love that is unconditional. It is a love that never abandons.

And, if we love one another with His love, it proves we are His disciples. There was certainly no evidence of this love in the lives of our religious leaders. Their achievement was their mastery of the Scripture, but Jesus was telling us our true achievement was in how we love one another. It wouldn't be the miracles we perform or the eloquence of our words, it would be the love we extend to others and to one another.

As I sat and wondered why Jesus was giving a "new commandment," it came to me – Jesus was birthing something new. He was birthing His Kingdom. He was instructing the apostles, who would be the first shepherds of His flocks in His Kingdom. He was instructing all of us to whom He had given the assignment to go and make disciples. But before He talked about how we were to accomplish that, He told us we had to love each other. Before we could follow Him beyond this point, we had to love one another.

We were all a little concerned when Jesus said, "I will be with you only a little longer. ...You will search for Me, but you can't come where I am *going."*[12] Where was He going? Why couldn't we come with Him? How soon was this going to occur? To put it mildly, we were troubled and confused. We couldn't understand what He was telling us. We were thinking about positions for ourselves in His kingdom, and now Jesus was telling us He was leaving.

Then Jesus said, *"Don't let your hearts be troubled. Trust in God, and trust also in Me. There is more than enough room in My Father's home. If this were not so, would I have told you that I am going to prepare a place for you? When everything is ready, I will come and get you, so that you will always be with Me where I am. And you know the way to where I am going."*[13]

Thomas spoke first, but honestly, he was really speaking for all of us when he said, *"No, we don't know, Lord. We have no idea where You are going, so how can we know the way?"*[14]

Jesus answered him, saying, *"I am the way, the truth, and the life. No one can come to the Father except through Me.*[15]

"Besides, where I am going there is more than enough room for each one of you. I am going to make the way for your arrival. I am going to make preparations for you. If I don't go, you won't be able to follow. But if I go, then, after everything is ready, I will be able to come and get you when the time is right.

"From then on, we will always be together. You will be where I am. I will be where you are. We will never again be separated. And you know where that is. It's the Father's house. And you know the way!" Jesus was speaking words of assurance. He was speaking truth we could hold onto in the midst of tumultuous times.

. . .

"Thomas, I am THE WAY. I am not a way; I am the only way. Don't be deceived into trying another way or make the mistake of trying to follow your own way. I am the only way. Only My way leads to the Father's house. Other ways may seem right in your own thinking, but those ways will take you where you don't want to go. Like you said, you've never seen the Father's house. But I have! You don't know the way there. But I do! And I'm the only one who does. Trust Me, Thomas – and all of you – I am THE WAY!

"And Thomas, I am THE TRUTH! I am not a truth. My word is absolute. My word is without error. My truth does not change based upon season or whim. It is not situational. It is not relative. It is absolute! You will never know the truth of any situation, or trial, or circumstance, until you hear from Me. I existed before the beginning of time. My truth has been the same from before the beginning and will remain beyond the end of time. My truth is ageless. My truth is matchless. And my truth is beyond reproach. If you need an answer, I am the One to ask. I am the only One to ask! Trust Me, Thomas – and all of you – I am THE TRUTH!

"Lastly, Thomas, I am THE LIFE! In Me, through Me, and by Me have all things been created. All life comes from Me. I am the Creator of life and the Defeater of death. Through Me – and Me alone – you can experience life, abundant life, to the maximum! Only through Me can you escape the chains of sin and death. Only through Me can you experience unfettered life. I am the only One who can make that promise. Trust Me, Thomas – and all of you – I am THE LIFE!

"And no one comes to the Father except through Me! I and the Father are one. If you have seen Me, you have seen the Father. For this is how the Father loved the world, He gave His one and only Son, so that everyone who believes in Him will not perish but have eternal life. There is no other plan! I am the only way to the Father.

. . .

"Trust Me, Thomas – and all of you – as you continue to follow Me, I alone am the Way. I alone am the Truth. I alone am the Life. Follow Me."

We were now walking through a vineyard in the Kidron Valley. We could see the vineyard around us when Jesus said, *"I am the true grapevine, and My Father is the gardener. He cuts off every branch of Mine that doesn't produce fruit, and He prunes the branches that do bear fruit so they will produce even more. You have already been pruned and purified by the message I have given you. Remain in Me, and I will remain in you. For a branch cannot produce fruit if it is severed from the vine, and you cannot be fruitful unless you remain in Me. Yes, I am the vine; you are the branches. Those who remain in Me, and I in them, will produce much fruit. For apart from Me you can do nothing."*[16]

Jesus was telling us we would wither and die, just like that withered fig tree, if we did not abide in Him. Thankfully, He made a way for us to be grafted into Him – the Vine – so we could have everlasting, abundant life.

Jesus told us this was the Father's plan. Much like a vinedresser, God didn't graft us onto the Vine so we might merely give the appearance of beauty; rather, He grafted us onto the Vine so that through us He can bear fruit. And the Vinedresser lovingly does in our lives all He needs to do to maximize the crop.

Our minds were reeling. Jesus was filling our minds and our hearts with more than we could comprehend. It was as if this was going to be His last time to teach us in this way, and He was telling us all of the "last things" He wanted us to know.

. . .

Then He said, *"There is so much more I want to tell you, but you can't bear it now. When the Spirit of truth comes, He will guide you into all truth. He will not speak on His own but will tell you what He has heard. He will tell you about the future. He will bring Me glory by telling you whatever He receives from Me. All that belongs to the Father is Mine; this is why I said, 'The Spirit will tell you whatever He receives from Me.'"*[17]

But who is this Spirit of truth? As we all looked at one another, we realized none of us fully comprehended all Jesus was teaching us. At that point, we didn't even know what questions to ask Him. But we knew one day He would make it clear. The hour was late. We were tired, and we simply could not absorb anymore.

We had arrived at the Mount of Olives at the olive grove called Gethsemane. Jesus told us all to remain here while He went a little farther with Peter, James, and John. The four of them walked another fifty yards, then Jesus told the three of them to wait while He walked about a stone's throw farther. We knew Jesus was going to talk to His Father.

I looked around to see if Judas Iscariot had rejoined us. He had not. Whatever he was up to was going to happen soon. I knew Jesus was troubled and we all knew we should be praying to the Father on His behalf. But we were exhausted, and soon, one by one, we all fell asleep.

* * *

28

"This is your moment, the time when the power of darkness reigns."[1]

* * *

S uddenly I was awakened by sounds that were growing louder and louder. I turned to see a large mob of men advancing in our direction. Some of the men were carrying torches and lanterns. As my eyes began to focus, I saw some of the men were Roman soldiers and some were Temple guards. Others were dressed in priestly robes. Many of them were armed – some with swords and others with clubs. The disciples around me now began to stir as well.

I glanced around in search of Jesus; He was standing over Peter, James, and John, who were also waking up. As I stood to my feet, I noticed the mob was moving briskly in our direction. It was then I saw Judas leading the group. When the mob arrived at our position, the captain of the Temple guards told some of the soldiers to remain with us, while the rest of the group continued on to the spot where Jesus was standing.

. . .

As Judas walked right up to Jesus, I heard him loudly exclaim, "*Rabbi!*"[2] and greet Him with a kiss. Judas acted as if he hadn't seen Jesus in quite a while and extended the traditional greeting for a respected teacher and mentor. But the action of the crowd was anything but cordial and respectful.

Then I heard Jesus respond, "*Judas, would you betray the Son of Man with a kiss?*"[3]

Immediately the captain of the guard told the Temple guards to take hold of Jesus and arrest Him. When Peter saw what was happening, he drew his sword. A man standing nearby looked ready to swing his club at Jesus or one of the disciples. Peter struck the man with his sword. His blade was true, and he sliced off the man's ear.

Before anyone else could react, Jesus shouted, "*No more of this! Put away your sword. Don't you realize that I could ask My Father for thousands of angels to protect us, and He would send them instantly?*"[4]

With that, Jesus reached out to the man, touching his ear. Immediately, the man's pain was gone. As he felt his ear, he knew Jesus had restored it. Amazed, he dropped his club to the ground and trembled before Jesus.

We all looked at one another. Jesus had just told us not to fight. Even if He hadn't, Peter and my fellow zealot Simon were the only ones among us with a sword. The size of the mob was overwhelming. Obviously, the religious leaders were not taking any chances on Jesus escaping their grasp tonight.

. . .

I was frightened and in shock by what had just happened. None of us ever anticipated they would send soldiers in the middle of the night to arrest Jesus. We had no idea what was going to happen to Him – or us. I am ashamed to admit we all abandoned Jesus and fled in different directions.

Even in my haste to get away, I heard Jesus ask His captors, *"Am I some dangerous revolutionary that you come with swords and clubs to arrest Me? Why didn't you arrest Me in the Temple? I was there every day. But this is your moment, the time when the power of darkness reigns. And since I am the One you want, let these others go."*[5]

By the time He finished speaking, He was standing alone in the midst of a mob who was there to arrest Him. Not one disciple remained – except Judas, the betrayer. We all had deserted Him!

Out of the corner of my eye, I saw John and Peter together running farther up into the Mount of Olives away from Jerusalem. I quickly decided to follow them. Since they were two of Jesus' closest apostles, perhaps they would have an idea about what we should do. Once it became obvious no one was following us, we stopped running. I caught up with Peter and John and we hid behind some trees so we could watch what was happening to Jesus. We didn't dare look each other in the eye – we were too ashamed that we had run away and left Jesus.

In a few minutes, the mob began to make its way back to the city with Jesus completely surrounded. Peter, John, and I followed at a distance so we could see where they were taking Him. They walked about a mile to the home of Annas, the former High Priest, in the southern part of the city. John expressed surprise they had taken Jesus to Annas' home and not the home of Caiaphas, the current High Priest.

John knew both men. He had spent time in both of their homes prior to following Jesus. He knew they were powerful and ambitious men who would go to any length to increase their own power and wealth. He knew that since Annas was no longer the High Priest, he had no legal standing under Mosaic Law for Jesus to be brought before him. But he also had a pretty good idea why Jesus was brought to Annas' home first.

John reminded us Annas was the overseer of the financial enterprises profiting from the buying and selling taking place at the Temple. Annas saw Jesus' actions against that trade as a direct attack on himself, his position, his authority, and on his financial livelihood. Though Annas had long ago recouped any short-term financial setback caused by Jesus' actions three years ago, he had not gotten over the affront to his position and power.

Though Annas did not act alone in having Jesus arrested, he was one of the principal plotters behind the arrest. John believed Annas had two reasons for having Jesus brought to him first. One, he wanted Jesus to know that he – Annas – was in charge, and though Jesus may have temporarily enjoyed an upper hand, today was Annas' day, and he was getting the last word. Where others had tried and failed, Annas had now succeeded – or so he thought at the time. Two, Annas considered himself to be craftier and cleverer than everyone else. The religious leaders had sent many emissaries in their attempts to entrap Jesus. All of them had failed. As one of the main architects of this plot against Jesus, Annas believed he was the best qualified to "catch" Jesus in saying something incriminating that could be used against Him in their mock trial.

. . .

John decided to risk entering Annas' home so he could witness what was taking place. After he gained entry, he spoke with the servant woman who was watching at the gate and arranged access for Peter and me. Peter decided to stay outside in the courtyard, while John and I went inside.

Annas asked Jesus to tell him what He had been teaching. Jesus had been speaking publicly for over three years and had repeatedly taught in the very Temple where Annas oversaw his enterprise. He was looking for Jesus to say something that could be used against Him in the trial. But Annas could have done that while Jesus was teaching in the Temple. Had Annas never taken the time to listen to Jesus personally? Had he merely relied on the accounts of others? But then again, truth had never been his motivation. Annas would never permit truth to stand in the way of his position or his fortune.

I remembered what Jacob had overheard a few nights ago – and it was now all much clearer – where Herod had failed in killing Jesus as a baby, Annas believed he would now succeed! He was a man set on an evil mission.

Everything that was being done to Jesus was illegal under Mosaic Law. Annas had no legal authority to detain or question Jesus. The law required there be witnesses before an arrest took place, but no witness ever came forward accusing Jesus of violating the law. No trial was ever to begin at night. A few moments ago, one of the guards had slapped Jesus across the face. Under the law, no prisoner was to be struck prior to being proven guilty.

.

Annas realized he could not keep Jesus indefinitely and he was not making any progress. He had Him bound and sent the group to take Him to the home of Caiaphas. As I walked out into the courtyard, I witnessed a brief exchange between Peter and the servant woman who had granted us entry. Peter was warming his hands with the household servants and guards around the fire.

The servant woman knew John was a disciple of Jesus, and she probably assumed Peter and I were as well. She wasn't one of the accusers, she was simply an inquisitive servant. She probably had heard about Jesus and simply wanted to know more about Him. Who better to ask than one of His disciples?

So she asked Peter, *"You're not one of that Man's disciples, are you?"*[6]

But rather than seeing it as an opportunity to tell her about Jesus, in the midst of the chaos and confusion taking place, Peter denied he was a disciple. Seeing the mob was taking Jesus elsewhere, he turned and hurriedly walked away. This time he did not join John and me.

It was only a short distance to the home of Caiaphas. John followed the mob into the house. I was not allowed to go in, so I found a spot in the courtyard near a window so I could see and hear what was taking place inside. Peter again remained by himself in the courtyard, warming his hands by the fire.

From where I was standing, I not only could see and hear what was happening in the house, I could also see and hear what was happening in the courtyard. Peter had always been near Jesus wherever they went. But today, it appeared he wanted to be as far away from Jesus as possible. It was not unusual for people to recognize Peter as one of Jesus' disciples.

· · ·

As he stood by the fire, the servants and guards were talking among themselves – they were certain he was one of the disciples. So, one of them asked him. It wasn't an accusation; it was an honest inquiry, just like that of the servant woman at Annas' home. But again, Peter, the one who had always spoken out boldly when others stood silent, was tongue-tied by fear and shook his head in protest.

Then after a few more minutes, someone else approached Peter. This servant was apparently a relative of the servant whose ear Peter had cut off. The story of the servant's ear being cut off and then restored by Jesus was already becoming well known.

Whether this servant's intention was to accuse Peter, or more likely, to hear an eye witness report of the healing, one more time he was asked, *"Didn't I see you out there in the olive grove with Jesus?"*[7] But for the third time, Peter adamantly denied even knowing Jesus!

Earlier that night, Peter had boastfully declared to Jesus he was willing to die with Him. To which Jesus had replied that Peter would deny Him three times before the rooster crowed the very next morning. I am certain Peter neither believed nor received what Jesus had said to him. But now, when the rooster crowed, Peter remembered Jesus' words and ran from the courtyard weeping bitterly.

John, Peter, and I weren't the only disciples at the home of Caiaphas that early morning. While Peter had been with the servants denying Jesus, Judas Iscariot had been standing near the religious leaders continuing to betray Jesus. He was standing close and watching carefully. He seemed to be very pleased with himself.

Judas fully expected Jesus at any moment to say "Enough!" and declare Himself the Messiah and establish His authority over everyone in the room. This was the moment for which Judas had been waiting. His three years of following Jesus were now going to pay off. These religious leaders who had treated Judas with such disdain were about to have the tables turned.

Jesus was about to establish His kingdom. Judas was about to step into his position of authority. And these religious leaders were moments away from having their authority stripped away. Judas was certain of how this was all going to end. Surely Jesus would be appreciative of how Judas had helped prompt the moment. Judas would have plenty of opportunity to talk through this with Jesus once He declared Himself. That's how blinded Judas had become by his own sin.

Then Caiaphas, Annas, and the entire High Council said to Jesus, *"Tell us, are You the Messiah?"*[8]

But Jesus replied, *"If I tell you, you won't believe Me. And if I ask you a question, you won't answer. But from now on the Son of Man will be seated in the place of power at God's right hand."*[9]

They all shouted, *"So, are You claiming to be the Son of God?"*[10]

And He replied, *"You say that I am."*[11]

"Why do we need other witnesses?" they asked. *"We ourselves heard Him say it."*[12]

With that, they shouted, *"Guilty! He deserves to die!"*[13]

. . .

Caiaphas directed the guards to take Jesus away. They locked Him in a room in the lower foundation of the home. Caiaphas told everyone who was not a part of the High Council to leave the room. From my place at the window, I could still hear their deliberations as they discussed their next steps. They knew they must present Him to Pilate in order for Him to be crucified.

I saw the expression on Judas' face change from smug satisfaction to terror in an instant! Judas couldn't believe his ears. Jesus was not taking control of the situation (or so Judas thought). Instead of declaring Himself and taking control, Jesus was allowing Himself to be bound, and the religious leaders were taking Him to Pilate to be crucified. And Jesus was going willingly. Judas' confusion quickly turned to the realization that Jesus had been condemned to die. And he, Judas, had been the one who betrayed Jesus.

At that moment, the scales that had blinded him from seeing his own treachery and deceit fell from his eyes. He realized he had been complicit in this plot to murder Jesus, the Messiah. He was overcome with remorse, but regrettably, he did not repent. Repentance would have led to forgiveness of his sin. Repentance would have led to restoration of his relationship with Christ, and through Christ, with the Father.

But, instead, he fell short and stopped with remorse. It is a guilt and regret that is inconsolable. I knew that remorse could be so terrible a person could "drown" in their guilt, shame, and regret. Remorse left unattended leads to death. Repentance on the other hand, though it begins with a sincere regret or remorse, is a turning point – a turning to God for forgiveness, receiving His forgiveness, and walking according to His righteousness. I knew firsthand that repentance leads to life – a life free of the bondage of remorse.

But Judas never made that turn. He verbalized his sin to the religious leaders, but he never sought the forgiveness of God. He laid down the thirty pieces of silver before the religious leaders and declared, *"I have sinned for I have betrayed an innocent man."*[14]

The callous religious leaders responded, *"What do we care? That's your problem,"*[15] leaving no doubt they were anything but men of God. Judas fled from the house filled with terror and agony. Soon afterward, we learned his remorse had led to his death – physically. He had immediately gone out and hung himself. But his remorse also led to his death – eternally. Since he never repented and sought forgiveness, he died eternally separated from God.

The entire council made ready to lead Jesus to Pilate. Everything was going according to their plan, or so they thought. But as I would later learn, this plot may have been hatched in the minds of Annas and Caiaphas ... furthered through the treachery of Judas ... and birthed from the heart of Satan ... but it was allowed to unfold because it was permitted by the Sovereign Almighty Father. Nothing would thwart His redemptive plan!

* * *

29

"I am innocent of this Man's blood. The responsibility is yours!"[1]

* * *

Pontius Pilate and King Herod Antipas were both very familiar with the ministry of Jesus. They were well aware of His growing popularity among the people. I am certain Pilate, being a military leader with the responsibility of keeping peace and order, had kept track of Jesus' movements and actions through his centurions and soldiers. And Herod, being the puppet leader over Galilee, certainly received reports of the miracles Jesus had performed and the crowds that were gathering around Him.

But neither ruler had ever shown any concern Jesus was a threat to their rule. They obviously viewed Him as a religious leader and not a political leader. They were certainly aware of the disdain the religious leaders had for Jesus. They knew the religious leaders viewed Him as a threat to their own power. But neither Pilate nor Herod saw Him as a threat to their power. If they had, they would have arrested Him a long time ago.

John and I followed the mob, along with a growing crowd, as the religious leaders brought Jesus before Pilate. We had no idea where Peter was. He had fled from the home of Caiaphas and we had not seen him since.

When I had been at the fortress two days earlier to visit Barabbas in prison, I never imagined I would be back watching Jesus being brought here as a prisoner. When the religious leaders arrived with Jesus before Pilate, they made three claims about Him. First, that He was telling the people not to pay their taxes. Second, that He was claiming to be their king, with a plan to overthrow Roman rule. Third, that He was inciting the people to riot.

It was clear by Pilate's response he knew all of these claims were false. He knew the real motivation of the religious leaders. He knew they were threatened by Jesus' popularity. He saw this as a religious dispute.

It was no secret Pilate didn't much care for the religious leaders. He knew they abhorred his religious beliefs, and he held theirs in equal contempt. As prefect, his primary role was to keep law and order utilizing a small force of soldiers, to collect the imperial taxes due Rome, and to oversee limited judicial functions. Beyond that, the local municipal council – the Sanhedrin – under the leadership of the High Priest Caiaphas was to attend to all other administrative matters.

Pilate saw this as an administrative matter, and he did not want to get drawn into one of their religious debates. He could find no reason for

Jesus to even be brought before him, let alone find any guilt in Him. Whatever Jesus had done, he saw no cause for Him to be put to death.

But he also could not permit an uprising of the people under his watch. The soldiers at his disposal could not restrain the large crowd that had gathered in Jerusalem this week if a riot broke out. Obviously, the religious leaders were not going to take "no" for an answer, and the crowd that was with them was beginning to become animated. As he looked for a way to keep himself out of the middle of this matter, and at the same time keep the crowd from rioting, he was presented with an opportunity.

Since Jesus was a Galilean, this was Herod's problem and Pilate welcomed the opportunity to refer the matter to him. Since Herod was also in Jerusalem for the week, Pilate sent the whole group to him to adjudicate. Pilate was very pleased with himself for having thought of this solution.

Herod Antipas would have been a young man of sixteen or seventeen years of age when Jesus was born. He would have been an understudy of his father, King Herod the Great, when the wise men arrived from the east seeking the birthplace of *the* King. He would have witnessed how his father directed the wise men, and his father's rage when the wise men failed to return with news of the baby's location.

Over thirty years had passed since that time, and Herod the Great had long been dead. Herod Antipas, now as ruler over Galilee and Perea, began to hear about the ministry and miracles being performed by Jesus in Galilee. I wondered if Herod had ever considered that the baby his father tried to kill was this same Miracle Worker he was now hearing about.

· · ·

Joanna and Chuza had reported to Herod how Jesus had healed their son. They had even hoped Herod would become a follower of Jesus. But he had shown no interest. They told us that when Herod heard about everything Jesus was doing, he was puzzled. Some were reporting to him that John the Baptizer had been raised from the dead. Herod knew John had never performed any miracles. But if this really was John, had he returned to life with extraordinary powers? And if so, what did that mean for Herod?

Having had John beheaded, Herod's conscience was no doubt convicting him. Had God sent John back from the dead to judge him? Herod wanted to see Jesus to determine once and for all who He was. But his pride would never permit him to travel into the countryside to seek Him out.

Now as the religious leaders brought Jesus before him, he was delighted at the opportunity to finally see Jesus perform a miracle. Again, it was obvious Herod did not view Jesus as a threat, he viewed Him more as a curiosity – a performer. So, he asked a series of questions intended to elicit a miraculous act from Jesus. But to his consternation, Jesus remained silent. Jesus was not there to "perform" for Herod. Neither was He there to prove Himself to Herod. Herod was not seeking truth; he was seeking entertainment.

John and I watched as the priests and teachers, who had earlier been unsuccessful in manipulating Jesus with their idle threats, now turned their attention to manipulating Herod with their false accusations. And Herod was easily swayed. Instead of seeking truth, or attempting to stand on truth, he was more concerned with the public opinion being expressed by the priests and teachers. He soon joined in ridiculing the one true King in the room. In an attempt to gain even more approval from the religious leaders, Herod decided to have one of his old robes placed on Jesus as a mockery.

. . .

While he may have been responsible for the execution of John the Baptizer, Herod decided he would not be responsible for this Man's death. He craftily deferred the matter back to Pilate.

Since the leaders in Judea were seeking the death of Jesus in Judea, it must be decided by the prefect of Judea. Pilate had attempted to avoid making a decision by sending Jesus to Herod. But Herod's action was seen as an act of deference to the authority of Pilate, and though it placed the issue of what to do about Jesus back in Pilate's lap, it actually strengthened the political alliance between the two leaders. Herod not only relieved his own conscience, he also created a stronger alliance with Pilate and, by joining in the mockery, he gained political capital with the religious leaders by refusing to take any action regarding Jesus.

When we returned to the courtyard outside of the praetorium, Pilate continued trying to sidestep making a decision about Jesus – but he could not. He announced for a second time that he did not find Jesus guilty of any charges brought by the religious leaders. Pilate knew that Herod had not found any fault with Jesus, either.

He also knew that the fair and just decision was different from the politically correct decision the religious leaders were after. Pilate knew a Jewish uprising under his watch would bring a hasty conclusion to his political and military career. He was not prepared to sacrifice his own well-being for this Jew – even though he knew Jesus was innocent. In reality, it was Pilate who was on trial, not Jesus. Jesus was not trying to escape from the decision, Pilate was.

A prevailing custom called for the prefect to commute one prisoner's death sentence at the time of Passover. Barabbas was scheduled to be crucified this day. If there was one thing the Romans and Jews could agree on, it was that Barabbas deserved to be crucified. Pilate was confident that given the choice between Barabbas and Jesus, the crowd would definitely call for the release of Jesus. He knew the religious leaders' motivation for seeking Jesus' execution was their envy of His standing with the swelling multitude of people.

But he underestimated the ability of the chief priests and elders to persuade the crowd to cry out for the release of Barabbas. The Pharisees had craftily made sure this crowd was made up of the religious leaders of the nation. This crowd – or jury, if you will – was by no means impartial or representative of the crowd that had shouted "Hosanna" and surrounded Jesus when we had entered Jerusalem on Sunday. This crowd was made up of people who felt threatened by Jesus. As the crowd cried out for Jesus to be crucified, Pilate feared a riot was about to break out.

As we watched, Pilate carefully questioned Jesus again, and even trembled at His answers. But now the truth didn't matter – it was all about Pilate's selfish ambition. He chose being popular over being right. He chose expediency over character, and compromise over what was just. There is at least one moment in everyone's life where he or she must stand up for what is right. This was Pilate's moment, and he failed miserably.

Barabbas had no idea all this was taking place. He had been found guilty by a legal tribunal and had been condemned to death. There was never any question as to his guilt – in the minds of his condemners or in his own mind. He knew he deserved a death sentence. He knew at any moment the Roman soldiers would take him from his prison to the hill of execution outside the city walls to be crucified on a cross. There would be no appeal. There would be no mercy. His sentence had been issued and his fate was sealed.

Off in the distance, he heard the crowd shouting his name. It began as a dull roar, but the shouts quickly grew louder. Then he heard them repeatedly shouting, *"Crucify him!"* [(2)] The crowd was obviously shouting for his blood. The time of his execution had arrived. The soldiers took him from his cell and led him out still bound. But to his surprise, instead of heading to Golgotha under the weight of his cross, he was led to the courtyard outside of the praetorium to stand before Pilate. There was another Man, also bound, standing there as well. Then the unimaginable took place.

I could not believe what was happening before my eyes. The man clothed in unrighteousness who deserved to be crucified for his transgressions was being set free, and the Man clothed in righteousness – the One without sin – was undeservedly being condemned by Pilate to be crucified. The criminal Barabbas was released, and the Savior Jesus was condemned.

I watched Barabbas closely. He knew he deserved to die. He had resigned himself to the fact he would die on a cross today. And at the last moment, he had been set free. Another would endure his cross. And Barabbas knew it was Jesus. He knew Jesus didn't deserve to die. He knew Jesus was taking his place undeservedly. Jesus was paying the price for his release.

Pilate directed the centurion to remove the chains and ropes binding Barabbas. As the last one fell, I saw his gaze settle on me. Pilate told him he was free. Barabbas knew better than to tarry. He immediately began to make his way out into the crowd. The crowd parted before him, partly out of fear and partly out of amazement.

· · ·

Barabbas made his way to where John and I were standing. He stood in front of me looking shocked. I could tell a change was overcoming Barabbas. Although we needed to talk, we both knew this was neither the time nor the place. He told me he was headed out of Jerusalem to Emmaus and asked me to come see him there. I promised to do so, and then he left. My gaze turned back to Jesus. The ropes that had been removed from Barabbas were now being placed on Jesus. Pilate made one final attempt to keep Jesus from being crucified by ordering the centurion to have Jesus flogged.

Pilate had Jesus scourged in the hopes it would satisfy the religious leaders and the crowd. The Romans had made scourging a macabre art. The scourge was a short whip made of two or three leather thongs or ropes connected to a handle. The thongs were knotted with pieces of metal or bones at various intervals, with a hook at the end.

The scourge was intended to quickly remove flesh from the body of the victim stopping just short of death. But even after putting Jesus through that pain and torture, the religious leaders and the crowd continued to cry out for Jesus to be crucified. Pilate acquiesced to the religious leaders and turned Jesus over to the soldiers to be crucified.

Roman soldiers were the brute force used by Rome to maintain law and order over its subjects. Though many had been locally recruited, they were a constant reminder to the Jewish people of their oppressive Roman ruler. Jewish people therefore viewed them with disdain and disrespect. But because they were not Roman citizens, they were also looked down upon by their Roman leaders.

The rank and file soldiers were not selected for their good character; they were selected for their sadistic brutality and fighting ability. Most of the time, they were forced to control their growing hatred for the

Jewish people. But this time, Pilate released Jesus to this group – and there were no constraints on their actions, except that they had to deliver Him to Golgotha for crucifixion.

I cannot fully comprehend the unbridled brutality, torture, and humiliation these men unleashed on Jesus as they sought to satisfy their sadistic appetites. I had heard of a "game" the Roman soldiers often played called "hot hand." The soldiers would each hold up a fist in the face of their victim. Then they would blindfold him, and each soldier would hit him in the face. They would beat their victim until his face was unrecognizable. Then they would remove the blindfold, and the victim was to identify which fist had not hit him.

The prisoner was never able to identify the right one; even if he did, the soldiers wouldn't admit it. So, the blindfold would be put back on him, and the "game" would continue. Even the mockery of the robe placed on Jesus' shredded flesh and the crown of thorns pressed into His brow were intended to subject Him to more brutality and torture.

But our Savior quietly suffered and did not speak out or fight back. By a single command, He could have called a multitude of angels, like those I had seen that night outside of Bethlehem, to remove Him from the suffering. With a simple thought, He could have reduced the soldiers to a pillar of salt. By a single word, He could have said, "Enough!" and brought it all to an end. But He did not. He stood there and suffered the depravity of His fallen creation on our behalf, according to His Father's plan.

They humiliated Him. They ridiculed Him. They spat on Him. They taunted Him in mock worship until they got bored. Then they led Him away to be crucified.

. . .

I was numb. I could not believe what I was witnessing. Pilate had sent for a bowl of water and was washing his hands before the crowd as he said, *"I am innocent of this man's blood. The responsibility is yours!"*(3) And somehow I felt the responsibility belonged to all of us. Somehow, I felt no one was innocent that day – except the One about to be crucified.

Jesus was never the victim of human decisions. He wasn't the victim of the treacherous disciple who betrayed Him. He wasn't the victim of the corrupt high priests who orchestrated His arrest. He wasn't the victim of the Sanhedrin who condemned Him. He wasn't the victim of the crowd who shouted for Barabbas' release. He wasn't the victim of the soldiers who brutalized Him. Nor was He the victim of Herod or Pilate, who ultimately had Him executed.

He was God's chosen Lamb in His redemptive plan. The Shepherd had now become the unblemished sheep. God had determined before the beginning of time He would die as the atonement for our sin. But nonetheless, each of these corrupt and tragic characters played a role in the murder of the Son of God. They could not escape their personal responsibility.

But I realized none of them really determined the destiny of Jesus. What they did with Jesus determined *their* destiny. None of them really condemned Jesus; but each one condemned himself. It wasn't Jesus on trial that day; it was they who were on trial. And they all damned themselves.

* * *

30

"This Man truly was the Son of God!"[1]

* * *

It was still morning. Everything was moving in slow motion. It was only last night we all had dinner together. And now somewhere inside the fortress, Roman soldiers were beating Jesus and preparing to crucify Him.

The women who had prepared last night's supper had returned to Bethany when Jesus led the rest of us to the Mount of Olives. Most of the disciples had fled to the home of Lazarus when Jesus was arrested. They reported to Lazarus and the women all that had happened. The group was in shock. What should they do? The Teacher had been taken by a mob of soldiers and religious leaders.

Lazarus announced he was going to Jerusalem to see if his testimony could help get Jesus released. But the disciples and his sisters discouraged him. They reminded him of the rumors that the religious leaders were plotting to kill him, as well. Now that they had taken Jesus, they wouldn't hesitate to kill Lazarus. There was nothing to be gained by his going to Jerusalem. He must remain in Bethany.

The remainder of the disciples had fled to Bethany because they, too, feared for their own lives. What could they possibly do? Already they had been overwhelmed by the mob when Jesus was arrested. They weren't soldiers; they were fishermen and tradesmen. And they were afraid they might also be arrested if they returned to Jerusalem. They felt helpless and frightened.

Mary, the mother of Jesus, pulled herself together and decided to return to Jerusalem to see her Son. The remaining women agreed they would accompany her, except Martha and Mary, who stayed in Bethany to keep a watchful eye on their brother.

John and I felt helpless as we waited outside the fortress. John had sought out two of the Pharisees – Nicodemus and Joseph of Arimathea – to see if there was anything we could do to dissuade the religious leaders from having Jesus crucified. Both men said they and a few other Pharisees had tried to talk the High Council out of taking this action. But they had failed. And now that the death order had been granted by Pilate, there was nothing that could be done to reverse it, short of an edict from Caesar himself.

Mary and the other women, including John's mother and my mother, had arrived from Bethany and found us outside the fortress.

The other day when I visited Barabbas, the centurion Gaius Marius had treated me kindly. He appeared to be sympathetic to the threats being made about Jesus. I attempted to see if I could get an audience with him to seek permission for Mary to see her Son. But soon the soldier who had taken my message to the centurion returned and told us he could not permit her to do so.

"The city is in an uproar over Jesus. No one is permitted to see Him. His mother will need to speak to Him as he hangs on the cross," was the message we received.

Soon after, a cohort of soldiers exited the fortress. In their midst were three men, each one carrying his own cross. According to Roman law, one who was found guilty and condemned to death was required to carry his cross, or at least the cross beam, to the place of his crucifixion. The first two men were apparently two of the prisoners I had seen in the prison on Wednesday. The third Man was Jesus. But He was barely recognizable.

His face had been pummeled. He was wearing a crown of thorns thrust into his scalp. Blood was streaming down His face and neck, saturating his clothing, particularly the back of His garment. All three men had been beaten, but it was obvious that Jesus' beating was the most severe. If we had not known Him, we would not have recognized Him. Mary cried out at the sight of her beloved Son.

Given His weakened condition, Jesus struggled under the weight of the cross. The soldiers decided He needed help, so they seized a man in the crowd and forced him to carry Jesus' cross. None of us knew who he was, but later we found out more about him and his story. His name was Simon from Cyrene. He was a Hellenistic Jew who had come to Jerusalem to observe Passover. Little did he know the Father had planned for him to be transformed that day – and the impetus was the Roman soldiers forcing him to carry Jesus' cross.

. . .

Simon's immediate reaction was resentment. Of all the people on the road that day, why were the soldiers singling him out to carry the cross for this Man? He was already weary from traveling. His pilgrimage to Jerusalem had taken more than three weeks, and he had only just arrived — which meant he had no idea who this Man was. The soldiers commanded him to carry the cross, and to refuse would have been fatal for him.

As they continued along the path, Simon heard the shouts from the crowd. He heard the grief-stricken cries of Mary and the other women as they trailed behind. He heard the crowd calling out the Man's name – some in disbelief, others in ridicule. At some point, it became clear to him who this Man was. He had heard of Jesus.

Then He heard Jesus turn to the women and say, "*Daughters of Jerusalem, don't weep for Me, but weep for yourselves and for your children.*"[2]

Jesus then briefly bore witness to what would occur in the end times. Even as He was being led to His death, Jesus was speaking as One in authority.

When the soldiers and prisoners arrived at the place of execution, Simon's task was finished, and he was free to go. But he felt compelled to remain at the foot of the cross. That is when I first met him. He told me he felt drawn to Jesus. Something had occurred in his heart as he carried that cross. He couldn't explain it. He had heard of Jesus the Miracle Worker, but that morning he realized Jesus was so much more. As John, the women, and I gathered at the foot of the cross, Simon remained with us.

. . .

The place of crucifixion was called Golgotha. It was located just outside the city wall along the trade road leading into Jerusalem. The Romans conducted their executions by crucifixion near a road with high visibility. It was part of the death penalty that the victim die in the most conspicuous and humiliating way possible. It also served as a deterrent to those considering breaking the law.

The three prisoners were nailed to their crosses – Jesus in the center with the other two men on either side. One of the other men called out to Jesus, *"So You're the Messiah, are You? Prove it by saving Yourself – and us, too, while You're at it!"* [3]

But the other criminal said, *"Don't you fear God even when you have been sentenced to die? We deserve to die for our crimes, but this Man hasn't done anything wrong."* [4]

Then he said, *"Jesus, remember me when You come into your Kingdom."* [5]

And Jesus replied, *"I assure you, today you will be with Me in paradise."* [6]

It was common for the victim's crime to be written on a sign and hung on the cross – also a further deterrent. The sign was written in the three main languages of the region so the majority of people were able to read it. It was written in Hebrew, the language of religion. It was written in Latin, the language of law and order. And it was written in Greek, the language of culture and education.

In Jesus' case, Pilate had instructed that the sign say, "The King of the

Jews." Little did Pilate know, or the rest of us at the time, the Romans were unknowingly proclaiming some of the first written words of the gospel message in ways that people from many tongues and tribes could understand.

The religious leaders attempted to have the sign changed. But Pilate denied their request in defiance of the way they had manipulated him into having Jesus executed. So, in an effort to counteract the message of the sign, the leading priests, the teachers of religious law, and the elders mocked Jesus by standing nearby and scoffing. *"So He is the King of Israel, is He? Let Him come down from the cross right now, and we will believe in Him!"* [7]

The soldiers overseeing the crucifixion were permitted to confiscate and share victims' personal belongings. All that Jesus possessed were a pair of sandals, a girdle, an outer robe, a head covering, and a seamless tunic. Each soldier took one of the first four items of clothing; then each man gambled for the tunic. This act also fulfilled prophecy: *"They divide My garments among themselves and throw dice for My clothing."* [8]

Jesus looked down from the cross and saw His mother standing beside John. His eyes were filled with compassion as He honored and completed His responsibility as the firstborn son of His earthly mother.

First, He was assuring her salvation. Mary needed to come to faith in Christ just like everyone else. Jesus was dying on the cross for the sins of the entire world – and that included Mary. He was making the way for her to be saved. She, too, had to believe, accept, and follow Him as her Savior.

Second, through His coming resurrection, He was clearing her name forever. For thirty-three years her reputation had suffered the injustice of gossip and innuendo regarding His birth. Only the Son of the Living God could overcome death. At last, she would be vindicated.

Third, as her firstborn son, He was making sure she would be cared for after He was gone. This responsibility He gave to John, whom He loved as a brother.

I was curious why Jesus had not asked one of Mary's other sons – James, Joseph, Jude, or Simon – to watch over her. James, as the next oldest son, would normally be given the responsibility by Jesus to care for His widowed mother.

But after thinking about it some more, I came to two conclusions. First, James and the other brothers had not yet believed in Jesus. They were not like-minded, and He would not entrust His mother to anyone who was not. Second, none of His brothers were present at His crucifixion. They chose to stay in Jerusalem for the observance of Passover instead of following Him to the cross. I didn't know whether they feared retribution because they were family, whether it was due to their unbelief in Him, or maybe because they were embarrassed over the way He had sullied the family's reputation.

However, I did know this. As He hung on that cross, with His mother as His only immediate family member present, Jesus entrusted her to John's care.

At noon, the Father caused a veil of darkness to fall across the whole land as His Son hung on that cross. There was a transaction that took place that day between the Father and the Son. It was a transaction for the sins of the world – something that none of us could ever truly comprehend. The only thing we could do was watch in sorrow.

Jesus was "spent." His physical body was dehydrated; He was parched. He could only whisper the words, "I am thirsty."[9] I had watched earlier as He refused to drink the pain-deadening wine the soldiers extended to Him. Offering the narcotic was not an act of compassion; it was meant to lengthen the time Jesus would suffer the humiliation and brutality of the cross. The excruciating pain accelerated the onset of death. Deadening the pain slowed it down. The Romans intended that the suffering leading to death last as long as possible.

This time, however, He allowed one of the soldiers to hoist a sour, wine-soaked sponge on the end of a branch and hold it to His lips. Even the Messianic prophecy of "… they offer me sour wine to satisfy my thirst"[10] – was fulfilled. That bit of moisture didn't quench Jesus' thirst, but it was all He needed to speak His last words in triumph: "It is finished!"[11]

My heart was heavy, and I could not process all that was going on. But in retrospect, that day on Golgotha must have seemed like a triumph to Satan. He had bruised the heel of the woman's seed as foretold in Genesis 3. The religious leaders considered Jesus' death to be a victory. The threat to their position and power had been eliminated forever. And to a watching world, it was a brutal murder – to many, an injustice. But to the Father, it was the only way His creation would ever be able to cross the sinful divide back to Him.

Jesus' physical suffering on the cross was over. But that wasn't the only suffering and pain He endured that day. During the three hours of darkness from noon until 3 p.m., Jesus felt the full wrath of God as He poured out the sins of the world onto His Son. And Jesus experienced complete separation from the Father for the first and only time in His existence.

None of us could understand the pain and suffering He endured by that separation and isolation. But He suffered because the Father loved us and the Son loved the Father – so He persevered to the end.

The prophecies foretelling His incarnation and death were now fulfilled. The sacrifice for our sin was now complete. It was finished! As He bowed His head and gave up His Spirit, the curtain in the sanctuary of the Temple was torn in two, from top to bottom. The earth shook, rocks split apart, and tombs opened. The earth quaked and the centurion Gaius Marius, who had overseen the crucifixion, declared, *"This Man truly was the Son of God!"* [12]

Yes, it was finished! Our redemption was made complete. Jesus had met the righteous demands of the holy law. He had paid our sin debt in full. Jesus had completed the work the Father had given Him to do.

From the day of His incarnational birth there in the stable until this day on Golgotha, Jesus had been on a mission given to Him by the Father. I had the unique perspective of being with Him on both of those days. I had witnessed firsthand His faithfulness. Surely this wasn't the end. The Son of God could not die! In my spirit, I knew there had to be more to come. But my heart was heavy with grief. I fell to my knees and wept.

* * *

31

"Peace be with you!" [1]

* * *

According to custom, it was the responsibility of Jesus' family and friends to arrange for His burial. But there had been no time to make plans. These events had all unfolded in less than twenty-four hours. Burial arrangements were the furthest thing from our minds.

Most of His family and followers had scattered out of fear, and those of us who remained were just barely coping with our sorrow and grief.

We had all traveled to Jerusalem from Galilee and now that Judas was gone, we didn't even have the little amount that was in our treasury. We had nothing at our disposal with which to bury Jesus' body. But the Sabbath was rapidly approaching. The bodies of the victims of crucifixion were usually left to be eaten by birds and wild animals, or thrown like worthless garbage into the dumping area in the Kidron

Valley and burned. But that would not be the case for the Son of God. Gratefully, His Father had a plan.

Joseph, the Pharisee from Arimathea, knew something needed to be done with Jesus' body quickly. He went to Pilate and requested the body, knowing his action would not be popular with Caiaphas, Annas, and most of the members of the High Council. In fact, his deed would be considered an outright act of betrayal by most of his Sanhedrin brothers.

It was political suicide for Joseph, jeopardizing his position on the Sanhedrin, his influence in the community, and his personal wealth. I admired the courage and strength of character it took for him to go to Pilate to arrange for a suitable burial for Jesus. Joseph provided the newly hewn tomb in which His body would be laid, as well as the linen cloth with which His body would be wrapped.

The Pharisee Nicodemus also assisted in the burial. He brought the embalming ointment to prepare Jesus' body. The Sanhedrin would not have looked kindly on his participation, either. The two men acted quickly so Jesus' body could be laid in the tomb before the beginning of Sabbath at dusk.

Though Jesus had foretold He would rise again, not one of us was watching by faith with hopeful anticipation. We were overwhelmed by our grief and never contemplated that possibility. Interestingly enough, the only ones who remembered His promise were the religious leaders.

When they heard Joseph had made arrangements to place Jesus' body in his tomb, they petitioned Pilate to post guards at the tomb entrance.

They were fearful we, as His followers, would remove His body and make the claim He had risen from the dead. We hadn't even thought about burying His body, let alone arranging a false resurrection!

Simon the Cyrene had stood quietly at the foot of the cross in reverence until Jesus declared, *"It is finished."*[2] Then he remained there weeping and worshipping. Now as Joseph and Nicodemus prepared to take Jesus' body to the tomb, Simon carried Him. Simon had carried His cross to Golgotha, and now He would carry His body to the tomb.

Mary Magdalene, Mary (the wife of Clopas), Salome, Joanna, and my mother volunteered to help prepare Jesus' body for burial. However, they were unable to do so before the sun set. They would have to delay going to the tomb until after the Sabbath.

Later, I was able to look back at this event and see the sovereign hand of God. The Father's plan was perfect. He didn't need the women to be at the tomb when Jesus' body was placed. They were to arrive at the tomb at another time for a totally different purpose!

As the women were preparing to leave Golgotha for Bethany, Clopas joined us at the foot of the cross. He had come to accompany his wife and the other women back to the home of Lazarus. He asked John and me if there was anything else he could do.

In the midst of my sorrow, I remembered I had promised Barabbas I would come to Emmaus to speak with him. I questioned whether I had the strength to have that conversation, but I knew I was supposed to go. And I knew I needed to talk to Barabbas sooner than later. I asked Clopas if he could accompany me on Sunday following the Sabbath.

He agreed and we arranged to meet in Bethphage early Sunday morning.

Earlier that day, when Peter realized he had denied Jesus, just as Jesus had told him he would, Peter was devastated. He ran away from the home of Caiaphas, but soon realized he didn't know where to go. He did not want to join the other disciples in Bethany. He did not want to see anyone. He decided to return to the upper room where we had all been together the night before. The room had been reserved for the week.

That was the last place he had been close to Jesus. It was there Jesus had washed his feet. No one would be looking for the disciples there. Peter spent the entire day on Friday by himself. He was not hiding out of fear; he was hiding out of grief and shame over his denial of Jesus. He had no idea what all was taking place. He knew it would end in death. Jesus had told us He would die. But Peter did not witness the trials or Jesus' death on the cross. He did, however, see the sky turn black at midday – and he knew that could only mean one thing. Peter was fully engulfed in his grief.

That was how John and I found him later that night. After Simon, Joseph, and Nicodemus had taken Jesus' body to the tomb, and the women had taken His mother back to the home of Lazarus, John and I went looking for Peter. We knew he had not gone to Bethany. He had obviously gone somewhere to be alone. We decided he was either at the upper room or the Garden on the Mount of Olives. We decided to check the upper room first.

The writer of Proverbs talks about a *"friend who sticks closer than a brother."*[3] That night and throughout the next day, I witnessed true friendship as John "stuck" with Peter, when Peter so desperately needed a friend. I realized God had appointed John to be the one through whom He ministered His redemption and restoration, so I watched as God used John as His vessel of ministry.

Peter was broken because of his denial of Jesus. His remorse was overwhelming. But gratefully, he didn't stop with remorse like Judas had. He was repentant of his sin. And he truly sought forgiveness. It would have been easy for John to judge Peter and cast him aside in light of his denial of Christ. I had seen other individuals who professed to be followers of Jesus do just that to those who had sinned. Instead of turning toward them in love, I had seen these "followers" turn away from them in judgment.

But John chose to love Peter. He chose to heed the words Jesus had spoken just the night before in this very room to *"love each other."* [4] God used John throughout Friday night and Saturday as He began His healing work to cleanse and repair Peter's heart.

The women had been able to prepare some of the spices and ointments in Bethany on Friday, just before the Sabbath began. They were then able to purchase the remainder and make their final arrangements after dark on Saturday night. They would need sunlight to do what they needed to do, so they waited until Sunday just before sunrise.

As the women were walking to the tomb, they realized the stone would be too heavy for them to roll away in order to gain entry. They hadn't thought through all of the details in advance. But fortunately, the Father had been planning the details for eternity, and He had not forgotten anything!

.   .   .

As the women approached the tomb, they saw the large stone had already been rolled away from the entrance. They immediately presumed someone had taken Jesus' body. Without even walking into the tomb, Mary Magdalene immediately left the other women to go and alert Peter, John, and me. She had rightly determined we were staying in the upper room in Jerusalem. She found us and told us the stone had been rolled away from the tomb. She was certain the religious leaders had taken Jesus' body. So, the four of us headed to the tomb to see what had happened.

While Mary Magdalene had gone to find us, the other women entered the tomb and encountered angels who told them Jesus had risen from the dead. The women could not believe their ears. They even wondered if the angels were false messengers. They fled from the tomb, trembling and bewildered.

Although Jesus had tried to prepare us by telling us He would rise again, even His closest followers couldn't quite believe it. We had all been there when Jesus called Lazarus to come out of the tomb, but we weren't expecting Jesus to call Himself out of the tomb. The women headed toward Bethany, to tell Mary (the mother of Jesus) and the other disciples what they had seen.

I found it ironic the religious leaders were concerned *we* would steal Jesus' body, and Mary Magdalene's first thought was *they* had taken His body. That thought just added to her grief. So, she let us run on ahead to the tomb. She wasn't in any hurry to see an empty tomb. She was now even more consumed by grief.

To be honest, we weren't truly expecting the resurrection of Jesus any more than Mary Magdalene had been. We thought she was mistaken in what she saw. Perhaps, she had gone to the wrong tomb. We were not running to the tomb expecting to find Jesus alive. We were expecting to uncover Mary's error and find His body.

John was the fastest runner. He got to the tomb before Peter and I did (remember, John was the youngest of the three of us). But John stopped at the doorway looking in. Peter arrived next and charged past John right into the tomb. I arrived last. There we saw the linen wrappings neatly rolled up. It was at that moment John would later tell me *"he saw and believed."*[5] He couldn't yet prove Jesus was risen, but He believed it with all his heart. He believed Jesus had risen according to the Scriptures, and he believed once and for all Jesus truly was God in the flesh.

Peter and I had not yet come to that place. Not knowing what else we could do, we decided to leave the tomb. I made my way to Bethphage to meet Clopas for our journey to Emmaus. John and Peter decided to return to the upper room. As we walked toward our respective destinations, we pondered what we had just seen.

Peter and John passed Mary Magdalene as they walked back to Jerusalem. They told her what they had seen. She decided to continue on to the tomb. When she arrived back at the tomb, she remained outside weeping. Then she stooped and looked into the tomb for the first time. She saw two angels who asked her why she was weeping.

"The religious leaders *have taken away my Lord, and I do not know where they have laid Him."*[6]

She turned and saw Jesus standing there. But she was so overcome with grief, she did not recognize Him. Thinking He was the gardener, she again sought an answer from Him as to where Jesus' body was laid. At that moment, Jesus spoke her name and she knew! Having seen Jesus, she believed! Off she went to deliver the good news and His instructions to Peter and John.

In the meantime, Jesus appeared to the other women – Mary (the wife of Clopas), Salome, Joanna, and my mother – as they were running back to Bethany. Imagine their reaction! They had not expected to encounter the living Lord Jesus; they had expected to anoint His body. As terrified as they were when they saw the angels, can you just imagine how they felt when they saw Jesus? And Jesus told them, *"Don't be afraid!"* [7]

Emmaus was a small village seven miles northwest of Jerusalem. I walked from the tomb to Bethphage to meet up with Clopas. Before I arrived, Clopas' wife (Mary) and the other women had just been there and told him about the empty tomb. (Apparently the women had not yet encountered Jesus when they reported this news to Clopas.) They had given an amazing report that they had seen angels who said Jesus was alive. But the women had been somewhat hysterical, so it was difficult to discern what they really had seen or heard. I shared with Clopas what Peter, John, and I had seen at the tomb, and that Jesus' body really was gone. But the question that still remained was – where was the body of Jesus?

Clopas and I discussed all of these things as we walked along. I told him what had happened when Jesus was arrested, then the stops at the homes of Annas and Caiaphas. I did not tell him about Peter's denial of Jesus. That was not my story to tell. I told him about the trials before Herod and Pilate. And I told him about the surprising release of Barabbas, and my brief visit with him in prison on Wednesday.

Then we continued to discuss everything that had unfolded. We didn't know what to make of it all. There was no question Jesus was the Son of God who did powerful miracles. And, without question, He was the mightiest Teacher either of us had ever heard. We believed He was the Messiah who had come to rescue Israel.

But the leading priests and religious leaders had been successful in their scheme. They had manipulated Pilate to condemn Him to death, and He had been crucified. Now all of our hopes He was the Messiah had been dashed. His death made no sense. We had faithfully followed Him for three years. What were we to do now? Had we been wrong? What would I say to Barabbas?

As we walked along, discussing these things, Jesus joined us – though we did not recognize Him. He was a stranger to us. Remember, we weren't looking for Him, either. We thought He was dead and gone. We were blinded to who He was by our grief and our doubts.

As we continued together, our fellow traveler began to explain the prophecies regarding the Messiah to us, one by one, with great clarity. When we arrived in Emmaus, we prevailed upon Him to join us for a meal. We would look for Barabbas after we ate with this stranger. Then as Jesus took the bread and broke it – just as He had many times before when we had all eaten together – our eyes were opened! I looked into His eyes – and I saw my Lord and my Savior! And I saw a twinkle in His eye as He saw I recognized Him. Then at that very moment, He disappeared! We could not contain our joy! We knew we must find Barabbas and immediately return to Jerusalem.

As we walked outside, Barabbas approached us. I quickly explained to him that we had just seen Jesus. Interestingly enough, he was less shocked by that statement than we had been. He told us that on Friday morning when he had been set free he knew Jesus was to be crucified in his place. He knew he owed his life to Jesus. And he knew he must do whatever he had to do to follow Him.

As Barabbas had looked into the eyes of Jesus that morning, he had seen and known He truly is the Son of God. So, he knew the grave would never be able to hold Jesus. He knew the Son of God could never remain dead. He knew he had surrendered his life to a living Lord. Clopas and I looked at one another. Through that one encounter with Jesus, Barabbas had demonstrated more faith than any of the rest of us who had followed Him for years. I was looking into the eyes of a man whose life had been transformed by Jesus! I invited him to come back to Jerusalem with us. Within the hour, the three of us began our way back to the upper room to tell the others what we had seen and heard.

Jesus also appeared to Peter that day. It occurred after Peter and John had visited the empty tomb. John, remembering that Jesus had given him the responsibility to care for His mother Mary, decided he needed to go to Bethany to check on her. Peter went back to the upper room. He didn't know what to believe. His judgment was still clouded by his remorse over his denial of Jesus.

Neither Peter nor Jesus ever told us what they said to one another when Jesus appeared to Peter in the upper room. Whatever conversation they had remained private. There was something that needed to be reconciled between the two of them. There was a personal and private transaction of healing that took place between Peter and his Lord.

Jesus knew He needed to correct Peter, but before that could take place, healing needed to occur. And that healing also needed to happen before Jesus and Peter were together with the other disciples.

Jesus met with Peter to extend His grace, His mercy, His love and His forgiveness.

That night, we all gathered back in that upper room. Three days had now passed. This was the first time all of us were back together since the night of His arrest, with the exception of Judas Iscariot (the betrayer) and Thomas (whose absence from this gathering was inexplicable). But two additional people had joined us – who weren't in the room three nights earlier – Simon the Cyrene and Barabbas. Everyone had looked at Clopas and me suspiciously when Barabbas followed us into the room. We quickly helped him tell his testimony of transformation. And Simon told his own. After they had done so, everyone welcomed them into the room.

We had gathered in secret, and the door to the room was locked. The room was abuzz with all of the reports. Mary Magdalene told the group about how Jesus had spoken to her as she stood outside the tomb. John shared how he and Peter had witnessed the empty tomb, and his belief that Jesus truly was the Son of the Living God. Mary, Joanna, Salome, and my mother relayed their encounter with the angels in the tomb, and then how Jesus had appeared to them on their way to report to the disciples. Peter told them Jesus was alive and had appeared to him earlier in the day. Finally, Clopas and I shared how Jesus had appeared to us as we were walking along the road.

The disciples' heads were spinning. They kept hearing these reports from brothers and sisters whom they respected, but this was all still hard to believe. How could this possibly be true? Jesus had been subjected to unspeakable brutality and had died on the cross. They had witnessed it, albeit from a distance after they scattered. Could this be a part of the religious leaders' plot to not only murder Jesus, but to defame His teachings and His miracles? Was this all part of the plan to now draw out His close followers and arrest us as well? At that moment, there was still more fear than faith present in that room.

Then, all of a sudden, Jesus appeared – out of nowhere! And the door was locked! If there had been any windows in the room, some of the men would have jumped out! They thought they were seeing a ghost. So, it is no wonder the first words out of Jesus' mouth were, *"Peace be with you!"* [(8)]

Be at peace, the One – the only One – who can make sense of it all is now in the room! Jesus calmed all of our fears and gave us assurance. He ate a piece of broiled fish to assure us He wasn't a ghost. He showed us the wounds in His hands, His feet, and His side to prove to us He who was dead was now alive. The work the Father had given Him to do was now complete.

Gradually everyone's fear and anxiety turned to peace and joy! I watched as Jesus' and Peter's eyes knowingly locked for a moment as they saw the rest of the disciples gradually coming to that place of peace. Peter had experienced that same emotional upheaval earlier that day – and I am certain his was even more turbulent.

Then for a second time, Jesus said to us, *"Peace be with you."* [(9)] But this time it wasn't a word of peace for us, it was a word of peace we were now to go and share with a world that desperately needed peace. As the Father had sent Him, He was now sending us!

To this day, I do not know why Thomas was not in the room that night. But later when he arrived to join us, he refused to accept our word Jesus was alive. He held to the conviction that since he wasn't there to see it, it must not be true. Thus, we started to call him "Doubting

Thomas." Sadly, his skepticism and faithlessness robbed him of joy for eight more long days before Jesus again appeared in our midst and stood among us. This time, Thomas was present.

Jesus again declared, *"Peace be with you,"*[10] but this time He added a rebuke to Thomas with a truth all of us would do well to embrace – "Don't believe simply because you see; believe because of Who I am and what I have said!"[11]

Jesus is alive! He has risen! He has risen, indeed!

* * *

32

"Take care of My sheep."[1]

* . * . *

After Jesus arose from the tomb, He appeared and disappeared at
will. One moment He was there with us, another He was with
His Father in heaven. As the days continued, we saw Jesus less
frequently. We never knew when He would appear, so we had to
remain alert.

He explained He was preparing us for the time He would no longer be
with us in bodily form. He was preparing us for the coming of the
Helper who would be with us at all times. He was using these visits to
prepare us for the assignments He had for each one of us. Such was the
day He came to us along the shore of the Sea of Galilee.

We remained in Jerusalem and Bethany for over a week after His resurrection. Jesus appeared to us twice there as a group. He instructed us

to go to Capernaum in Galilee and wait for Him there. We waited for several days. Peter, not being one to just sit around and wait, decided he wasn't going to miss a good opportunity to go fishing.

He enlisted the other fishermen in the group to join him – Andrew, Philip, Thomas, Nathanael, and the brothers James and John. These men had grown up on the sea and fishing was "in their blood," so they were easily persuaded. They would fish all night, then rest during the day. The rest of us slept each night and found other things to do each day in the village to pass the time.

One morning, the fishermen had been out on the sea all night with no success. It was now dawn and they were preparing to return to shore. Simon (the zealot), Barabbas, and I woke up early and were walking along the shore. At a distance, we saw someone else standing on the shoreline. He was looking out toward the boat. The sun was just coming up, and the boat was still a good ways out.

Suddenly, the Man called out to the fishermen and told them to throw out their net on the right-hand side of the boat one more time. Even though they didn't have any idea who was calling out to them, something told them to obey. As they did, the fish struck the net. There were so many fish they couldn't haul them all in. As a matter of fact, like the good fisherman he was, John later told us they had caught one hundred fifty-three large fish. Miraculously, the net didn't tear under the weight.

Peter and John were reminded of that day almost three years earlier, at almost that exact same spot, when Jesus had told them to do the same thing. And the catch that time had been more than one boat could bring to shore. Suddenly, that memory prompted John to say, "It's the Lord!"[2]

. . .

He knew his Lord's ways – and though he couldn't recognize His form and He hadn't recognized His voice, he knew it was Jesus! This time, Jesus didn't need to tell Peter to come. Hearing from John it was their Lord, he quickly jumped into the water and headed for Jesus. By that time, we also recognized Jesus, so Barabbas, Simon, and I ran toward Him as well.

Although I didn't know it at the time, this was the last miracle Jesus would perform as part of His earthly ministry before He ascended to the Father – nets full of fish. It was just like His first miracle that day in Cana – water pots full of wine. Jesus never did anything halfway! When Jesus showed up there was abundance – perhaps not always in fish or wine – but abundant life, abundant joy, and abundant mercy.

When I reached Jesus, He was already cooking some bread and fish over a charcoal fire. He told Peter to bring some of the fish they had caught and add it to the fire. He was preparing breakfast for us. Soon, all of the disciples – those from the boat and those who had been sleeping in the village – were gathered there on the shore.

Jesus was getting us ready to go out into the world and share His gospel message, making disciples who would in turn make other disciples. Jesus was even using breakfast to teach us. We were like the fish He had already prepared on the fire. He had called us and taught us, but now there would be others who would be added through the work He would do through us – just like the fish we now added to the fire.

He would show us where to cast the net. The harvest would be His. We would be His laborers. Over the past three years, He had called us to follow Him bodily. He had instructed us each step of the way. Now, He

was reminding us He would continue to instruct us as we follow Him
– not bodily – but by His Spirit.

On their first meeting, Jesus had given Simon, the son of John, a new
name. From then on, Peter had been called "the rock." Jesus had later
said, *"upon this rock I will build My church, and all the powers of hell will
not conquer it."*[3]

Jesus was preparing to build His church and He was giving us – and
the others we would disciple – the assignment to disciple and lead this
new church. Principal among those of us to whom He was giving that
assignment was Simon Peter, the rock. But Jesus knew … and Peter
knew … and many of us knew … that Peter had denied knowing Jesus
the night before He was crucified.

We knew on the day of His resurrection, Jesus had appeared to Peter.
We knew it had been a personal and private time of healing and
forgiveness for Peter. Peter had sinned against His Lord, and that sin
had created a separation between him and Jesus. But gratefully, Jesus'
shed blood on the cross covered that sin – and so much more. So there
needed to be that moment when Peter confessed his sin, sought
forgiveness and received it from Jesus.

I am certain on the day of His resurrection, Jesus took Peter in His
arms as Peter confessed his sin and wept in the embrace of his Lord
and Savior. I am sure of this because I remember the day Jesus took me
into His arms and did the same for me.

Peter's confession was not for Jesus' sake, it was for Peter's sake. The
moment Peter was forgiven, his relationship with Jesus was reconciled.

He no longer needed to walk in grief and shame. He had been forgiven, and His sins were forgotten; He was set free.

Jesus promised, "*If we claim we have no sin, we are only fooling ourselves and not living in the truth. But if we confess our sins to Him, He is faithful and just to forgive us our sins and to cleanse us from all wickedness.*"[(4)]

Because Peter had been forgiven, he could boldly declare to us that night in the locked upper room before Jesus appeared that He was alive! Peter could wholeheartedly welcome Him into the room that night. He could, without any hesitation, jump into the water and make a beeline for Jesus that morning at the shore. He was no longer shackled by sin.

But there is a public side to sin – Peter's denial of Jesus had become well-known among the followers. That meant Peter's confession and forgiveness needed to be as equally well-known. For Jesus to work through Peter in the newly forming church, Peter needed to be held accountable as a leader.

So, Jesus asked him, "Peter, *do you love Me more than these?*[(5)] Do you love Me above all others? Do you love Me in a way that causes your love for everyone else to pale in comparison?"

I could tell Jesus' question caught Peter off guard. He hastily replied, "Of course, I love You, Jesus. How could You think otherwise?"

But then Jesus asked him a second time. This time his response was in greater earnest, wanting to leave no doubt of his love for Jesus. When

Jesus asked him a third time, it was obvious Peter was deeply wounded by the question.

"Lord, You know everything. You know that I love You,"[6] Peter replied.

Peter wanted to assure Jesus he loved Him with all of his heart, soul, and mind. But why did Jesus keep asking the same question? And then it dawned on me – Jesus asked that question once for each of the three times Peter had denied Him.

Peter needed to confess his love for Jesus – and he needed to confess it with his whole heart. And the rest of us needed to hear Peter confess his love that way. Jesus was making sure there would be no lingering doubt in anyone's mind as to Peter's love for his Lord.

Then, in response to each of Peter's answers, Jesus replied: *"Feed My lambs," "Take care of My sheep,"* and *"Feed My sheep."*[7] Jesus was publicly restoring Peter to his apostleship and leadership. He was reminding this fisherman – and each one of us who was surrounding them – that He was calling each of us to be shepherds caring for the sheep, protecting the sheep, and nurturing the sheep.

In fact, we were to be under-shepherds, walking in obedience to Him, under His authority and His leadership as the Good Shepherd, the Great Shepherd, and the Chief Shepherd. And as an under-shepherd, the most important thing we could do was love Jesus with our whole heart, soul, and mind.

Then Jesus told Peter, *"Follow Me."*[8]

• • •

This was one of the last times Jesus would stand in front of Peter physically and tell him to *"Follow Me,"* but He would continue to do so through His Spirit. Peter's journey with Jesus was not ending here on the shore of the Sea of Galilee. His journey with Jesus would continue throughout eternity – for a finite period on this side of glory, and for an infinite period on the other side of glory.

Right after that, Jesus told Peter how he would die. Peter turned around and spotted John. He then asked Jesus, *"What about him, Lord?"*[9] (referring to John). Jesus rebuked Peter and reminded him his job was to follow, not to be focused on the paths of other believers. Jesus then turned His attention to all of us gathered around Him, telling us we each have a path the Master has laid out for us to follow. We are to keep *"our eyes on Jesus, on whom our faith depends from start to finish."*[10] He cautioned us not to be distracted by others, our circumstances, or even ourselves.

Throughout my time with Jesus, I had learned that though He was always on His mission, He was never hurried. He never rushed about, like so many of us tend to do. He always had plenty of time to do what He needed to do. And He never wasted time.

On numerous occasions, Jesus took time with each of us to answer our questions and to help us understand. We never once felt Jesus was too busy or that we were bothering Him – and we always had His undivided attention.

That day by the Sea of Galilee was another one of those occasions. Jesus lingered and spent time with each one of us personally, just as He had done with Peter. It was mid-afternoon when He invited me to walk with Him along the shore.

. . .

He looked at me with that knowing look and smiled as He asked, "Shimon, you have questions you want to ask Me, don't you?"

"Yes, Master," I replied. "Even before that day in the stable when You came to earth, You knew all that would come to pass leading to this day. You knew the cross that awaited You. You knew all of us would fail You. On that early morning of Your arrest, we all would abandon You. Peter would deny You. Judas would betray You. And yet, knowing that, You still invited all of us to follow You. How could You do that, knowing what we would do?"

"The Father gave each of you to Me," Jesus explained. "Each of you – except Judas – has repented of your sin and each of you belongs to Me, and all who are Mine belong to the Father. So I knew from the beginning you would bring glory to both the Father and the Son. Judas, however, was an instrument of Satan as foretold by the Scriptures."

Jesus went on to explain how even Judas had been given by the Father for His divine purpose. And yes, Jesus had known from the beginning. With great sadness He told me some of the thoughts Judas had during our time at the home of Lazarus and that night in the upper room – a result of his blindness to the truth and the selfish ambition in his heart.

"But now I am preparing to go," Jesus continued, "and I will send My Spirit to empower you, guide you, and shepherd you in all truth. For a time, I will not be with you physically, but I will never leave you or forsake you. You are My sheep, and I will always be your Shepherd."

Then, later that evening, Jesus departed.

. . .

A short while later He told us to gather in Bethany. It had been forty days since He had risen from the grave. Our group of followers had grown to be one hundred twenty people. Each one of us had been transformed by the work of our Lord and Savior. We came from many different walks of life. Over there were the fishermen – Peter, Andrew, James, John, Philip, Bartholomew, Thomas and Zebedee.

There were the tax collectors – Matthew and Zacchaeus. There were the Pharisees – Joseph and Nicodemus. There were the carpenters – Clopas, James and Thaddeus. There were Jesus' half brothers who, since His resurrection, had also come to believe – James, Joseph, Jude and Simon. There was the one who later would be chosen to replace Judas as the twelfth apostle – Matthias.

There were the criminal and former zealot – Barabbas and Simon. There was the man who had carried His cross – Simon the Cyrene. There was the man born blind who had been given sight, as well as his parents. There was Lazarus who had been raised from the dead, as well as his sisters, Martha and Mary. There were the women whom He had healed and touched – Mary Magdalene, the woman with the issue of blood, and the woman who had been caught in adultery.

There were two shepherds – who had now been taught how to shepherd His sheep – my brother Jacob and me. There were my mother and a host of other men and women whose lives He had also transformed for eternity.

As He stood there in our midst, He reminded us that we, as His followers, had been given an assignment to *"tell people about Him everywhere – in Jerusalem, throughout Judea, in Samaria, and to the ends of the earth."* [11] This was to be accomplished through our actions as well as our words – and with our very lives. He told us we are to be His witnesses, making *"disciples of all the nations, baptizing them in the name of the Father and the Son and the Holy Spirit."*[(12)]

Jesus told us the Father had given Him all authority, and He would send His Holy Spirit to indwell, equip, and empower each one of us to carry out His assignment. This was the purpose for which He was leaving us, He said.

Even as He disappeared from our midst and ascended into heaven that day, He exhorted us to continue in the work He had given us. He told us as His followers, our lives were no longer about our own desires, circumstances, or situations; our lives were now to be about Him, His gospel, and His glory!

Our Master had gone away, but like the story He told us, we now had talents to invest for His Kingdom. He will return one day, and He will call on us to give an accounting. He left us to be shepherds among His sheep. I pray that upon His return He will find I have been faithful. And I pray the same for you!

* * *

EPILOGUE

"Therefore, go and make disciples of all the nations, baptizing them in the name of the Father and the Son and the Holy Spirit. Teach these new disciples to obey all the commands I have given you. And be sure of this: I am with you always, even to the end of the age."[1]

* * *

While the disciples were standing there on the mount, Jesus was taken up into a cloud. As they continued to look up into the sky, two angels stood in their midst and said to them, *"Why are you standing here staring into heaven? Jesus has been taken from you into heaven, but someday He will return from heaven in the same way you saw Him go!"*[2] The group of one hundred twenty followers returned to the upper room where they met and prayed together for ten days.

On the tenth day, there was a sound from heaven that suddenly began like the roaring of a mighty windstorm. It filled the house where they were meeting. The Holy Spirit – the Helper that Jesus had promised –

had now come upon them. For three years prior, God had enabled them to watch and follow His Son as He taught and prepared them.

Now, God had provided His Spirit to indwell within them to equip and enable them to do all Jesus had taught them. Apart from the cross of Christ, they, and we, would still be separated from God by our sin. He paid the price for the forgiveness of our sin! Apart from the Spirit of Christ, they, and we, would be incapable of living the life Jesus called us to live. His Holy Spirit living inside of us makes that possible!

Throughout this story, we have seen men and women whose lives have been redeemed through the shed blood of Jesus. Some of the stories of redemption are told through fictional characters like Shimon and his family members. Some of the stories of redemption have been fabricated for this novel about persons who lived in that day. For example, Scripture never tells us Simon the Cyrene or Barabbas became followers of Jesus.

i pray they did, but we will not know until we get to heaven. Other stories included in the novel come straight from Scripture and are testimonies to the grace and mercy of the redemptive work of our Lord. Each life that has been redeemed has been forever changed. As the apostle Paul writes, each one *is a new creation. The old has passed away; behold, the new has come.*[3]

Repeatedly we have seen the way the Father ordered His Son's steps throughout His incarnational life and ministry according to His perfect timing. Not one of His encounters was accidental or by chance. Not one moment was ever wasted. Not one circumstance was unexpected by the Father. The Father had known it all from before the beginning of time. And He had ordered the steps of His Son to fulfill His perfect redemptive plan.

. . .

The Father not only ordered the steps of His Son, He has ordered the steps of His Son's followers. He ordered Peter's steps in the work He had prepared for him in the furtherance of His gospel. Peter was the first to preach the Good News on that day when the Holy Spirit came upon them, when three thousand believed and were baptized. He was the first to proclaim the gospel to the Gentiles. He suffered persecution, imprisonment, beatings, and crucifixion – all for the sake of the gospel.

John fulfilled his assignment to care for Mary, the mother of Jesus, and then went on to be the leader of the church of Ephesus. He was persecuted in Rome by being cast into boiling oil, and then was exiled on the island of Patmos. The paths of each of the disciples were very different. John's brother, James, was the first disciple to be martyred, and John was the last one of the original twelve to die.

Each of their paths was unique, just as ours are unique. As we walk in the steps the Lord has set before us, we will experience very different circumstances. Some will experience extreme persecution. Some will experience severe health challenges. Some will experience painful losses. Some will experience abundant blessing. Some will experience abundant loss.

Whatever the path is that He has set before us, as we follow Jesus, we need to remember the words of our Savior to Peter – *"As for you, follow Me."* [(4)] Our times are in His hands. Our circumstances are in His hands. Our very lives are in His hands. And He has permitted it all. He has ordered our steps through it all.

Heed the words of the prophet Isaiah: *"Forget the former things; do not dwell on the past"* – or even the present! *"See, I am doing a new thing!*

Now it springs up; do you not perceive it? I am making a way in the wilderness and streams in the wasteland."[5] Our God is in control – and He who began the good work, *"will continue His work until it is finally finished on the day when Christ Jesus returns."*[6]

Though the shepherd Shimon is a fictional character, our Good Shepherd Jesus is our *"very present and well-proved help in trouble."*[7] He sacrificed His life for us – His sheep. He knows each and every one of us. Listen for His voice. We are His flock. Each one of us is precious in His sight – in and through the eyes of our *Good* Shepherd.

Now may the God of peace who brought again from the dead our Lord Jesus, the Great Shepherd of the sheep, by the blood of the eternal covenant, equip you with everything good that you may do His will, working in us that which is pleasing in His sight, through Jesus Christ, to whom be glory forever and ever. Amen.[8]

PLEASE HELP ME BY LEAVING A REVIEW!

i would be very grateful if you would leave a review of this book. Your feedback will be helpful to me in my future writing endeavors and will also assist others as they consider picking up a copy of the book.

To leave a review, go to:
amazon.com/dp/B07THHDTFD

Thanks for your help!

* * *

THROUGH THE EYES OF A SPY

COMING SPRING 2020

A Novel
about the faithfulness of God

* * *

For more information

https://wildernesslessons.com/through-the-eyes-of-a-spy

WildernessLessons

TIMELINE

* * *

Chapter 1 (15-14 BC)
    Marriage of Moshe and Ayda
    Spring 14 BC – birth of Shimon

Chapter 2 (13-4 BC)
    Birth of Shimon's siblings:
    11 BC – Sister–Hannah; 9 BC – Brother–Jacob; 7 BC – Sister–Rachel
    4 BC -- Brother–Eliezer
    Two days later – incarnational birth of Jesus

Chapter 3 (3-2 BC)
    Massacre of children by Herod's soldiers

Chapter 4 (2BC-20AD)
    A shepherd becomes a zealot

Chapter 5 (21 AD)
    The life of a zealot

Chapter 6 (22-25 AD)
A zealot becomes a disciple of John the Baptizer

Chapter 7 (Fall 25 AD)
A shepherd becomes a follower of Jesus

Chapter 8 (Fall 25 AD - Spring 26 AD)
Shimon returns home to Bethlehem
The first Passover of Jesus' earthly ministry

Chapter 9 (Summer 26 AD)
An encounter with the Samaritan woman and an official's son is healed

Chapter 10 (Summer 26 AD)
A leper and a paralytic man are healed
The twelve are chosen

Chapter 11 (Summer 26 AD)
A widow's son is raised from the dead; Mary Magdalene is set free

Chapter 12 (Fall 26 AD – Early 27 AD)
John the Baptizer is imprisoned and beheaded

Chapter 13 (27 AD)
Jairus' daughter is raised from the dead; a woman is healed
Jesus is rejected in Nazareth

Chapter 14 (Winter 27 – 28 AD)
The seventy-two are sent out

Chapter 15 (Spring 28 AD)
Five thousand are fed; Jesus walks on water; a coin in a fish's mouth

Chapter 16 (Summer 28 AD)

The account of the good Samaritan; the lost sheep
Dining at the home of Mary and Martha

Chapter 17 (Summer 28 AD)
Ten lepers are cleansed; a rich young man turns away

Chapter 18 (Fall 28 AD)
Attending the Festival of Tabernacles; the adulterous woman and the religious leaders

Chapter 19 (Fall 28 AD)
The man born blind receives sight

Chapter 20 (Fall 28 AD)
A visit to Bethlehem

Chapter 21 (Winter 28–29 AD)
Lazarus is raised from the dead

Chapter 22 (Spring 29 AD)
A visit to the home of Zacchaeus

Chapter 23 (Spring 29 AD)
Dinner at the home of Lazarus

Chapter 24 (Spring 29 AD Passion week)
The triumphal entry into Jerusalem; Barabbas is arrested

Chapter 25 (Spring 29 AD–Passion week)
The fruitless fig tree; the cleansing of the Temple
Healing, teaching, and testing in the Temple

Chapter 26 (Spring 29 AD–Passion week)
A visit in prison; the Last Supper

Chapter 27 (Spring 29 AD–Passion week)

Journeying from the upper room to the Mount of Olives (the Olivet Discourse)

Chapter 28 (Spring 29 AD–Passion week)
Jesus is arrested in the Garden and taken to the High Priest's home

Chapter 29 (Spring 29 AD–Passion week)
The trials before Pilate and Herod

Chapter 30 (Spring 29 AD–Passion week)
The crucifixion of Christ

Chapter 31 (Spring 29 AD–Resurrection Sunday)
The burial of Jesus' body; the empty tomb; the road to Emmaus
That night in the upper room

Chapter 32 (Spring 29 AD–after Jesus' resurrection)
At the Sea of Galilee
Jesus' ascension

* * *

LISTING OF CHARACTERS

* * *

Fictional Characters

    Shimon – *shepherd, narrator, zealot rebel, disciple of John the Baptizer, disciple of Jesus*

    Moshe – *shepherd, father of Shimon, husband of Ayda*

    Ayda – *mother of Shimon, wife of Moshe*

    Hannah – *younger sister of Shimon*

    Jacob – *shepherd, younger brother of Shimon*

    Rachel – *youngest sister of Shimon*

    Eliezer – *youngest brother of Shimon*

    Unnamed husband of Hannah – *shepherd, Shimon's brother-in-law, Jacob's partner*

    Unnamed wife of Jacob – *Shimon's sister-in-law*

    Unnamed husband of Rachel – *carpenter, Shimon's brother-in-law*

    Unnamed relative of Elizabeth – *Essene who became guardian of John the Baptizer*

    Jonathan – *young boy born deaf, lived in Chorazin with his mother and shepherd father*

    Unnamed Samaritan man – *was living with the Samaritan woman* *when Jesus came to Sychar, subsequently assisted an injured traveler on the road to Jericho*

Hiram – *merchant, father of Zacchaeus*

Lydia – *mother of Zacchaeus, wife of Hiram*

Joshua – *merchant, brother of Zacchaeus*

Gaius Marius — *centurion at the Antonia Fortress*

* * *

Historical Characters

Note: Italicized portion of character description indicates either a historical assumption not confirmed in Scripture, or story elements of this novel that have been added to this character.

Jesus – the Good Shepherd, the Son of God, Savior, Redeemer, Lord, King of Kings

Joseph – carpenter, husband of Mary, earthly father of Jesus

Mary – mother of Jesus

James – half brother of Jesus

Joseph – half brother of Jesus

Jude – half brother of Jesus

Simon – half brother of Jesus

Anna – the prophetess in the Temple in Jerusalem

Simeon – man in the Temple in Jerusalem

John the Baptizer — the voice crying in the wilderness

Zechariah – priest, father of John the Baptizer

Elizabeth – wife of Zechariah, mother of John the Baptizer

Peter (Simon Peter) – fisherman, apostle, older brother of Andrew

Andrew – fisherman, apostle, younger brother of Peter, disciple of John the Baptizer

James – fisherman, apostle, son of Zebedee, older brother of John

John – fisherman, apostle, son of Zebedee, younger brother of James, *disciple of John the Baptizer*

Philip – fisherman, apostle

Bartholomew – fisherman, apostle (also known as Nathanael)

Thomas – fisherman, apostle (also known as the Twin)

Matthew – tax collector, apostle (also known as Levi)

James (the Less) – apostle, *carpenter, older brother of Thaddeus, son of Clopas*

Thaddeus – apostle (also known as Judas), *carpenter, younger brother of James, son of Clopas*

Simon (the zealot) – apostle, *zealot rebel with Shimon, disciple of John the Baptizer*

Judas Iscariot – one of the twelve, betrayer of Jesus; *all other depictions and assumptions in this novel about him are fictional or conjecture to advance the story line*

Barabbas – criminal that was released by Pontius Pilate, *zealot rebel with Shimon, appears in scenes throughout novel – all depictions of him are part of the fictional story line*

Judah, the Galilean – zealot leader, led raid on armory of Herod's palace, *all other depictions of him are fictional to advance the story line*

Zadok, the Pharisee – zealot leader, *all other depictions of him are fictional to advance the story line*

Zebedee – fisherman, business partner with Simon Peter, father of apostles James and John, husband of Salome

Salome – wife of Zebedee, mother of apostles James and John, one of the women who traveled with Jesus

Clopas – *brother of Joseph (the earthly father of Jesus),* husband of Mary, one to whom Jesus appeared on the road to Emmaus, *carpenter, father of apostles James the Less and Thaddeus*

Mary – wife of Clopas, one of the women who traveled with Jesus, *mother of apostles James the Less and Thaddeus*

Chuza – husband of Joanna, household manager of Herod Antipas, *father of son healed by Jesus*

Joanna – wife of Chuza, one of the women who traveled with Jesus, *mother of son healed by Jesus*

Lazarus – brother of Martha and Mary, friend of Jesus, raised from the dead, *also known as Simon the leper, leper healed by Jesus, owned vineyards outside Bethany*

Martha – older sister of Lazarus, friend of Jesus, often hosted Jesus and His followers

Mary – younger sister of Lazarus, friend of Jesus, often hosted Jesus and His followers

Mary Magdalene – out of whom Jesus cast out seven demons, *woman who anoints Jesus' feet at home of Simon the Pharisee,* one of the women who traveled with Jesus, the first person to whom Jesus appeared after His resurrection

Susanna – one of the women who traveled with Jesus, *widowed mother of son Jesus raised from the dead*

Unnamed young man Jesus raised from the dead – *son of Susanna*

Zacchaeus – tax collector in Jericho who hosted Jesus in his home; *all other depictions of him are fictional to advance the story line*

Simon the Cyrene – seized by Roman soldiers to carry Jesus' cross; *all other depictions of him are fictional to advance the story line*

Unnamed Samaritan woman – encountered Jesus at Jacob's well, was used by God to bring spiritual awakening to Sychar and other parts of Samaria

Unnamed paralytic man and his four friends – healed by great faith

Unnamed woman with issue of blood – healed by great faith

Jairus – leader of synagogue whose daughter Jesus raised from the dead

Unnamed girl Jesus raised from the dead – daughter of Jairus

Unnamed ten lepers, including one Samaritan who returned – healed by Jesus

Unnamed blind man who was given sight, and his parents – healed by Jesus, *followed Jesus*

Unnamed adulterous woman – forgiven by Jesus

High Priest Annas – father-in-law of Caiaphas, former High Priest

High Priest Caiaphas – son-in-law of Annas, current High Priest

Pharisee Simon - hosted Jesus for dinner, *lived in Magdala*

Pharisee Nicodemus – *presumed to have become a follower of Jesus*

Pharisee Joseph of Arimathea – provided a tomb for the burial of Jesus' body, *presumed to have become a follower of Jesus*

Herod the Great – tetrarch ruler at the time of Jesus' birth, ordered the massacre of all boys two years and under living in and around Bethlehem

Herod Archelaus – ruler of Judea, Samaria, and Idumea after Herod the Great's death

Herod Antipas – ruler of Galilee and Perea after Herod the Great's death, second husband of Herodias, ordered the imprisonment and beheading of John the Baptizer, a principal in the mock trials of Jesus

Herod Philip II – ruler of Ituraea, Trachonitis, Gaulanitis, Paneas after Herod the Great's death

Prefect Valerius Gratus – fourth prefect of Iudaean province after Herod Archelaus was deposed

Prefect Pontius Pilate – fifth prefect of Iudaean province after Herod Archelaus was deposed, ordered the crucifixion of Jesus

Caesar Augustus, Roman emperor – ruled Roman empire 27 B.C.–14 A.D.

Caesar Tiberias, Roman emperor – ruled Roman empire 14 A.D.–37 A.D.

* * *

SCRIPTURE BIBLIOGRAPHY

* * *

Much of the story line of this book is taken from the Gospels according to Matthew, Mark, Luke, and John. Certain fictional events or depictions of those events have been added.

Specific references and quotations:
Preface
[1]John 20:31

Chapter 1
[1]Micah 5:2
[2]2 Samuel 23:16
[3]Proverbs 18:22
[4]Leviticus 12:3
[5]Leviticus 12:6-8

Chapter 2
[1]Luke 2:1
[2]Deuteronomy 6:4-9 (ESV)

r

(3)Psalm 127:3-5
(4)Luke 2:10-11
(5)Luke 2:14
(6)Luke 2:15
(7)Luke 2:25-35

Chapter 3
(1)Jeremiah 31:15
(2)Matthew 2:18

Chapter 4
(1)Matthew 2:16

Chapter 5
(1)Luke 3:1-2, Acts 5:36-37

Chapter 6
(1)Acts 5:37, Luke 3:2-3
(2)Matthew 3:7-12
(3)Luke 3:10-14
(4)Luke 3:16

Chapter 7
(1)John 1:35-37
(2)Matthew 3:10
(3)Matthew 3:14-15
(4)Luke 3:21-22
(5)John 1:29-31
(6)John 1:36
(7)John 1:38
(8)John 1:39
(9)John 5:39, 46
(10)Deuteronomy 18:15-18
(11)John 17:1
(12)John 1:42 (HCSB)
(13)John 1:43

(14)John 1:45-46
(15)John 1:47-50
(16)John 2:4
(17)John 2:10
(18)John 2:5

Chapter 8
(1)John 2:13-14
(2)John 1:29
(3)John 2:16
(4)John 2:19-20
(5)Matthew 4:17, 5:3-12, 43-48
(6)Isaiah 53:5-6
(7)John 3:14-21
(8)John 3:26-36

Chapter 9
(1)John 4:25-26
(2)John 4:7
(3)John 4:9
(4)John 4:10
(5)John 4:11-12
(6)John 4:13-14
(7)John 4:15
(8)John 4:16
(9)John 4:17-18
(10)John 4:19
(11)John 4:20
(12)John 4:21-24
(13)John 4:25
(14)John 4:26
(15)John 4:29
(16)John 4:32, 34
(17)John 4:35-38
(18)John 4:42
(19)John 4:48

(20)John 4:49
(21)John 4;50
(22)John 4:52
(23)John 4:53

Chapter 10
(1)Luke 5:24b
(2)Luke 5:4
(3)Luke 5:5
(4)Luke 5:8
(5)Luke 5:10
(6)Luke 5:12
(7)Luke 5;13
(8)Luke 5:14
(9)Luke 5:20
(10)Luke 5:21
(11)Luke 5:22
(12)Luke 5:27

Chapter 11
(1)Luke 7:14
(2)Luke 7:13
(3)Luke 7:14
(4)Luke 7:16
(5)Luke 7:40-42
(6)Luke 7:43
(7)Luke 7:44-47
(8)Luke 7:48,50

Chapter 12
(1)Luke 7:20
(2)Luke 7:20
(3)Luke 7:22
(4)Isaiah 35:5-6,10
(5)Luke 7:23
(6)Luke 7:28

(7)Luke 7:35 (CEV)
(8)Mark 6:22-23
(9)Mark 6:25

Chapter 13
(1)Mark 5:28
(2)Mark 5:23
(3)Mark 5:30
(4)Mark 5:31
(5)Mark 5:34
(6)Mark 5:35
(7)Mark 5:36
(8)Mark 5:39
(9)Hebrews 11:6
(10)Mark 5:41
(11)Mark 6:2
(12)Mark 6:3
(13)Mark 6:4

Chapter 14
(1)Luke 10:3
(2)Luke 10:2-5, 7, 9, 16
(3)Luke 10:13
(4)Isaiah 9:6-7
(5)Luke 2:10
(6)Luke 10:19-20
(7)Luke 10:21
(8)Luke 10:23-24

Chapter 15
(1)Mark 6:34
(2)Luke 9:12
(3)Matthew 14:16
(4)John 6:5
(5)Mark 6:37
(6)Mark 6:38

(7)John 6:9
(8)Matthew 18:3-4
(9)John 6:10
(10)John 6:12
(11)John 6:14
(12)John 6:20
(13)Matthew 14:28
(14)Matthew 14:29
(15)Matthew 14:30
(16)Matthew 14:31
(17)Exodus 30:11-16
(18)Matthew 17:27

Chapter 16
(1)Luke 10:29
(2)Mark 12:28
(3)Mark 12:29-31
(4)Luke 10:29
(5)Luke 10:30-35
(6)Luke 10:36
(7)Luke 10:37
(8)Luke 10:37
(9)Luke 15:7
(10)Luke 19:10
(11)Luke 10:40
(12)Luke 10:41-42
(13)Matthew 11:15

Chapter 17
(1)Luke 18:22
(2)Luke 17:13
(3)Luke 17:14
(4)Luke 17:17-18
(5)Luke 17:19
(6)Luke 18:18
(7)Mark 10:18

[8]Mark 10:19
[9]Mark 10:21
[10]Mark 10:23-25
[11]Mark 10:26
[12]Mark 10:27
[13]Mark 10:28
[14]Mark 10 :29-31
[15]Luke 16:19-31

Chapter 18
[1]John 8:10-11
[2]Malachi 3:1
[3]John 7:17-18
[4]John 7:25-27
[5]John 7:28-29
[6]John 7:31
[7]John 7:40
[8]John 7:41
[9]John 7:41-42
[10]John 7:45
[11]John 7:46
[12]John 7:47
[13]John 7:48-49
[14]John 7:51
[15]John 8:4-5
[16]Leviticus 20:10
[17]John 8:7
[18]John 8:10
[19]John 8:11
[20]John 8:11
[21]John 8:12
[22]Ecclesiastes 3:11
[23]Isaiah 53:6

Chapter 19
[1]John 9:36

[2]Mark 8:27
[3]Mark 8:28
[4]Mark 8:29
[5]Mark 8:29
[6]John 9:2
[7]John 9:3
[8]John 9:4
[9]John 9:5
[10]John 9:7
[11]John 9:8
[12]John 9:9-11
[13]John 9:16
[14]John 9:24
[15]John 9:25
[16]John 9:27
[17]John 9:28-29
[18]John 9:30-33
[19]John 9:34
[20]John 9:35
[21]John 9:36
[22]John 9:37
[23]John 9:38
[24]John 9:39
[25]John 9:40
[26]John 9:41

Chapter 20
[1]John 10:11
[2]John 10:1-5
[3]John 10:7-10
[4]John 10:11-16
[5]John 10:17-18
[6]John 10:20
[7]John 10:21
[8]Psalm 23:1-6

Chapter 21
[1]John 11:43
[2]John 10:22
[3]John 10:25-30
[4]John 11:3
[5]John 11:4
[6]John 11:7
[7]John 11:11
[8]John 11:12
[9]John 11:14
[10]John 11:16
[11]John 11:21-22
[12]John 11:23
[13]John 11:24
[14]John 11:25-26
[15]John 11:27
[16]John 11:28
[17]John 11:32
[18]John 11:34
[19]John 11:34
[20]John 11:39
[21]John 11:39
[22]John 11:40
[23]John 11:41-42
[24]John 11:43
[25]John 11:44

Chapter 22
[1]Luke 19:5
[2]Luke 19:5
[3]Luke 19:8
[4]Exodus 22:1

Chapter 23
[1]Matthew 26:13
[2]John 12:5

(3)Mark 14:6
(4)Matthew 26:11-13

Chapter 24
(1)Luke 19:40 (NKJ)
(2)Matthew 21:2-3
(3)Matthew 21:3
(4)Zechariah 9:9
(5)Matthew 21:9
(6)Luke 19:39
(7)Luke 19:40
(8)Matthew 21:10
(9)Matthew 21:11

Chapter 25
(1)Mark 11:28
(2)Mark 11:14
(3)Luke 19:46 (ESV)
(4)Matthew 21:15
(5)Matthew 21:16
(6)Matthew 21:16-17
(7)Matthew 2:4-5
(8)Zechariah 4:7a
(9)Mark 11:28
(10)Mark 11:30
(11)Mark 11:33
(12)Luke 20:21
(13)Luke 20:22
(14)Luke 20:24

Chapter 26
(1)John 13:16
(2)Exodus 12:15
(3)Luke 22:10-13
(4)John 13:6
(5)John 13:7

(6)John 13:8a
(7)John 13:8b
(8)John 13:9
(9)John 13:10
(10)John 13:12-17
(11)Luke 22:21-22
(12)John 13:24
(13)John 13:26
(14)John 13:27
(15)Luke 22:19
(16)Luke 22:20, 17-18

Chapter 27
(1)John 14:6
(2)Luke 22:25-30
(3)Luke 22:26
(4)Luke 22:27
(5)Matthew 19:28
(6)John 13:33-35
(7)Matthew 22:37
(8)Matthew 22:39
(9)John 13:34
(10)Mark 3:35 (NASB)
(11)1 Corinthians 13:4-7
(12)John 13:33
(13)John 14:1-4
(14)John 14:5
(15)John 14:6
(16)John 15:1-5
(17)John 16:12-15

Chapter 28
(1)Luke 22:53
(2)Mark 14:45
(3)Luke 22:48
(4)Luke 22:51; Matthew 26:52-53

[5]Luke 22:52-53; John 18:8
[6]John 18:17
[7]John 18:26
[8]Luke 22:67
[9]Luke 22:67-69
[10]Luke 22:70
[11]Luke 22:70
[12]Luke 22:71
[13]Mark 14:64
[14]Matthew 27:4
[15]Matthew 27:4

Chapter 29
[1]Matthew 27:24
[2]Mark 15:14
[3]Matthew 27:24

Chapter 30
[1]Matthew 27:54
[2]Luke 23:28
[3]Luke 23:39
[4]Luke 23:40-41
[5]Luke 23:42
[6]Luke 23:43
[7]Matthew 27:42
[8]Psalm 22:18
[9]John 19:28
[10]Psalm 69:21
[11]John 19:30
[12]Matthew 27:54

Chapter 31
[1]John 20:19
[2]John 19:30
[3]Proverbs 18:24
[4]John 13:34

(5)John 20:8
(6)John 20:13
(7)Matthew 28:10
(8)John 20:19
(9)John 20:21
(10)John 20:26
(11)John 20:29 (paraphrase)

Chapter 32
(1)John 21:16
(2)John 21:7
(3)Matthew 16:18
(4)1 John 1:8-9
(5)John 21:15
(6)John 21:17
(7)John 21:15-17
(8)John 21:19
(9)John 21:21
(10)Hebrews 12:2
(11)Acts 1:8
(12)Matthew 28:19

Epilogue
(1)Matthew 28:18-20
(2)Acts 1:11
(3)2 Corinthians 5:17
(4)John 21:22
(5)Isaiah 43:18-19 (NIV)
(6)Philippians 1:6
(7)Psalm 46:1
(8)Hebrews 13:20-21 (ESV)

* * *

OTHER BOOKS WRITTEN BY KENNETH A. WINTER

* * *

The Lessons Learned In The Wilderness series

There are lessons that can only be learned in the wilderness experiences of our lives. As we see throughout the Bible, God is right there leading us each and every step of the way, if we will follow Him. Wherever we are, whatever we are experiencing, He will use it to enable us to experience His Person, witness His power and join Him in His mission.

Each of the six books in the series contains 61 chapters, which means that the entire series is comprised of 366 chapters — **one chapter for each day of the year.** The chapters have been formatted in a way that you can read one chapter each day or read each book straight through. Whichever way you *choose, allow the Master to use the series to encourage and challenge you in the journey that He has designed uniquely for you so that His purpose is fulfilled, and His glory is made known.*

The Journey Begins (Book #1)

God's plan for our lives is not static; He is continuously calling us to draw closer, to climb higher and to move further. In that process, He is moving us out of our comfort zone to His land of promise for our lives. That process includes time in the wilderness. Many times it is easier to see the truth that God is teaching us through the lives of others than it is through our own lives.

"*The Journey Begins*" is the first book in the "*Lessons Learned In The Wilderness*" series. It chronicles those stories, those examples and those truths as revealed through the lives and experiences of the Israelites, as recorded in the Book of Exodus in sixty-one bite-sized chapters.

As you read one chapter per day for sixty-one days, we will look at the circumstances, the surroundings and the people in such a way that highlights the similarities to our lives, as we then apply those same truths to our own life journey as the Lord God Jehovah leads us through our own wilderness journey.

The Wandering Years (Book #2)

Why did a journey that God ordained to take slightly longer than one year, end up taking forty years? Why, instead of enjoying the fruits of the land of milk and honey, did the Israelites end up wandering in the desert wilderness for forty years? Why did one generation follow God out of Egypt only to die there, leaving the next generation to follow Him into the Promised Land?

In the journeys through the wildernesses

of my life, i can look back and see where God has turned me back from that land of promise to wander a while longer in the wilderness. God has given us the wilderness to prepare us for His land of promise, but if when we reach the border we are not ready, He will turn us back to wander.

If God is allowing you to continue to wander in the wilderness, it is because He has more to teach you about Himself – His Person, His purpose and His power. "**The Wandering Years**" chronicles through sixty-one "bite-sized" chapters those lessons He would teach us through the Israelites' time in the wilderness as recorded in the books of Numbers and Deuteronomy.

The book has been formatted for one chapter to be read each day for sixty-one days. Explore this second book in the "**Lessons Learned In The Wilderness**" series and allow God to use it to apply those same lessons to your daily journey with Him.

Possessing the Promise (Book #3)

The day had finally arrived for the Israelites to possess the land that God had promised. But just like He had taught them lessons throughout their journey in the wilderness, He had more to teach them, as they possessed the promise.

And so it is for us. Possessing the promise doesn't mean the faith adventure has come to a conclusion; rather, in many ways, it has only just begun. Possessing the promise will involve in some respects an even greater dependence upon God and the promise He has given you.

"**Possessing the Promise**" chronicles the stories, experiences and lessons we see recorded in the books of Joshua and Judges in sixty-one "bite-sized" chapters. The book has been formatted for one chapter to be read each day for sixty-one days.

Explore this third book in the "**Lessons Learned In The Wilderness**" series and allow God to use it to teach you how to possess the promise as He leads you in the journey with Him each day.

Walking With The Master (Book #4)

Our daily walk with the Master is never static – it entails moving and growing. Jesus was constantly on the move, carrying out the Father's work and His will. He was continuously surrendered and submitted to the will of the Father. And if we would walk with Him, we too must walk surrendered and submitted to the Father in our day-to-day lives.

Jesus extended His invitation to us to deny ourselves, take up our cross and follow Him. "**Walking With The Master**" chronicles, through "sixty-one" bite-sized chapters, those lessons the Master would teach us as we walk with Him each day, just as He taught the men and women who walked with Him throughout Galilee, Samaria and Judea as recorded in the Gospel accounts.

The book has been formatted for one chapter to be read each day for sixty-one days. Explore this fourth book in the "**Lessons Learned In The Wilderness**" series and allow the Master to use it to draw you closer to Himself as you walk with Him each day in the journey.

Taking Up The Cross (Book #5)

What does it mean to take up the cross? In this fifth book of the *Lessons Learned In The Wilderness* series, we will look at the cross our Lord has set before us as we follow Him. The backdrop for our time is the last forty-seven days of the earthly ministry of Jesus, picking up at His triumphal entry into Jerusalem and continuing to the day He ascended into heaven to sit at the right-hand of the Father.

We will look through the lens of the Gospels at what taking up the cross looked like in His life, and what He has determined it will look like in ours. He doesn't promise that there won't be a cost – there will be! And He doesn't promise that it will be easy – it won't be! But it is the journey He has set before us – a journey that will further His purpose in and through our lives – and a journey that will lead to His glory.

Like the other books in this series, this book has been formatted in a way that you can read one chapter each day, or read it straight through. Whichever way you choose, allow the Master to use it to draw you closer to Him as you walk with Him each day in your journey.

Until He Returns (Book #6)

Moments after Jesus ascended into heaven, two angels delivered this promise: "Someday He will return!" In this sixth and final book of the *Lessons Learned In The Wilderness* series, we will look at what that journey will look like **Until He Returns**. No matter where we are in our journey with Him – in the wilderness, in the promised land, or somewhere in between – He has a purpose and a plan for us.

In this book, we will look through the lens of the Book of Acts at what that journey looked like for those first century followers of Christ. Like us, they weren't perfect. There were times they took their eyes off of Jesus. But despite their imperfections, He used them to turn the world upside down. And His desire is to do the same thing through us. Our journeys will all look different, but He will be with us every step of the way.

Like the first five books in this series, this book has been formatted in a way that you can read one chapter each day or read it straight through. Whichever way you choose, allow the Master to use it to encourage and challenge you in the journey that He has designed uniquely for you so that His purpose is fulfilled, and His glory is made known.

* * *

For more information about these books,
including how you can purchase them, go to
wildernesslessons.com or kenwinter.org

ABOUT THE AUTHOR

 Responding to God's call from the business world in 1992 to full-time vocational ministry, Ken Winter joined the staff of First Baptist Church of West Palm Beach, Florida, serving as the associate pastor of administration and global mission.

In 2004, God led Ken, his wife LaVonne, and their two teenagers on a Genesis 12 journey, that resulted in his serving with the International Mission Board (IMB) of the Southern Baptist Convention. From 2006 until 2015, Ken served as the vice president of church and partner services of IMB, assisting churches across the US in mobilizing their members to make disciples of all peoples.

From 2015 until 2018, Ken served as the senior associate pastor of Grove Avenue Baptist Church in Richmond, Virginia.

Today that Genesis 12 journey continues as Ken labors as a bond-servant of the Lord Jesus Christ in the proclamation of the gospel to the end that every person may be presented complete in Christ.

To read Ken's weekly blog posts go to kenwinter.blog

* * *

And we proclaim Him, admonishing every man and teaching every man with all wisdom, that we may present every man complete in Christ. And for this

purpose also I labor, striving according to His power, which mightily works within me.
(Colossians 1:28-29 NASB)

* * *

PLEASE JOIN MY READERS' GROUP

Please join my Readers' Group in order to receive updates and information about future releases, etc.

Also, i will send you a free copy of *The Journey Begins* e-book — the first book in the *Lessons Learned In The Wilderness* series. It is yours to keep or share with a friend or family member that you think might benefit from it.

It's completely free to sign up. i value your privacy and will not spam you. Also, you can unsubscribe at any time.

Go to kenwinter.org to subscribe.

* * *

Made in the USA
Columbia, SC
27 November 2019